KASHMIR RESCUE

SAS
OPERATION

Kashmir Rescue

DOUG ARMSTRONG

Harper
An imprint of HarperCollins*Publishers*
1 London Bridge Street,
London SE1 9GF
www.harpercollins.co.uk

This paperback edition 2016
1

First published as *Operation Takeaway* by 22 Books/Bloomsbury Publishing plc 1996

Copyright © Bloomsbury Publishing plc 1996

Doug Armstrong asserts the moral right to
be identified as the author of this work

A catalogue record for this book
is available from the British Library

ISBN: 978 0 00 815548 3

Set in Sabon by Born Group using Atomik ePublisher from Easypress

Printed and bound in Great Britain

MIX
Paper from
responsible sources
FSC C007454

FSC is a non-profit international organisation established
to promote the responsible management of the world's forests.
Products carrying the FSC label are independently certified
to assure consumers that they come from forests that are managed
to meet the social, economic and ecological needs
of present and future generations.

Find out more about HarperCollins and the environment at
www.harpercollins.co.uk/green

1

There were many kinds of exile. The old man realized that now. In fact, he wondered whether he had been unfortunate enough to experience them all in the course of his long life. As he ambled along the pavement bordering the busy road, the surface glistening with drizzle, he hunched his shoulders into the motionless cold and found himself thinking of his boyhood. That had been the first one. When he had been very small he had never been able to work out why he was exiled from the company of the other boys in his neighbourhood. Of course, he had heard the rumours of his parents, uncles and aunts, all speaking of Hindus and Muslims, and on holy days he saw how his own family went to pray at a different temple from the one attended by the other people in their street.

A passing lorry sprayed him with a fine film of muddy water as it shot by, heading south for the junction of the M4, which would already be thickening with traffic, even at such an early hour. By 9 a.m. it would have ground to a virtual standstill, clogged like an artery, the flow gradually stiffening to a halt in the moments before his death.

He hated his new country. He still thought of it as new, even though he had left the land of his birth nearly fifty years before. That had been another exile, more obvious than his boyhood solitude but stifling and bitter nonetheless. He looked around at the grey, sullen landscape of concrete, tarmac and red brick. It was barely light, and every house was closed as tight as a fist. Their owners had made pitiful attempts to differentiate their property from the one next door: a glass panel, the colour of woodwork, a cursory stab at flamboyance with a winding pathway. More noticeable, however, were the similarities, apart from the most obvious one of the houses' identical design: a front garden concreted over to provide parking for a clutch of cars; burglar alarms to keep at bay the increasing number of have-nots; and the satellite dish clinging under the miserly eaves like an extraterrestrial orchid, its brainwashing duties long completed but still reflexively cleansing the occupants of original thought.

The bench he usually rested on had been vandalized in the night. He stood before it, surveying the efforts of the mental giant who had spray-painted a swastika and racist slogans across the seat.

'If only I could go home,' he muttered to himself as he read the misspelt words. 'If only I could.'

He tested the paint with one cautious fingertip, and finding it dry, eased himself down, feeling a stab of satisfaction as his buttocks pressed into the swastika. He wondered briefly if the youth had been aware of the symbol's Indian origins. He smiled at the irony and took out a cigarette.

Against the background noise from the motorway he could hear the car alarms starting to go off around the district, each one welcoming its owner with the faithfulness of a dog, bleating an answering toot as a keyring was fired at it. Soon their drivers would be sitting in traffic jams and feeling the tension knot in the solar plexus at the prospect of being late for work.

The old man sat back and drew on his cigarette, glad to be out of it all, yet unable to resist the slightest twinge of regret that his own participation in the conduct of life was at an end. He had never become used to retirement, another one of the many exiles. Had his wife still been alive there might have been some solace in the spread of empty hours that extended from dawn to dusk. But she was dead – yet one more exile that he mentally ticked off on the tally he kept.

A growing roar overhead heralded the approach of the first morning flight into Heathrow. Moments later the fat silver fuselage broke through the low, swirling clouds like a bloated fly, sinking down to settle on a new-found corpse. The old man smiled grimly. He had seen plenty of those in his time. Too many. But that was all such a long time ago. He wondered sometimes if it had been a dream. Nightmare might be a better description.

He watched the plane disappear behind a prim row of houses, its great belly touching down out of sight on the soaking runway. The day had begun pretty much like every other since he had arrived in Britain. Perhaps later on he would go to the temple near his home in Southall, but he never knew whether or not he would actually go inside until he was mounting the steps and walking through the tinsel-adorned entrance hall. More often than not he simply passed by, unable to drum up the courage to face his conscience. He didn't believe in the gods any more. That had died a long time ago, but the temple had proved to be a place of brutally frank reflection and of late he found he preferred the cinema.

When he had finished the cigarette he contemplated smoking another but decided instead to heed his doctor's warning and cut down. By evening he would have finished the packet which had been new when he had got out of bed, unable to sleep, to dress and set off on his walk.

So how would he spend the day? He could go and visit any one of the restaurants, but then his son-in-law would think he was interfering and by midday his daughter would be on the phone, whining at him to give them space. They were so bloody sensitive, the younger generation. They had no concept of respect. All they thought about was themselves and their own selfish fulfilment. Self-sacrifice was an unknown land, and the notion that age had a certain wisdom to offer was as alien as the other planets.

If not the restaurants, what then? He was beginning to regret handing over the management of his little empire to his son-in-law. But he had to admit that the lad had improved their efficiency more than he would have thought possible. He was always spouting the jargon gleaned from the MBA course he had attended after university. 'Total quality management', 'customer care' – stuff like that. In the old man's day it had been enough simply to be the best in the neighbour-hood, to crush the opposition by fair means or foul and fill the resulting power vacuum. Now it was all graphs and figures. There didn't seem to be any room for intuition.

He pushed himself off the bench and set off for home. As he walked the drizzle began to harden into rain and he cursed himself for not taking his umbrella. He was a creature of habit and always liked to return by a roundabout route past the cinema, but as he felt the sting of cold water lash against his cheeks he decided to go back the way he had come, taking the shorter path through the park. 'Park' was a grand description for a miserable patch of grass, largely trampled to mud at this time of year. From the far side a narrow path crept between the side of an old Victorian terraced house and a row of fenced-off garages, beyond which a single road cut in front of his own house. He glanced at his watch, trying to shield the glass from the rain. It would take him at least fifteen minutes, enough time to get thoroughly soaked. Perhaps he would go back to bed once he got home. That would solve the problem of what to do with himself. But no. That way lay a quick death. He would take to his bed only when he knew his end was near, and not before.

He approached a row of shops. Built in the early 1960s, they exuded all the charm and grace of an empty cornflakes packet. White wooden boards coated the upper floor and the lettering identifying each of the shops was in stark black plastic, the occasional letter missing. There was a launderette, a newsagent who served also as confectioner and postmaster, a greengrocer, a hairdresser and a chemist, every one of them Indian. It was extraordinary, the old man reflected. If their noble ancestors could see them now and witness what they had become, making their living in such an unpleasant foreign land. They had forsaken the wide, sweeping continent of their forebears, the ancient land of gods and sagas, of princes, fables and legends, to retreat to a dank, miserable corner of the globe that had been civilized for barely a millennium.

The newsagent was winding up his metal blinds and squinted suspiciously at the old man in the gloom.

'You should keep your spectacles on,' the old man called across. 'One day you'll be robbed.'

The newsagent grinned with relief as he recognised the old man's voice. 'You're up early, Mr Sanji.'

'As ever, as ever,' the old man said with a dismissive wave of the hand.

'You should get some sleeping pills from Dr Gupta.'

'Why hasten matters? We'll all be sleeping soon enough, and for as long as any man could wish.'

The newsagent shook his head in bemusement. 'You are always joking, Mr Sanji. Always joking.' He went inside and reappeared seconds later with a paper. 'Do you want to take this with you?' he asked. 'You know what that delivery boy is like. Quite, quite useless. Always late, always idling.'

The old man nodded appreciatively and accepted the paper, glancing briefly at the headlines and then folding it away inside his coat out of the rain. 'Thank you. I expect it's all bad news anyway.'

Chuckling to himself, the newsagent wagged a finger at him and went inside. A moment later there was the flicker of neon and the inside of the shop was illuminated in the garish whiteness. The old man walked on.

By the time he reached the edge of the park the rain had become too heavy for him to ignore it. For a moment he toyed with the idea of pressing on and accepting the inevitable drenching, but his daughter would scream with horror at the sight of him and then fuss for the rest of the day. His son-in-law would likewise protest, but more from a sense of good manners. In his heart, the old man knew, his son-in-law would be wishing upon him a speedy death by pneumonia. There was no love lost between them. Politeness concealed their mutual hatred.

The entrance porch to an old church provided partial shelter from the rain. The old man squeezed up against the shuttered door and turned up his collar, but the rain slanted in, soaking the toes of his shoes. He turned them in like a pigeon but the water still found them, feasting on the cheap leather until he felt it penetrating to his socks. Strangely, the cold moisture between his toes reminded him of walking

6

barefoot as a boy during the monsoons in the backstreets of Delhi. It was comforting now, knowing that warmth and proper shelter were a short distance away. Not that he had been deprived as a child. But confronted with the poverty of others, he had never felt the security he now took for granted.

Up above, the grey sky was lightening almost imperceptibly. Great swathes of cloud banked and rolled overhead, seeming so close he felt he could reach out and touch them. Another jet loomed out of the sky, the undercarriage down, lights blinking at the wingtips. Inside, he could imagine the passengers tut-tutting at the British weather, peering grimly through the thick windows at the disastrous-looking scene beneath them. The pilot would perhaps have made an attempt at humour and would now be concentrating on the path of lights before him, peeling open as he steadied the aircraft into its lowering approach run, and, perched on their seats, the stewardesses would be touching up lipstick and eye-shadow in readiness for the chorus of farewells by the exit door.

However dark the sky, when he looked back at the surrounding streets the old man felt as if night had fallen again by comparison. It seemed there was not going to be any let-up in the rain and suddenly he felt exasperated at the delay. It was so pointless. So much was pointless these days. He stepped out of the porch and set off as briskly as he could towards the park entrance, darting across the street and passing between the bent railings and the notice warning of the fine for owners who allowed their dogs to foul the pathways. Pointless.

The next instant he thought of his granddaughter and smiled. She at least gave some meaning to his life. She at least would be bright on this dismal, depressing day. But even there all was far from perfect. Her parents had consented to her wishes to be allowed to go to university. The old man had protested. Eli was the delight of his old age, he had said. Her place was at his side. Naturally it had been his son-in-law who had countermanded his order. Theirs was a modern family, he said proudly, not bound by the traditions of the past. Eli would go to university and that was an end to it.

Of course the old man knew that his son-in-law didn't care a jot for his daughter's emancipation. He was simply taking delight in thwarting the old man and depriving him of the only pleasure he had left. But Eli had come to see him and had promised to write at least once a week, and deep down he realized that, however much he resented it, the times had changed. He would be the last one to hold her back. They would see how modern and British his son-in-law was when Eli came back one weekend and announced her own choice of husband. The old man could well imagine the uproar that would create, and then he would be the one to support her decision. Then he would delight in the torment of his son-in-law.

He was about to emerge from the path at the far side of the park when he noticed the car. The windows were clouded with mist and it was impossible to recognize the people inside. He could just make out two figures, both in front. It was some kind of Ford, cheap-looking and obviously an unmarked police car. He smiled to himself. Perhaps his son-in-law had been cooking the books as well as the curry and the Inland Revenue was about to haul him away for interrogation. The old man prayed it would be a long and brutal affair.

More likely, he imagined, it was part of another of the anti-terrorist exercises that the police conducted from time to time on the outskirts of the airport. The idiots had left their windows tightly shut and the engine and heater turned off, until the car looked as though it had just been removed from a giant fridge. They couldn't possibly see through the glass. The buzz and hiss of a radio receiver from inside the car confirmed his suspicion that they were policemen. He sighed and started towards the park exit.

The sound of another engine stopped him. Although he had nothing to fear from the police, having always kept out of trouble, he drew aside into the inadequate cover of the scrawny bush and watched, more out of idle curiosity than anything else. Sure enough, the grubby white Ford Transit that cruised slowly round the corner at the top of the road seemed to be involved in the same exercise. Unlike the car's occupants, the driver of the van had kept the windows clear, and the old man could see the face peering at the houses as if searching for a particular number.

A cold drop of rain found its way down the old man's neck and tumbled down his spine, but the shiver that wriggled through his bones was caused by something altogether different. The van had stopped outside his own house, and through the back of the vehicle he could just see another man leaning over the driver's shoulder. They appeared to be arguing, and behind them he could make out other figures, perhaps half a dozen in all.

He looked anxiously at the unmarked police car again. What was going on? Perhaps he hadn't been so far from the truth about his son-in-law after all. But there was something very wrong, although he couldn't put his finger on it. For a moment he considered crossing the road and going straight indoors, ignoring the police and leaving them to get on with their exercise. But before he could move he heard the rear doors of the van opening and the sound of booted feet jumping to the ground. He watched in horror as the men moved purposefully towards his house and went to the front door, three of them striding down the pathway and the other four or five jogging down the drive. He almost cried out as one of them kicked open the side gate and disappeared towards the kitchen door, which gave on to the back garden.

In the police car the figures didn't move. Then one of them leaned forward and scrubbed a hole in the mist. Through the circle of misted breath the old man could see the surprise on the face and with another bolt of horror he realized that though they were indeed most likely policemen, they were nothing to do with the intruders breaking into his house.

He looked back at the van, where the man next to the driver was stepping on to the road. The engine was still ticking over and the man signalled for the driver to gun the accelerator and prepare for a speedy departure. Until then his face had been turned away from the park, but as the man gave the order to the driver, the old man saw him clearly and his heart missed a beat. There was something about the features that alerted him to the man's lineage. He had hoped to have done with the lot of them but it was obviously not to be. After all these years they had found him at last. Now it would begin all over again.

'Was that you?'

Colin Field grinned sheepishly. 'Sorry. It was that curry last night.'

'Jesus Christ.' Paul Robins screwed up his face and opened the car window a crack. Instantly a gust of frosty, damp air buffeted its way in, relieving the strain on his nose but reminding him that they had been freezing all night in an unheated vehicle. Reluctantly he closed the window again.

'What a bloody night.' He reached for the glove compartment and hunted around until he found his pack of cigarettes. It was empty. He scrunched it up and tossed it over his shoulder on to the back seat.

'What time do we finish?' Colin asked.

'Don't ask me. Ask that pan-faced git from Hereford. He's supposed to be running the package.'

'Do you reckon he'll give us the run-around again? You know, pretend the exercise has ended and then fuck us off to another task?'

'If he does I'll tell the force they can stick their sodding job. I'll volunteer to go back on the beat and leave special duties to heroes like you.'

Colin nodded sagely. 'Beats me why our own training organization can't run the course. Why do they have to bring in outsiders?'

'Haven't you heard? They're sodding bloody supermen. I guess the boss is hoping some of it'll rub off on us.' He stared hard at Colin, appraising him. 'Some bloody hope.'

'Here, what do you mean?' Colin asked, an expression of confused hurt on his face.

'Nothing.' Paul decided it was best to let it go. They had already had a couple of set-tos during the night and with tempers frayed from lack of sleep he could do without another. Colin eased sideways on his seat cushion and Paul noticed the tell-tale signs. 'Don't you bloody dare!'

'Give us a break. It's either this or I'll have gut-ache for the rest of the day.'

'Make it gut-ache then, but one more of those and you're out in the rain.'

Muttering under his breath Colin sat upright. He looked at his watch. 'Couldn't we call in? Perhaps the ex is over and they've forgotten to tell us.'

Paul laughed. 'Don't be a bigger dick than you already are. Can you imagine Don sodding Headley screwing up like that?'

The radio crackled and a terse message was sent to one of the other teams. Spread in a vast ring around Heathrow, they were taking part in an anti-terrorist exercise that had already been going on for nearly three days. The floor of the car was littered with all the detritus of a stake-out: cigarette packets, hamburger cartons, newspaper reeking of old fish and chips, drink cans, crisp packets, sweet wrappers and heavily thumbed copies of several tabloids, the pages no longer in any sort of order and not one crossword more than a third completed.

Captain Don Headley of the SAS had kept them on the go ever since his initial briefing, and all the teams were longing for the exercise to end. Those who passed were due to proceed to the next stage of training, but Paul and Colin were having serious doubts about their original decision to transfer to the new anti-terrorist squad that was being set up.

'You know what I can't stick?' Colin said after a while.

'What's that?'

'The way Don manages to go without sleep for days on bloody end and still keep his cool.'

He wiped his brow with the back of his hand. 'Me, I feel shagged after one night out.'

Paul grinned. 'He's a right smooth bugger, isn't he? Still, with a little luck he'll sod off back to Hereford soon and leave us in peace.'

The rain lashed against the car window and drummed on the roof. Colin shivered and slid deeper into his leather jacket. The zip was open to the waist and his stomach bulged over his belt. Paul looked at him with distaste.

'In a way it's kind of cosy in here, isn't it?' Colin said, hunting around on the back seat for a paper to read.

'Speak for yourself.' Paul eyed the debris. 'If this is your idea of cosy I can imagine what your house looks like. It explains why your wife left you.'

'Nah, silly cow was worse than I was. You should have seen the kitchen. Looked like a shagging bomb had hit it.'

Paul could well imagine. He had seen the food stains on the walls and ceilings of Colin's office. The man was a walking disaster area.

He rubbed a hole in the breath misting the windscreen. Outside it was starting to lighten. Rain came down vertically, bouncing on the tarmac and rushing in the gutters. He sighed, misting the peep-hole, then looked at his watch for the umpteenth time.

'When do you reckon we'll be ordered to move?' Colin asked.

Paul shrugged. 'Your guess is as good as mine.'

They had been carrying out a series of surveillance tasks in their assigned area, but after their last one they had been directed to their present location to await retasking. It looked a prosperous residential street. The houses were mostly large, with trim hedges, large front gardens and no doubt even larger gardens to the rear.

At the end of the street he saw the large, white shape of a Transit turn towards them. It cruised slowly closer, stopping some thirty yards away. With the water coursing down the windscreen it was impossible to see it distinctly, but he wasn't bothered. It was probably just a plumber or decorator arriving early for a job in one of the houses.

However, the next moment he made out the vague outline of figures bundling from the back of the van and running towards one of the larger houses.

'What do you make of that?'

Colin grunted, not lifting his eyes from the nude in the paper. Her lips were peeled back in a provocative smile, eyes half-closed, breasts thrust out as if someone had just shoved her hard in the small of the back and she was about to topple downstairs.

'Colin, I'm fucking talking to you. Look.'

Reluctantly Colin made his own peep-hole with his sleeve and peered through it at the house. He was just in time to see one of the men kick his way through the side gate.

'Fucking hell!' He dropped the paper. 'It must be another part of the bloody exercise. That bastard! He sent us here for a break and then hits us with an incident. What the fuck do we do?'

Paul thought for a moment. 'Hang on,' he said, playing for time while he ordered his thoughts. 'They're probably supposed to be terrorists. It'll be a safe house or something.'

'Don't be daft. They wouldn't go bundling in like that, kicking in doors if it was a safe house, would they?'

Paul cursed himself silently. He liked to think of himself as the brighter of the two, but for once Colin was right.

'Then they're probably seizing the house to use as a base for the duration of an attack on the airport.'

'Yeah!' Colin chirped, becoming enthusiastic. All of a sudden their fatigue was forgotten and they sat up and kicked aside the debris littering the floor of the car as they tried to work out how they were expected to react.

'Perhaps they're planning to fire a shoulder-launched anti-aircraft missile from the back garden, or something?' Colin said, his tongue hardly able to keep pace with his ideas.

Paul thought about it and rubbed his chin. 'Could be. We're right under the main flight path all right. Yeah, that's probably it.'

'So what do we do then?' Colin blinked at him, lost for a solution.

'There's too many of them for us to do anything. I reckon we report in and wait for backup.'

'Good thinking. Will you do it or shall I?'

Paul reached for the radio. 'It's my turn. You bogged up the last one.'

He pressed the transmitter switch and spoke slowly and clearly, reporting the incident and requesting support. The message was acknowledged and when he had replaced the handset he sat back with a self-satisfied smile.

It was a couple of minutes before the radio buzzed into life again and the voice of Don Headley rasped into the stagnant air of the car.

'Echo Two, what's all this about a van? Over.'

Paul and Colin swapped grins. 'He's playing dumb,' Colin whispered, as if Don himself were actually in the car.

Paul repeated his report. There was another pause before Don came back and said, 'It's nothing to do with the ex.'

'Yeah, yeah,' Paul crooned easily. 'Look, just log it down that we did the right thing and asked for backup. I know a bunch of terrorists when I see one.'

Don sounded amused. 'If that's the case I suggest you get the hell out of there. I repeat, there are no exercise activities planned in your area for the rest of the day. Out.'

The line went dead. Paul and Colin sat staring at one another.

'Reckon they could be decorators or something? Builders perhaps. They looked fit buggers.'

Paul laughed uneasily. 'They can't be terrorists, can they? Can you imagine it? Here in the middle of bleeding Southall?'

Colin nodded and scrabbled around on the floor for his discarded newspaper.

Suddenly, from inside the house they heard a muffled crack. They stared at each other again, but this time their faces paled.

'Did you hear that?'

'What the fuck was it?'

There was a second crack, and then a third.

'Oh, shit. That's a bloody shooter.'

Colin opened his door and started to pull himself out of the car. Paul snatched at his sleeve and tugged him back.

'Where do you think you're going, Humphrey sodding Bogart? In case you've forgotten, we don't carry firearms.'

'Well, we can't just sit here.'

Paul grabbed at the radio and called the station where the exercise control had been established.

'Get me the guv. And be quick about it!' he snapped.

'He's in a meeting. He told me he was not to be interrupted,' the duty operator replied.

'Listen, you tit, I don't give a fuck. We've got a real incident here. There's shooting in Bramley Road. Tell them to get some armed assistance here on the double. Got that?'

There was a pause before the operator asked nervously, 'This is part of the exercise, right?'

Paul almost slammed the handset against the dashboard in frustration. 'No, it fucking isn't! This is for real. Now do as I say or I'll crawl down the sodding air waves and rip your throat out!'

'So it's not part of the ex?'

Colin swore and started out of the car again.

'No,' Paul persevered with all the self-control he could muster. 'Now pass my message, right?'

'Roger. Out.'

He looked up to see that Colin was almost at the driveway, then quickly got out and rushed to join him. It was only

16

when they were opening the gate that they noticed the man still standing beside the dirty white van. He appeared to be unconcerned by the gunshots from inside the house and when they caught his eyes he smiled pleasantly.

'Hang on, let's ask the geezer what's going on. Maybe it's nothing.'

They went towards him and as they drew near Colin whispered, 'It's a Paki.'

'Brilliant, Watson. Any more deductions?'

The man stepped towards them. 'Can I help you?'

They were taken aback by his Oxford accent.

'Excuse me, sir, but is this your van?'

The man turned round as if to check it was still there. 'Yes,' he said, then, as an afterthought, 'May I enquire who's asking?'

Remembering procedure and feeling suddenly a bit stupid, Paul fumbled in his jacket pocket and produced his identity card. 'Police,' he said.

The man smiled. 'Splendid. How can I help you?'

Becoming impatient, Colin said, 'Was that a gunshot we heard just now?'

The man's eyes widened theatrically. 'A gunshot? I certainly hope not.'

'Well, what was it then?'

'I really couldn't say. I didn't hear anything.' He turned to the driver, who had got out of the van and joined him. In contrast to the two policemen they were both tall, lean and fit.

Paul glanced back at the house. 'Would you come with us, please, sir?'

The man shrugged. 'If you insist, officer.' He said something quickly to the driver in a language that the policemen could not understand.

Keeping the man in front of him, Paul walked down the driveway towards the house. As the front door was shut they veered towards the side gate. 'After you, if you don't mind, sir,' he said. Again the man shrugged politely, still smiling.

A window showed into the kitchen and although the room itself was empty they could hear something being smashed elsewhere in the house. Before they could ask any more questions the man turned and explained, 'We're doing some construction work, you see. A really wealthy fellow, the owner. He wanted all sorts of alterations done.'

Colin relaxed, whispering, 'I thought so. Sodding builders. The boss is going to roast us alive when the heavies turn up and find out. We'll be the laughing-stock of the whole bloody force.'

They reached the back of the house and saw a large, well-kept garden stretching down to a tall hedge at the bottom.

'Come on,' Paul said miserably. 'Let's get this over with.' He turned to the man. 'We'd better check it out if you don't mind.'

For the first time the man's calm smile faltered and a second later it died altogether. His eyes chilled and narrowed and he sighed heavily. 'Of course. I understand. I very much regret the inconvenience to you though.'

Paul chuckled pleasantly. 'It's no bother, sir. Just a peek and then we'll leave you in peace. So as we can say we did our duty.'

'Naturally. Duty,' the man said, his voice low and matter of fact. He seemed to be searching for something in his pocket and when he pulled out a small automatic pistol Paul and Colin stared at it dumbly, the shock not even registering.

'We all have our duty to perform,' the man said. He took a single step backwards, widened his stance and shot Colin in the solar plexus with a rapid double tap. Colin staggered against the wall, his mouth opening and shutting like a fish out of water, and then sank to the floor. Paul watched in mesmerized horror as the smoking muzzle flicked on to its new target. Behind it, the man seemed almost apologetic for what he had just done, and, more particularly, for what he was about to do.

'If only you'd stayed in your car and minded your own business. But you know what they say about curiosity and the cat.'

Paul held out his hand as if ordering a car to stop, as the first of the bullets spat straight through his palm and hammered into his ribcage. He clutched at the wound and his knees gave way.

'You bastard,' he muttered, his words sounding distant and garbled. He didn't seem able to get his tongue around the syllables he had used so often in the past. 'You fucking . . .'

He fell on to his back and stared up at the foul grey sky. Rain stung his face but it was strangely refreshing, a counter to the ache he was just beginning to feel. Suddenly the sky filled with the man's enquiring face looking down at him. Then he saw the muzzle again, lowering, getting monstrously large until he felt its warm metal pushing into his mouth. He tried to speak, to plead, but the cold muzzle was being forced upwards, pressing into the roof of his mouth, the line of the short, hard barrel aiming directly through the slim bone and into the brain.

There were words in his head, something about being so terribly sorry. Wrong place and wrong time. The man's voice was calm as if talking about the weather. The weather. It was a shit-awful day to die, Paul thought, as the pistol flinched at the sudden pressure being applied to the trigger.

2

By the time Don Headley received the news the phones in the ops room were already buzzing with enquiries from the press. At first he couldn't believe what had happened. Reality had broken into the middle of his exercise and two men were dead.

As soon as he could he got away from his desk and drove to Bramley Road. It was mid-morning and the traffic was heavy. On all sides drivers drummed their steering wheels in frustration as the long queues edged slowly forwards. The rain had stopped and a harsh winter light percolated through the thick layers of cloud, muting the colours into one contin- uous semblance of grey. It was a part of the country Don particularly hated, the dense belt of urban wasteland spread thickly around central London. Successive decades had added to it, pushing it out ever further until towns that had once counted themselves lucky to be outside the city now found themselves being sucked in, not enjoying full membership but rather taken on board as second-class citizens in a dubious club.

Hounslow, Isleworth, Sunbury, Feltham – the names rolled past, each representing an identical sprawl of little red houses and car-packed residential streets. It wasn't so long ago that such roads would have boasted hardly a single vehicle parked at the kerbside, but increasing prosperity had combined with thoughtless marketing by the car manufacturers, whose eyes were solely on profit, and it had resulted in nearly every household owning at least one vehicle. Along either side of every road parked cars were jammed in nose to tail. It struck Don as a case of suicide by self-strangulation on a national scale. No one individual was prepared to sacrifice his car, not even with the prospect looming of the next generation gassing itself. Public transport was overcrowded and stank, so what was the incentive?

For an incentive to work and change a lifestyle it had to produce a more immediate threat. But then with smoking even that hadn't worked, Don reflected as he waited impatiently behind a lorry that was belching obnoxious blue fumes. It was almost possible to predict to a smoker the year in which his habit would bring about his agonizing death, and yet nine times out of ten he would continue. What was the answer? Don was buggered if he knew. Perhaps the species was on track for extinction and it was as simple as that. Self-destruction had replaced self-preservation as the prime motivation in the human psyche, and no one had even noticed. He grinned sardonically. They had probably been too busy watching *Gladiators*.

It was another half hour before he drew up outside the house. A policeman came to his window to wave him on but he produced a pass and was allowed to go in search of a parking space. The curtains in the neighbouring houses twitched as inquisitive eyes followed him out of the car and down the driveway. The couple in the house on the opposite side of the road were less circumspect and stood at their open doorway, mugs of tea in their hands, interested to find their mundane existence disrupted by something as exciting as a murder.

Chief Inspector Rod Chiltern met Don at the front of the house.

'The SOCO's round the back with his lads. Be careful not to touch anything.'

Don scowled at him, resenting the caution. Nevertheless, he was only there as an observer. It was police business and had nothing to do with the SAS. So far.

He followed Chiltern down the narrow path. The first thing he saw when he emerged at the back outside the kitchen door was the body of Colin Field. It was propped up against the wall as if he had just sat down for a rest. His legs were splayed, the scuffed trainers out of sync with the portly figure of their owner. His head was cocked heavily to one side, the eyes open a slit, lips pursed. A trickle of blood had dried to a crack of dark purple running from the corner of his mouth to his chin, but the real sign of damage was the blood on the red brick of the wall, splashed liberally as if a child had flung a can of paint at it.

A couple of yards from him, Paul Robins lay on the crazy-paving terrace. Don noticed the shattered hand and could imagine how Paul had received the wound. The wound in his chest was bad but he judged it had probably not been fatal. That had been reserved for the head shot.

He moved carefully round to the far side.

'Jesus,' he whistled.

Chiltern nodded. 'Not much chance of giving him the kiss of life, is there?' he said.

The explosion of the gun in the confined space of the mouth had blown out most of the teeth, propelling them through the thin wall of the cheeks. But where the bullet had exited through the top and back of the skull there was a gaping hole. It had taken the larger portion of the brain with it and slammed it in a rough fan shape on the paving stones.

'How well did you know them?' Chiltern asked.

Don shrugged. 'Reasonably. They'd been on my course for a while and you get to know the guys quickly that way.'

He was being polite, tempering his opinion because he knew that Chiltern had worked with both the dead men for several years. In truth Don had found them to be a couple of no-hopers, overweight, inefficient, dim-witted and bungling. Just the stupid sods, in fact, to walk straight into the middle of an armed gang without so much as a catapult. But no one deserved to die like this, he thought. Not even these two.

He crouched down beside them and looked around. The scene-of-crime officer had done a thorough sweep and every-thing that might be needed as evidence was circled with a thin chalk line. Principal among these items were several cartridge cases. Don asked if he might have a closer look at one of them and the SOCO nodded.

'Don't bugger up the prints, and put it back where you found it,' he snapped, busy with a measuring tape, marking the distance from Colin's body to the point where he estimated the firer must have been standing.

Don took a pair of gloves from his pocket and slipped one of them on. Carefully, he picked up the nearest of the cases and examined it. It was 9mm calibre. Powerful enough to silence a full-grown man, especially at almost point-blank range. No wonder Colin had been flung against the wall with such force, he thought.

But there was something unusual about it and a moment later Don realized what it was. He had come across its kind only once before. Several years ago he had been on secondment to the Sultan of Oman's army. The Sultan's quartermaster had done some shopping around on the open market for ammunition in an effort to cut costs. British ammunition had proved the most expensive, and he had finally opted for a batch of Pakistani-made rounds, both 7.62mm and 9mm. They hadn't performed as effectively or as consistently as the British-made ammunition, several of the rounds misfiring and causing stoppages owing to an insufficient charge of powder in the brass case. But they had done the job and Pakistani ammunition had been used a great deal thereafter.

Turning the cartridge case in his fingers, Don was convinced that this was from the same source. He replaced it in its white chalk circle, where it looked as if it was about to be part of some Satanic ceremony.

He voiced his opinion to the SOCO, who grunted and said, 'Right now I couldn't give a stuff. But thanks all the same. I'll get the lads on to it back at the lab. If you're right they'll be able to tell you the exact factory it came from, right down to the postcode.'

Don went into the kitchen, where Chiltern was receiving a report from one of his men. He looked up as Don came in. 'Nice mess, isn't it?'

'That's what happens when you get in the way of a 9mm bullet or two.'

'Well, there's another two dead upstairs,' Chiltern added, shaking his head. 'Right sodding blood-bath this is turning into.'

He led the way into the hall and up the stairs. Everywhere were signs of the intruders' recent presence. Furniture had been overturned, pictures ripped from the walls and ornaments smashed.

'It looks like my own place after the kids have had a party,' Chiltern said, grinning.

They found the next body sprawled on the landing. It was the body of a middle-aged man of Indian appearance. A bullet wound in the back of the left leg indicated that he had been brought down trying to run away from his attackers. Thereafter someone had made a crude attempt at interrogating him. A heavy metal file had been applied to the surfaces of his teeth until they were almost completely rubbed level with the blood-soaked gums.

'That's an old Spetsnaz trick,' Don said in amazement.

'Who?'

'Spetsnaz. Soviet special forces.'

Chiltern winced at the gruesome spectacle. 'What the fuck would they be doing in Southall?'

Don shrugged. 'I don't know, but during the Cold War they sent training teams abroad, just like we did.'

'Passing on their techniques, you mean?'

'Exactly.'

The man's eyes were wide open and staring, bulging out of their sockets with the agony. A cloth had been stuffed at the back of his mouth to prevent him screaming and he had been finished off with a bullet to the back of the head.

'Who was he?' Don asked.

'Just a guy who ran a chain of curry restaurants in the area,' Chiltern replied. 'I've ordered takeaways from them myself. Bloody good they were too.'

'Any idea why anyone would want to do this to him?'

Chiltern shrugged. 'Not a clue.' He smirked. 'Perhaps someone got Delhi belly after his vindaloo.'

Don ignored the wisecrack. 'You said there were a couple of bodies?'

The policeman pointed to an open door. From inside Don could hear the click and whirr of an automatic camera. He stepped over the dead man and went on down the corridor. The bare legs were the first thing he saw, protruding from behind the bed. The police photographer looked up.

'Nasty. Very nasty. It's as clinical as an execution.'

He moved aside to allow Don a clear line of sight to the body. It was a woman. Presumably the man's wife. They seemed to Don to be of a similar age. She was dressed in a bright-blue sari trimmed in gold. Expensive. He studied the room. It was obviously the home of a well-to-do family.

Unlike her husband's, the woman's eyes were tightly shut; clenched, as if trying to shut out some unpleasantness. One hand was clasped to her throat in shock and the other held a candlestick.

'Looks like she tried to defend herself,' Chiltern said.

A single bullet between the shoulder-blades had thwarted any such attempt, ending her life immediately.

While Chiltern spoke to the SOCO, who had now finished in the garden and climbed up the stairs to start work in the house, Don wandered out on to the landing again and explored the other rooms. There were two bathrooms, a guest bedroom, tastefully decorated but unlived in, and a large room clearly belonging to an older man. There were smashed photograph frames on the floor, and a walking stick snapped in two.

But it was the last room that caught his attention most. Posters hung off the walls, pictures of pop stars and horses. The furnishings were in pinks and pale, gentle shades, and the clothes torn from the ransacked drawers were those of a young woman. More interestingly, there was a single small stain on the carpet close by the door. Don stooped and examined it. The next moment he shouted down the landing to the SOCO.

'I think you'd better take a look at this.'

The SOCO and Chiltern padded down the corridor towards him.

'What is it?'

Don pointed at the stain. 'Looks like blood, if you ask me.'

The SOCO sighed in exasperation. 'Is that all? The whole sodding house is awash with blood, and you raise the alarm over one tiny stain.'

'Yes, but look at the room. Someone's been in here recently.'

'Brilliant! I can tell you're army.' The SOCO shook his head.

But Chiltern saw what Don was getting at. 'Don's right.'

'Thank you,' Don said. 'Have you found the body of a girl yet?'

The SOCO blanched. 'No.'

'Then I suggest you start looking for her because there was a girl in this room less than an hour ago. Look.' He pointed at the dressing table. 'The make-up's open. Don't tell me the intruders wanted to touch up their lipstick.'

'Shit,' Chiltern hissed. 'If they've taken her we could have a hostage crisis on our hands as well as a quadruple murder. What the hell's going on here?' He turned on his heel and marched back to the stairs. 'Don, you come with me. This is police business now. I shouldn't have allowed you in here in the first place. Your assistance and interest are much appreciated, but I'll handle things from now on. Oh, and by the way, I suggest you end that exercise of yours. Reality's got in the way. Thanks for everything, but you can return to Hereford. Send me a report on the guys you think might have passed when you've got a moment to write them up.'

He led Don to the front door and ushered him out into the front garden. It had started to rain again and as he sauntered back to his car Don turned up the collar of his jacket and hunched his shoulders against the sharp cold. He had seen more than his fair share of action, but the sight of the murders had shocked him. There was something particularly repulsive about the sight of a dead body in an otherwise normal setting. It was bad enough on the battlefield, but in a comfortable house in the middle of suburbia it smacked of the most appalling decay. Two of the men on his course had been butchered in cold blood and in a way he felt responsible for it. They had radioed in to report their sighting of a van and although it had been a police responsibility to dispatch assistance, Don had noticed that there had been little sense of urgency. No one had really believed Paul's message, assuming it to be just another part of the exercise programme. Because of the delay they were dead.

He unlocked the door of his car and got in, turning the key and gunning the accelerator as the engine fired. He glanced at the clock on the dashboard. He could be home in Hereford by teatime. All of a sudden he wanted nothing more than to be out on the motorway and burning up the miles of tarmac between London's dismal outskirts and the fresh air of the Severn estuary, the green hills of Wales beckoning from beyond.

Chiltern had been right. It was a police matter and nothing to do with a soldier. Don's job had simply been to run the exercise and help the police with their anti-terrorist training. What could such an occurrence possibly have to do with him? It was just bad luck that Colin and Paul had got caught up in the middle of something that was too big for them. They were dumb for getting involved.

Blanking it out of his mind, he headed for the nearest junction of the M4, just east of Heathrow, and threaded his way out into the traffic. The rush hour was tailing to a close but it was always busy on this stretch. Within half an hour, however, the spaces between the cars expanded and soon he had his foot flat on the floor, feeling the miles being eaten up beneath his wheels.

No doubt there would be the usual hearty jokes in the mess when he got back to the barracks. The older he got the more the humour grated. It was all very well when you were young but after a while you started to see that there wasn't much to laugh about in death. Perhaps that was the time to quit.

But as he drove he found his mind flicking back always to the same thing. Not to the bodies of Colin or Paul, the exploded brains on the paving stones and the blood on the wall, nor the body on the landing or in the bedroom, the candlestick clasped pathetically in its small, tight fist. But rather to the empty bedroom with the posters and the untouched make-up jars. Somewhere, if he was right, a young woman had been taken hostage. And although the matter was out of his hands he couldn't shake off the feeling that somehow he hadn't heard the last of it. Somehow he knew that he would be involved with it again.

'Are you sure she can breathe?'

'Don't worry.'

'I'm not worrying,' Ceda Bandram said slowly, glowering over his shoulder at Ali Shaffer, who sat sprawled across the back seat. 'I don't want to arrive only to find that she's suffocated.' He stabbed a finger at Ali. 'You would be held personally responsible. Remember that.'

Ali sniggered and waved a large, nonchalant paw. 'I drilled holes in the underside of the boot. A shame considering the newness of the car, but it couldn't be helped, I suppose. It'll all be charged to the expense account.'

Bandram stared ahead at the slow-moving traffic. Since the events at the house he had changed into a sweatshirt, slacks and moccasins. The van had been dumped in a lock-up garage that had been hired for the purpose and he estimated it would be a good many weeks before it was discovered. By then they would be several thousand miles away.

The team had split up and were now travelling by separate routes and methods of transport to the next rendezvous and the next leg of their onward journey. For himself, Ali and the driver, there had been a waiting BMW and of course he had ensured that the hostage had been brought with him. Every man in the team had been hand-picked but even so he made a habit of never trusting anyone but himself with the most delicate part of any mission.

The only man whom he had not selected was Ali. There was nothing he could do about it, however. Ali had been forced upon him by the boss. He was another relation, although Ceda had never known much about him. But that was the way with families in Pakistan, complex networks of relatives with every so often the discovery of some hidden black sheep. And Ali was such a cupboard skeleton if ever there was one. Ceda had been disgusted with the evident glee with which Ali had conducted the interrogation at the house. It was not that he was squeamish, but there were ways of doing things. One didn't have to enjoy the more unpleasant tasks of the business. Some unfortunate things might always be necessary, but maintaining a sense of propriety kept one separated from the beast. In Ceda's view Ali had crossed that threshold. He glanced back at him again, but Ali was staring happily out of the window humming to himself. His torture of the poor individual at the house seemed to be completely forgotten.

Ceda consoled himself with the thought that there were a great many pitfalls before the team finally reached safety. There would be plenty of opportunities for a fatal accident to befall Ali. Ceda for one would not mourn his loss.

The driver coughed and nodded towards a lay-by. A police car and motorcycle were parked at the roadside, the men scanning the traffic. They had already flagged down two white vans and were attempting to attract the attention of a third. Ceda smiled to himself. He was due to switch vehicles at least once more before the final RV and was confident that even if the police discovered the original van they would be unable to track him in time.

He reached down the side of the seat and pulled out a road map, unfolded it on his lap and began studying the markings he had made earlier. Bored with his humming, Ali leaned forward, crossing his arms on the back of Ceda's seat and peering over his shoulder to get a look at the map.

'Where to now, cousin?' he asked sarcastically.

'Don't call me that,' Ceda said coolly.

Ali shrugged. 'I thought blood was supposed to be thicker than water?'

'You ought to know. You've seen enough of it.'

'You didn't do so bad yourself, you hypocrite. Dropping those two cops like that.' He shaped his hand like a gun and put it to Ceda's head, mimicking the shooting. 'Bang, bang. You're dead. Nice work. A bit cold and clinical for my liking, but professional. Uncle would approve.'

'I didn't do it for Uncle's approval. In fact I didn't want to do it at all.'

'Oh no, of course not. I forgot. You're the ex-army officer. Death before dishonour, and all that. I'm sorry.' He sat back with a derisory laugh. 'You're full of shit.'

Ceda gritted his teeth, resisting the urge to go for the gun in his belt. The driver glanced nervously across at him and he relaxed. He was responsible for the whole team, not just for himself. He couldn't afford to lose his temper, and certainly not over a dick-head like Ali.

'Where's the next switch?' the driver asked, keen to divert the conversation away from the rivalry between the two men. It had been evident to most of the team members from the outset but they all knew and trusted Ceda, and were confident that he would see them safely through.

'Not the next service station but the one after that. The cars have been left in the car park. I've got the registration numbers here.' He patted his breast pocket.

'It seems such a waste just to ditch the car,' the driver added, stroking the dashboard lovingly. 'She's a beauty.'

Ceda smiled. 'That's business. Just be thankful you're not footing the bill.'

Ali perked up from the rear. 'Talking of beauties, how do you intend to transfer the cargo?' He jabbed a thumb at the boot. 'You can't just lift her out in full view of everyone.'

'Don't worry. That's been seen to. The car'll be parked in a nice private spot. No one will see.'

He turned on the radio to cut short any further talk with Ali, pressing the automatic tuning button and watching the digital display purr rapidly through the frequencies. There was some traffic news warning of jams on the M4, and he checked the map to see if it would interfere with their escape.

'Problem?' the driver asked.

'Could be. It's after the next switch. It could have cleared by the time we get there, but it might be wise to make a detour.'

'Won't that confuse the others?'

'It might, but it'll be better than getting stuck in a tailback and waiting for the police to catch up with us. Every extra hour we spend in this miserable country increases the chance that they'll be on to us.'

There was a metallic click from the back of the car and Ceda glanced around to see Ali playing with his pistol.

'Personally I don't care if they do catch up with us,' Ali said. He aimed down the barrel of his gun. 'Just let them try and take me.' He squeezed the trigger and the hammer clicked shut on an empty chamber.

'Keep that bloody thing out of sight,' Ceda snapped. The traffic was light on the present stretch of road but there was always the chance of another motorist seeing the gun and reporting it to the police.

It was another half an hour before they saw the sign advertising the service station. The driver waited for Ceda's confirmatory signal before indicating and pulling over into the slow lane. Ceda adjusted the wing mirror beside him and checked that they were not being followed. The lane behind was clear. No other car appeared to be coming after them.

The car slowed as the driver worked down through the gears, tracing the white arrows marking the route for cars wanting the main car park. It was moderately busy. Rows of large lorries were drawn up in line and in the other section the only available spaces were the ones farthest from the restaurant and shops. They cruised up and down until Ceda said, 'There it is. The grey Ford.'

'That's a bit of a come-down,' Ali drawled from the back. Ceda ignored him. 'Park next to it.'

Two orange plastic cones had kept the adjacent space free of cars and as the car slowed, Ceda darted out and moved them, waving the BMW forward until it was close alongside and the driver cut the engine. The boots of the two cars were angled away from the main public areas and were shielded from view by a screen of trees.

Ceda cursed.

'What's the matter?' the driver asked as he got out and stretched, his muscles cramped after the long drive.

'Those idiots who did the recce. They must have come here in the summer. The trees would have been covered in leaves then. Now look at them.'

He was right. The leaves had long since fallen, washed into a brown pulp by prolonged heavy rain, and it was possible to see the shopping area through the bare branches.

'Well, it can't be helped.'

'Do you want us to transfer the girl now?' the driver asked nervously.

'No. We'll wait until the others get here and then do it. I want to have a look around in any case.'

'Good, I'll come with you,' Ali said brightly.

Ceda considered telling him to forget it, but decided not to.

'You stay here,' he ordered the driver. 'If you see any of the others don't make it obvious that we're together.'

'Got it.'

Trying to forget that Ali was beside him, Ceda walked briskly towards the main building. His familiarity with Britain was one of the reasons he had been selected for the mission. In his army days he had been sent for training to Sandhurst and since then he had been back to attend further courses in the country. During those times he had used the opportunity to travel widely. Later, after his resignation, he had worked briefly in Britain, staying with relatives in London and Birmingham. He felt comfortable moving through the rail and road networks, while still maintaining the psychological distance of the visitor. On the present mission that distance was a vital safeguard against carelessness. Familiarity might well breed contempt, but complacency was a far more dangerous by-product.

After a trip to the toilets they went into the concourse and stood for a moment surveying the array of shops and eating places. There was the choice between a sit-down restaurant, a hamburger takeaway bar and a cafeteria. Without asking Ali which one he preferred, Ceda pointed towards the cafeteria and grunted.

They each took a tray and tagged on to the short queue. Plastic-wrapped sandwiches and salads were stacked behind a glass-fronted cabinet, and at the next counter a selection of hot dishes steamed under heat lamps.

'What'll it be, love?' the waitress asked when their turn came.

Ali flashed her a disarming smile. 'The All Day Breakfast looks impossible to resist . . .'

The waitress reached for a plate and started to shovel on bacon and eggs.

'. . . but I'll go for the cottage pie.'

She glared at him and with a heavy sigh tipped the bacon and eggs back in their containers. 'Cottage pie? Are you sure?' she asked, taking a clean plate.

Ali hummed. 'Yeees,' he said slowly. 'I think so.'

He felt a sharp dig in his ribs and looked round to find Ceda staring hard at him.

'Yes, cottage pie,' he said with an air of finality.

In an attempt to placate the waitress Ceda helped himself, bustling Ali along to the till, picking up two coffees on the way. When they had paid and were sitting at a table he leaned across and said threateningly, 'Try that again and I'll shoot you, in public or not.'

'What have I done?' Ali said innocently.

'Drawn attention to yourself, that's what. She'll remember you now, you idiot. If you'd kept your stupid mouth shut you'd be just another customer. But oh no, not you. When the police start asking questions she'll be able to give them a full description of the two of us. Are you satisfied?'

'Don't worry about it. We'll be long gone by then.'

Afraid lest he lose his temper, Ceda started his food, eating more quickly than he would have liked to, feeling as if the eyes of everyone in the place were upon them. This is not good, he thought. This moron could jeopardize the whole team.

The moment he had finished his food he drained his coffee cup and prepared to leave.

'Hang on. I'm not ready yet,' Ali protested.

'I don't give a shit. We're going.'

While they had been eating, Ceda had noticed the rest of the team members arriving in twos and threes. Each group sat alone, acknowledging each other with only the most cursory of glances. When they saw Ceda make a move, they moved too.

Ceda was just making his way out towards the entrance when Ali stopped.

'I need a leak.'

'Again? Be quick about it.'

The other teams walked on past, looking at Ceda with sympathy. There was no love lost between any of them and Ali. Through the glass entrance doors Ceda could see the teams making their way towards their new cars. It would all be over soon, he consoled himself. They would soon be out of the country and in the clear, and as soon as they were back home he would speak to the boss and tell him how the choice of Ali had been a disastrous one.

It was the raised voices that first alerted him to the approach of trouble. From inside the toilets Ceda heard a shout followed by scuffling. He moved rapidly towards the entrance but as he rounded the tiled corner a single gunshot rang out.

The sight that greeted him when he burst through the swing door stopped him in his tracks. A man in the blue overalls of a lorry driver lay sprawled across the floor, blood spreading from his chest across the white lino of the floor. Standing over him, Ali looked up at Ceda. In his right hand he held his pistol, smoke seeping from the muzzle.

'He went for me,' he said simply, as if that explained everything.

Against the far wall, three other men backed away in horror. The door to one of the cubicles opened and a man came out, his face frozen in fear.

'You idiot!' Ceda roared and made a grab for the pistol. But Ali snatched it out of reach, his eyes warning him not to try again.

'He insulted me, I said. No one calls me names and gets away with it.'

Without stopping to listen Ceda spun on his heel and made for the exit. 'Come on,' he shouted at Ali.

In the space of seconds the whole painfully prepared escape procedure had collapsed about him. The pre-positioned cars, the garage hideaway, the recced routes – everything. All to no avail. Within minutes the police would be on to them. Speed was now their only chance – and even that might not save them.

3

Don Headley swerved on an impulse into the slow lane, carving up a lorry in the process. The driver blew his horn and Don waved an apology as he veered off the motorway and headed up the exit road into the service station. He had been driving for well over an hour and felt in need of a strong coffee. Because of the exercise with the police he had not had a decent night's sleep for several days and his eyes had started to blink shut as the motorway unfurled beneath him, its rhythmic pulse on his tyres soothing his nerves and lulling him into a fatal sleep. He had to wake himself up if he was to make it to Hereford in one piece.

Some way back he had wound down his window, letting the cold air blast in. For a while it had worked, but since he was well used to exposure to the elements even that had eventually been blunted by his fatigue. Now, only a substantial intake of caffeine would do the trick.

It was a service station he had used many times before. He had lost count of the number of times he had made the M4 trip between Wales and London, but over the years he reckoned he must have sampled the delights of every service station along the way. Most of them were pretty rough; various companies had bought them as part of a job lot, stamping each one with its own insipid identity. It had got to the stage where Don preferred to take his own sandwiches and a flask of coffee, and simply sit in the car park by himself before filling up with petrol and pressing on. That morning, however, there had been no time for such preparations, so he turned towards the restaurant and shops and looked for a parking place.

There was the usual assortment of visitors, families with young kids, sales reps in their Fords, Vauxhalls and Rovers, the occasional foreign tourist coping with the difficulties of driving on the left, and a variety of coaches and articulated lorries. An icy wind cut savagely across the car park, sweeping in across the surrounding open fields. He hurriedly wound up his window and shivered, deciding that he would need his jacket once out of the car.

He found a vacant space reasonably close to the buildings, swung his car in and switched off the engine. The car rocked in the stiff breeze that howled along the avenues of vehicles, struggling to get in. When he opened the door the wind grasped at it and tugged it wide. Don stepped out on to the tarmac and turned up his collar, then locked the door and set off towards the main entrance. He had gone only a few yards when he heard a commotion and looked up to see two men pushing their way out of the concourse. In their haste they shouldered aside an elderly couple, almost knocking the man to the floor.

'Bloody impatient bastards,' Don muttered. Everyone was in such a rush these days.

The old man staggered but managed to regain his balance, turning after the men and shaking a wizened fist at them. He shouted something but his words were lost in the wind.

But something else was happening. Through the double glass doors Don could see people throwing themselves to the floor while others scurried for cover. In his half-awake state, the images refused to order themselves in his brain. It failed to register that there was anything untoward about it all. He reached the doors and only then did he hear the shouting.

'He's got a gun!'

'Someone call the police!'

'Get a doctor! There's a man dying in here!'

Suddenly Don's head cleared. He took one look at the chaos inside the concourse and then spun to see where the two men had gone. A large lorry was just pulling to a halt, obscuring his view. He ran around it and scanned the car park. Two cars were tearing away from the service station, but through a thin screen of bare trees he just caught a glimpse of the men ducking into a waiting car. The engine was already turning over, white plumes of exhaust hanging in the cold air, and the next moment the wheels were spinning as it set off.

Don's hand went automatically to his chest and felt the reassuring bulge of the shoulder holster. There might just be time to head them off and get a couple of clear shots at the car before it disappeared past the petrol pumps.

He sprinted past the rows of parked cars. People stared at him in surprise and alarm, unaware of what had just happened in the restaurant area. Someone called out a warning and Don narrowly managed to avoid running head-long into an approaching van. He veered to one side, bouncing off the sides of it and regaining his balance with difficulty. On the far side of the car park he could see the car and its occupants accelerating away. It was heading in the opposite direction to the other two cars. In Don's mind the connection was quickly made. They were all part of the same team. He had seen that the men were Asian and could hardly believe what his instinct told him: that they were the ones from the Bramley Road incident.

However, unlike the two cars that had screamed away towards the exit, the one he was running after was making for a barrier that led out of the rear of the service station on to a minor road. It was a restricted entrance for use by the service-station staff only, and from it access could be gained to the local town and road network. Whoever was in charge of the car obviously had his head screwed on. The other two, by taking to the motorway, were in effect entering a potential trap. The next exit from it was several miles away and by then the police might be able to have a cordon in place. At the very least they would be able to position observers who could report on the cars' direction and progress to enable armed officers to pursue them.

The other car, by taking a back road, was not restricting itself in any such way. It would be able to go in any number of directions and so multiply its chance of escaping.

Don covered the last few yards to the end of one of the rows and as he reached the last parked car he skidded to his knees and drew his 9mm Browning pistol. Holding it in a two-handed combat grip, he steadied himself against the car door and brought the gun into the aim, waiting for his target to appear and enter his sights.

There was the sound of squealing rubber and the car roared into view, the tyres spinning as the driver swung it round towards the barrier. Don waited until he had a clear line of sight and then squeezed off a rapid double tap at the rear window, where he was able to make out the silhouette of a man sitting upright in the centre. He saw the glass frost as his bullets found their mark but the car continued towards the barrier.

He dropped his point of aim to the fuel tank and was about to fire another double tap when something stopped him, freezing his finger on the trigger's fragile second pressure. The image of the girl's room flashed through his mind. If they were indeed the same men from Bramley Road, then they had taken a hostage. Of course it was possible that she was in one of the other two cars, but there was also the chance that she was in this one. The last thing he wanted was to be responsible for the loss of an innocent life. He realized that the most obvious place for the girl would be in the boot, and even if he managed to avoid hitting her and got the fuel tank instead, it was possible that his bullets could start a fire. He couldn't take that risk.

He tried to sight on the tyres but it was no use. In his frustration he fired off another double tap through the rear window in the vague hope that one of his rounds might hit one of the kidnappers.

The next second the bonnet smashed through the flimsy barrier, splintering the wooden pole and breaking free on to the open road beyond. Don got to his feet and ran after it. As he reached the ruined barrier he tried to aim at the retreating car again but it was too late. He stared after the fast-dwindling target, the frosted rear windscreen now being punched out by the man who had been sitting in the back seat. In the last moments before it disappeared Don glimpsed a face grinning derisively at his failure.

Don cursed, easing off the hammer of his pistol and flicking on the safety-catch. He slid it back into his holster and turned back towards the restaurant. In the distance he heard the sound of a police siren and far down the motorway he saw a blue flashing light.

It suddenly occurred to him that he was probably the only one present who had made the connection between the various cars, recognizing them as all part of the same terrorist gang. The two that had taken the motorway could not have got far. There was still time to go after them.

He ran back to his car, slipped into the driving seat, gunned the accelerator and shot out for the entrance to the motorway. A hitchhiker stood at the roadside thumbing a lift. Don screeched to a halt and when the youngster jogged up to his car, instead of opening the door for him to get in he wound down the window and said, 'There's been a shooting in the service station. There's a police car coming up behind. Wave them down and tell them there are two cars on the motorway heading west and some of the men responsible are in them. Tell them to block the next exit and get a helicopter in the air. Another car crashed out of the back of the car park. Have you got that?'

The youth stared at him dumbstruck. Don repeated, 'Have you got that? I haven't got time to stick around.'

'A shooting?'

'That's it.'

The youth nodded. 'I'll tell them.'

'Good lad.'

Don put his foot down hard and sped away. The cars he was chasing had already pulled away out of sight, so he drew out into the fast lane and put the accelerator to the floor. It felt as though there was a hand in the small of his back pushing him along. He thought briefly of the car that had burst through the barrier. Perhaps he should have chased that one. But no. By the time he could have gone after it the driver could have veered off on to any one of a dozen minor roads. He had a far better chance of catching the cars that had stupidly chosen the motorway.

The road bent into a long, steady curve as it entered a cutting. When it emerged from the far side of the chalk hillsides he had a clear view for several miles ahead. Like a vast fat snake, the tarmac unfolded across the gently undulating countryside and there, way in the distance, he spotted the two cars, one blue and the other red. Both had now slowed to a more normal speed and he assumed that their occupants imagined they were in the clear. After all, it had been the men in the other car who had done the killing at the service station. It was unlikely that anyone had linked them to the shooting. Who could have known that they were all part of the same team?

Don knew. He eased back on the accelerator so as not to arouse their suspicion but continued to steadily close the distance. Mile after mile passed and all the while he drew closer until eventually he was barely three hundred yards behind the rear car. Out in front he could see the blue Honda Accord powering ahead, the red Ford Orion behind it and closer to him. The two cars were separated from each other by about a hundred yards, and Don could see the men in the rear of the Honda turning to exchange hand signals with the driver and front-seat passenger of the Ford. They appeared to be smiling and carefree, and he could make out their cheery waves.

'Enjoy it while it lasts, you murderous bastards,' he said quietly, closing the gap a bit more.

He was almost level with the Ford when in the distance behind him he caught the sound of a police siren.

'Bugger!' he growled.

He looked in the rear-view mirror and saw the blue light of a police car flashing far behind. It was a good couple of miles away and he wondered what on earth the police intended to do from that distance.

'Nice one, lads,' he said. 'You've just warned them you're coming.'

Sure enough, he looked at the Ford and saw the men in the back crane round at the sound of the siren. One of them pointed and said something to the driver, and the next moment the car surged ahead, pulling away fast. But as yet they were unaware of Don's presence and as they accelerated so did he. He knew it would not be long before he was noticed but he had to keep up with them. The driver of the Ford must have flashed his lights to attract the attention of the Honda in front, because the next thing Don saw was the Honda veering away as well. He eased gently up beside the Ford, keeping his eyes fixed on the road and trying not to look suspicious. But the police car was closing steadily and he knew that at any moment the two cars would have to give up all pretence of innocence and make a break for it.

He glanced at his speedometer and saw that the needle was touching ninety. Surely he couldn't escape their notice much longer?

The answer came a second later when the Ford swung across into the middle lane and almost rammed him. Don tugged the steering wheel hard to avoid a collision and almost lost control, as the driver of the Ford had intended. Struggling to keep on the road, he glanced across and saw the men in the Ford staring hard at him.

'Time to forget the pretence, fellas,' he said through gritted teeth, and steered straight towards them.

In response they accelerated, swerving to overtake an articulated lorry. Up in the cab the driver stared at the two cars in amazement and blew his horn as the Ford swung dangerously close to his front bumper.

To Don's horror he saw the rear window of the Ford opening and the next instant a pistol appeared, waving unsteadily in the blast of wind. The firer aimed it in Don's direction and pulled the trigger repeatedly. Over the noise of the engines Don heard the thin cracks of the gunshots and saw the puffs of blue smoke erupt from the muzzle. Although the firing was appallingly inaccurate he knew that there was always the chance of a lucky shot finding its mark. And it wouldn't even have to hit him. At that speed it would only have to rupture a tyre or other vital component to send his car spinning out of control.

He swung the steering wheel to bring himself directly behind the Ford, cutting the pistol's direct line of fire.

'If you want me now you'll have to smash your way through your rear window,' he said.

By now the police car had closed to within thirty yards of Don and the Ford, but to Don's surprise it headed straight for him, the policeman in the front passenger seat waving him to pull over and stop.

'Not me, you stupid fuckers!' he mouthed through the window. 'Them!'

He pointed at the Ford but the policeman ignored him, waving again for him to stop. Don shook his head in exasperation and put his foot full down on the accelerator, aiming straight for the rear of the Ford. Before its driver could react, Don's front bumper rammed into the boot. The car veered to one side and Don watched in satisfaction as the driver fought to regain control.

'Try some of your own medicine, pal.'

He readied himself to take evasive action as he was certain that the gunman would try to hit him again, but it was the police car that reacted first. Believing Don to be the aggressor, the police driver swung towards him, intending to knock him off the road.

'Get away, you arsehole!' Don roared. He stabbed a finger at the Ford again. 'They're the ones you're supposed to be after!'

Once more he surged forward and hit the rear of the Ford, and this time he provoked a reaction. One of the men in the back seat leaned out of the window, the pistol in his fist, and loosed off a couple of rounds at him. Don swerved but one of the bullets punched through his windscreen. A cobweb of cracks fanned out from the neat hole and the bullet buried itself harmlessly in the passenger seat.

He stared across at the police car. 'See what I mean, you gits?'

The policeman blinked back at him in confusion, looking from him to the Ford and back again. Don felt he could almost see the man's brain working.

'That's it,' he muttered as he saw the policeman reach for his radio. 'Who's a clever boy then?'

As the police car reported the gunfire to its control centre, the driver pulled back from the chase.

'Well, that's nice,' Don shouted at them. 'Leave it all to me.'

He looked up to see a sign flash past, announcing the approach of an exit. In the Ford he could see the men engaged in a frantic dispute. The driver clearly wanted to stick to the motorway but the others seemed to be against it. Sure enough, when the exit opened up before them several hundred yards further on, the car swung towards it and shot up the incline. Don followed hard on their heels but the police car was too slow to react and continued on past the exit.

By now the Honda had disappeared. Don had been so involved with chasing the Ford that he had lost sight of it. Nevertheless, he was resolved to catch at least part of the terrorist group. If he could only catch one of them an interrogation might reveal the whereabouts of the rest.

The last glimpse he had of the police car was of its brake lights stabbing on, smoke burning off the tyres as it screeched to a halt and the driver shot it into reverse to retrace his steps to the exit road. By that time the Ford was at the top of the incline, where a small roundabout forced it to slow down. The driver swung his car into the turn, heading off down the minor road that cut away across country. Keeping as close as he could, Don hoped that it wouldn't be long before the policeman's radio report yielded some help. He didn't particularly want to get involved in a fire-fight with four armed terrorists by himself. It was all he could do simply to track them.

The road stretched away in front, hedges bordering it on either side with farmland beyond. A low mist clung to the barren fields and everywhere looked bleak and desolate. Driving at high speed was more difficult on the narrow road after the expanse of the motorway, but the advantage was that it was more difficult for the men in the Ford to get a clear shot at him. Nevertheless, every so often one of them would give it a go. The shots all went hopelessly wide but it was unnerving all the same.

A cluster of roadside cottages came and went. He was aware of a couple of white, staring faces flashing past before they were out among open fields again. He felt a grudging admiration for the driver of the Ford. The man obviously knew his stuff. It was a long time since Don had done the SAS fast-driving course, but he reckoned that the man in front must have been through some kind of similar training. He appeared to possess all the skills, and it was all Don could do to keep up with him. The slightest lapse in concentration would mean a crash and, at that breakneck speed, instant death.

For a moment he toyed with the idea of trying to get in a couple of shots himself. He realized that the chances of actually hitting anyone or anything were remote, but he might just be able to distract the other driver enough to send him spinning off the road.

He waited until the chase entered a long stretch of straight road with no houses on either side and then wound open his window. Next he reached under his arm for his shoulder holster and drew his Browning. Keeping his left hand on the steering wheel, he put the barrel under its fingers, gripped it tightly and cocked it. Having flicked off the safety-catch, he put his arm out of the window and rested the base of his fist on the car's bodywork. Keeping the car aligned with the Ford in front, he fired off one round after another.

A small hole appeared in the Ford's rear window, then another and another. The car swerved and for a moment Don thought he had achieved his aim, but against all the odds the driver maintained his control on the wheel. In the back, though, he could see that one of the men had slumped across the back seat.

'Gotcha!' he shouted.

He fired again but a second later the hammer clicked on an empty chamber. He cursed. There were several spare clips of ammunition in the glove compartment, so, putting his pistol in his lap, he switched hands on the wheel and reached across to hunt for them. When he had one, he pressed the release button on the side of the butt and popped out the empty magazine, sliding in a fresh one, clicking it home on his knee and then cocking the gun as he had done before.

'A few more ought to do it,' he said out loud.

He steadied his hand out of the window again and continued firing, but the cars were entering a series of bends and for a while he had to use both hands on the wheel, clasping the pistol between his knees, the muzzle pointing down at the floor.

'Don't blow your balls away, Don lad,' he muttered to himself.

The bends were tighter than he had anticipated and he fought to keep the car under control, but at last they pulled clear of them and after another group of houses the cars were once again out on an open stretch of road. He took up his pistol and aimed through the window again.

'This time,' he said, willing himself to concentrate. 'This time.'

The first shot again found the Ford's rear window, and in the front of the car Don thought he saw the driver slump. He closed the distance a little and, sure enough, he saw that the man had removed one hand from the wheel and was clutching at his right shoulder.

'Bingo!'

The Ford started to slow, although in the front seat Don could see the passenger urging the driver on. For a minute or two it gathered speed again, but his bullet had clearly done its job, for the car was now veering all over the road.

'That's it, lad. No need to crash. Just pull over and give yourselves up. Nice and peaceful like.'

Going into a corner too fast, the driver was unable to hold the road. He lost his grip on the wheel and the car careered up a bank and ploughed straight through a thick hedge and into the field beyond. Crows burst into the wintry sky from the surrounding trees, startled by the interruption. Don hit the brake, pumping it gingerly to control his emergency stop. Pulling up on to the side of the bank some thirty or forty yards further on, he pushed open his door and leapt out on to the road, his pistol in his hand. He knew it would be dangerous to go back to the place where the car had entered the field. If any of the men had recovered from the shock they would be expecting him from that direction.

Instead he scanned the hedgerow until he saw a gap beside a tree where he reckoned he would be able to gain access without making too much noise.

He dropped on to his stomach and wriggled up the slope. An old barbed-wire fence threaded its way through the centre of the hedge and he rolled on to his back to work his way underneath the lowest strand. For a moment it snagged on the material of his jacket but he managed to work it free and slithered underneath. The ground on the other side dropped towards the edge of the field, the ploughed earth striped into furrows, hard and bare as iron. He rolled out from behind the cover of the tree, bringing his pistol into the aim as he did so. The Ford sat out in the open, its skid marks visible right back to the hole in the hedge. In the front he could see the driver, slumped over the wheel, unconscious or even dead. Beside him, the passenger had shot through the windscreen and his limp body hung across the bonnet, half in and half out of the car. His arms were splayed and there was blood on his face.

'That'll teach you to wear your seat-belt next time, mate,' Don whispered to himself.

The rear doors were both open and there was no sign of the men who had been in the back. He knew that he had hit one of them, but how badly? And that still left the man's companion unaccounted for as well.

Don's eyes scanned the line of hedgerow. He knew they couldn't have gone far and judged that they must have rolled clear as the car entered the field. Perhaps, once the driver had been hit, they had prepared themselves for just such an eventuality. If so, it had paid off.

As he wriggled out into the field Don caught sight of the men on the far side of the car. They were running towards a large copse, the one man helping his wounded comrade.

As they ran, they kept glancing back over their shoulders. The moment he identified them, Don sprang to his feet and sprinted towards the car, keeping it between himself and the fugitives to prevent them from getting a clear line of fire on him. One of the men nevertheless loosed off a couple of wild rounds as soon as he saw Don, but both snapped past him harmlessly, cracking in the air like a whip.

Flinging himself down beside the wrecked car, Don gripped his Browning in a two-handed combat grip and then spun round the side, hunting for his target.

'Stop! Army!' he shouted at the top of his voice.

In response the wounded man half turned and fired again. Don cursed under his breath and rattled off a double tap. It was as though the man had been slammed in the back with a sledgehammer. He hurtled forward, tearing from his companion's helping grip, and sprawled face down on the hard, rutted earth. He moved for a second and then was still.

'Stop!' Don shouted again. But the other man had made good use of the breathing space provided by Don's first shots. Instead of trying to fire back, knowing that Don was behind cover and therefore almost impossible to hit, he sprinted the last few yards towards the copse, zigzagging as he went. Don fired another two double taps, but his bullets all went wide, and the next instant the man disappeared from view, diving through the thick bushes and losing himself among the trees.

To reach the copse, Don decided to take a roundabout route along the hedgerow. To risk crossing the field the way the man had gone was far too dangerous as he could well have been lying in wait. It would be no joke getting caught out in the open without a shred of cover.

There was no sight of the police follow-up and he could only assume that they had taken a wrong turning.

Brilliant, he thought as he darted through the hedge and began to snake along its outer side. They've probably stopped to issue a few parking tickets along the way.

About fifty yards along, the hedge veered towards the copse, leaving only about twenty yards of open space between it and the nearest of the trees.

'That'll do nicely,' he whispered, crouching down when he reached the bend and slipping under the wire. His jacket snagged once again and he made a mental note to lose a few pounds. Better get in some runs, he thought. I've been with the cops too long. All that riding around in patrol cars does sod all for the waistline.

Without pausing he was on his feet the moment he was through the hedge, and sprinting for the trees. Expecting to be fired at every foot of the way, he zigzagged, but a moment later he pounded through a screen of low-hanging branches and found himself in the copse.

It was gloomy inside. The trees stretched away in every direction and in between them thick bushes and undergrowth sprouted. The floor was a mat of sodden brown leaves and he felt the water soak quickly through the knees of his trousers as he crouched down to lower his profile. He steadied his breathing and listened. After the shots the rural calm had quickly returned. Somewhere far away he could hear a tractor in another field, and overhead a flock of geese screamed raucously as they flew by.

Suddenly he heard the crack of a branch and swung towards the tell-tale sound. He lowered himself on to his stomach and crawled steadily forward, holding his Browning in one hand and using the other to sweep aside the brittle dead branches lest he give his own position away with a similar signal. In the pit of his stomach he could feel the knot of tension curl into a ball, pushing his heart into his mouth until he had to stop and calm himself.

'Steady, lad. You're behaving like some new kid on selection, for God's sake. Get a grip on yourself.'

With his new resolve he moved on, slower than before, forcing himself to relax into the stalk, prepared at any second for a flurry of deadly exchange shots. There was another crack, this time towards the other side of the copse. He frowned, puzzled how the man could have crossed so silently in front of him without being seen.

This bugger's good, he thought. Be careful, Don.

Painfully slowly he closed the gap between them, but as he drew closer he became puzzled. Where he had heard the crack of the twig he could now hear a shuffling. What the fuck's he up to? he thought. Is he digging a sodding trench or something?

But then he was on him. The sound was coming from just beyond the next tree. Drawing his legs up under him, Don rose stealthily from the ground and prepared to rush forward. He took a deep breath, and exhaled. Then one more breath before he burst round the side of the tree. To his astonishment he found himself face to face with a roe deer. For a split second the creature froze, its round, startled eyes fixed on his own, and then it was off, scudding away across the open field beyond the trees, its white tail bobbing furiously as it vaulted over the iron-hard furrows.

Don threw himself to one side, aware that he had just given away his position, furious with himself for having been so stupid. It was a drill he had used a hundred times, rolling twice and coming up in the ready position, but never before had it paid off as it did now.

As he was halfway through the second roll he heard the crack of a gunshot and felt the sting of blown earth on his face.

Bullets were ripping into the ground around him and when he came out of the roll, starting to return the fire even as he spun to face his attacker, he caught a fleeting glimpse of the man from the car, partially concealed behind a stout oak.

Don blazed at him, round after round, seeing them impact into the shattered bark until they found their target at last and the man was flung backwards. Without giving him time to recover, Don rushed towards him, his pistol aimed at the prone form. As he rounded the oak he saw the man was still alive.

'Freeze!' he shouted. 'Not one move or I'll drill you!'

The man's gun was a good yard out of reach, cushioned on a bed of leaves, still smoking.

'That's it,' Don said calmly, locking his eyes on the man's. 'There's been enough killing for one day. Don't make me shoot you.'

The man stared back fearlessly. His hands were under him and he seemed to be clutching something to his stomach.

'Show me your hands, mate. Nice and slow like.'

In answer, the man rolled slowly on to his back and Don gaped in horror at the hand-grenade he was cradling against himself. He had already pulled the pin and as Don watched he released the lever. It spun clear with a metallic crack and Don knew that he had only a second or two before the detonator exploded it, rocketing white-hot splinters towards him. Instead of throwing the grenade at Don, however, the man clutched it to his own stomach, simultaneously curling into a ball as if to wrap himself around the deadly object.

For a moment he locked his gaze with Don's. It was a mixture of triumph and anger, without the slightest trace of fear. The next instant Don whirled himself behind the oak, straightening himself taut against the thick trunk as the grenade exploded on the far side, firing out its shards harm-lessly into the surrounding undergrowth. But when he looked again, it was to see that the man had been blown almost in two. Where his stomach had been was now only a massive raw wound. He had died instantly.

'Jesus Christ,' Don murmured. 'Who the fuck are these guys?'

It was then that he heard the sound of a police siren, and a moment later the policemen were running across the field towards him.

4

They drove for the best part of two hours before Ceda Bandram indicated a sharp left turn to the driver. In the back of the car Ali sat miserably staring out of the window, watching the countryside roll by. Ceda hadn't said a single word to him since the shooting at the service station and Ali was beginning to wonder if he had gone too far. But what was he supposed to have done? The man had shouldered him aside from the wash-basin and Ali had distinctly heard the racist insult spoken under his breath. He was damned if he was going to let anyone get away with that.

They had heard police sirens as they sped away from the area surrounding the motorway but no one appeared to have followed them. All three of them had kept a careful watch for any sign of a tail but apparently the chase had been confined to the other two cars. Their own road had remained clear. At one point they had seen a police car coming in the opposite direction and they had all tensed themselves for a fight, but the car had sped past, continuing down the road in the direction they had just come. Ali had grinned and made a wisecrack, but Ceda had ignored it.

Studying his map, Ceda let the driver continue straight

ahead for a good five miles and then directed him to turn right.

'It's not much further now,' he said.

'What isn't?' Ali asked hopefully. It was true that, as a family member, he could not come to any harm at the hands of Ceda Bandram, but nevertheless he knew that Ceda was not a man to be trifled with. He would undoubtedly have words to say to their uncle and it could even mean that Ali would be barred from further participation in other such missions.

Ceda was concentrating on his map again as if he hadn't heard Ali's question. Rather than repeat it, Ali leaned forward, folding his arm on the back of Ceda's seat.

'Look, Ceda. Do you want an apology? Is that it?'

Instead of answering, Ceda spoke again to the driver, who glanced nervously from him to Ali and back again, terrified lest the tension erupt into violence. That was the last thing they needed. Enough had already gone wrong.

Ali sighed heavily and sank back into his seat, muttering to himself. Clearly there was going to be no rapprochement this side of Pakistan.

The first sign of where they were headed came a few moments later when he looked up and saw a bright-orange windsock fluttering at the end of a tall pole above a line of trees.

'So this is the airfield,' he said. 'A well-kept secret indeed.' He tried to inject a tone of flattery into his voice, although he suspected that Ceda was probably impervious to it. No harm in trying, he thought. The guy can't be totally bloody perfect.

It was a small private airfield, mostly used by light aircraft and gliders. However, as the car rounded a line of hangars that looked as though they dated back to the war they saw ahead of them a small, slim executive jet. Two men paced up and down beside it and when they heard the sound of a car engine they looked up eagerly.

To his immense relief Ceda noticed the Honda parked several yards away. The doors opened and the four men got out and jogged to meet him.

'Pull up over there,' Ceda instructed the driver, indicating a hangar. 'Park the car inside it and tell the other driver to do the same. We're going to need every minute we can get and if it takes the police a while to find our cars, so much the better.'

As he got out of the car he glanced around the airfield. It was virtually deserted. Only beside the entrance gate did a single watchman sit in his booth, idly stirring a mug of tea. In front of him a television screen flickered hypnotically.

'Are the others here?' Ceda asked the other team members as they reached him. He had been alarmed not to see the Ford and the expressions on the men's faces confirmed his fears even before they opened their mouths to speak.

'The police gave chase. Hari left the motorway and that was the last we saw of them. But there was this other bloke.'

'What do you mean?'

The man shook his head. 'I'm not sure who he was, but he tailed us all the way out of the service station. When the police car turned up I saw him ramming Hari. He followed the Ford off the motorway. I'd swear he was security forces or something.'

'What makes you say that?'

'I don't know. It was just the way he handled his car, the way he drove. He was totally confident. No ordinary man could have acted like that.'

Ceda nodded knowingly, guessing the answer. He described the glimpse he had had of the man he had seen in his rear-view mirror firing at him as they had burst through the barrier gate.

A light dawned on his comrade's face. 'Why yes, that sounds like him, although I couldn't be certain. We were some way ahead.' He looked suddenly worried. 'You don't suppose he could have tailed us all the way from Southall, do you? If so, perhaps they'll be here any minute.'

Ceda waved his hand dismissively, wishing at the same time that he actually felt the confidence he was aping. 'It was probably just a coincidence. If they'd been tailing us we'd have had to deal with a lot more than just one man. He was probably a special forces soldier or armed policeman who just happened to be using the same service station and was lucky enough to be carrying a gun.'

He looked all around him. For as far as he could see across the flat landscape the roads were empty. A quick check of his watch confirmed that they were already well past their scheduled departure time. The plan had gone completely to hell and he couldn't afford to delay another minute.

'Everyone on board. You two' – he pointed at his men – 'get the girl. Check she's all right before you carry her aboard. And try to be discreet. Don't let the gateman see what you're doing.'

The driver stared at him in disbelief. 'You're not thinking of leaving before the others arrive, are you?'

'We don't have any choice.' He glared angrily at Ali, who pretended not to have noticed. 'They knew the risks. If they get away from the police they know the contacts who will give them shelter. Because we fucked up the backup team's going to have to be retasked. If our guys get away they can join them.'

The men went to the boot of Ceda's car and opened it. Wide, frightened eyes stared up at them, blinking in the unaccustomed daylight. The girl was gagged with masking tape over her mouth, and her wrists and ankles had been tied with lengths of rope. They hoisted her out, first checking that no one could see. She thrashed and kicked as they carried her the short distance to the waiting plane and bundled her up the steps.

'Where shall we put her?'

Ceda strode across to them and hopped up the steps into the fuselage. 'Strap her into a seat at the rear and stay with her. I don't want her getting loose and giving the game away.'

He smiled at the girl, whose eyes flashed at him angrily. 'As soon as we're airborne I'll untie you and take the gag off, but for now please bear with us. It won't take long.'

She lunged at him with her bound feet and he only just managed to avoid the kick, deftly dodging aside.

As the men carried her into the plane, Ceda's driver came to his side. 'It's too bad about the old man.'

Ali overheard and chipped in, 'You bet it is. Uncle's not going to be very pleased.'

Ceda stiffened his jaw, keeping his fist in check. 'That's not all Uncle's going to be displeased with,' he said woodenly. 'And anyway, even if we did miss old Sanji I've got a plan. The game's got a long way to run. We'll have him yet.'

'I certainly hope so for your sake,' Ali chided.

When the last of the men were on board and the two pilots were starting the engines and running through their pre-flight checks, Ceda and Ali stood on the tarmac by the door and took one last look around in case the other team should suddenly appear. But there was nothing. The countryside was empty of life, barren at the start of winter.

'We'd best be going,' Ali prompted at last.

'OK,' Ceda agreed. He turned to get into the plane, but then, as if as an afterthought, he said, 'Oh yes, there's just one more thing . . .'

His movement was so fast that Ali never saw it coming, the balled fist slicing upwards and crashing into the underside of Ali's jaw. His head whip-cracked back and his body crumpled to the ground. Ali groped blindly, his mind swimming as he struggled on the edges of consciousness. Beside him, he was dimly aware of Ceda crouching down, level with his bleeding face. Through the haze Ali could taste blood and he spat out teeth, hearing them tinkle on the floor.

Ceda grabbed his collar in one large fist and wrenched his face close to his own until Ali found himself staring into his hard, cold eyes. 'If it was up to me I'd leave you here. Because of you four good men are probably either dead of captured. I trained them myself. Each one of them meant more to me than you do, relative or not.'

He pulled Ali's face even closer until Ali could feel Ceda's spittle on his cheeks. 'Don't you ever cross me again. Don't ever disobey an order. If you do, I'll kill you.'

He threw Ali away and wiped his hands as if trying to remove the stain of something unpleasant. Ali sprawled on the tarmac, trying to get to his knees but failing. As Ceda climbed into the plane one of the men popped his head out to see what was happening. He stared in surprise at the grovelling shape of Ali and at Ceda, who appeared as calm as ever.

'Help him aboard,' Ceda commanded. 'He slipped on the steps.'

When everyone was strapped into their seats, the plane lurched forward and one of the pilots taxied to the end of the runway. Ceda had chosen a place across the aisle from the girl and as the plane hurtled down the runway and lifted into the air he signalled to his men to remove her gag. Through the window he watched the fields and farm buildings shrink in size, the ground rushing past beneath them.

The jet was a slim fourteen-seater and up at the front he could see the pilots at work in the cockpit.

'How the hell do you think you're going to get away with this?'

Ceda looked across at the girl, who was rubbing her lips and cheeks where the gag had been.

He shrugged. 'We already have. Mind you, I'm sorry about our losses.'

She shook her head angrily. 'You must be absolutely mad. The police will stop you before . . .'

Ceda threw back his head and laughed. 'How? With a flying patrol car? A helicopter perhaps?'

'They'll use jet fighters or something. They'll force you down.'

He looked at her with sympathetic eyes. 'You're living in fantasy land, my dear. They don't even know who's in this aircraft. We've filed several different flight plans with the authorities, all false of course. By the time they figure out what happened to us we'll be well out of British airspace. Even if the civil police had some speedy means of liaison with the air force – which they haven't – we'd be over North Africa before they could scramble a fighter aircraft. They wouldn't dare push it that far. Certainly not for you.'

He sat back and relaxed, pleased with himself, although less with the overall planning of the operation than with the punch he had delivered to Ali. It had released the tension wonderfully and he had enjoyed it. He had been dying to see Ali flat on the deck ever since he had been ordered to take him along.

'Mind you, a few years ago in the days of the Cold War they might have been able to give chase. Then they used to keep pairs of fully armed fighters airborne twenty-four hours a day. But not any more.' He leaned back and folded his arms behind his head. 'Nowadays the aircrew sit in nice, comfortable rooms watching the television and drinking coffee. The last thing on their minds is a cross-country chase after some insignificant Indian girl.'

The girl bristled. 'I'm not Indian. I'm a British citizen. I was born here.'

Ceda laughed again and winked at her playfully. 'When did you last look in a mirror? You're as Indian as I am Pakistani.'

She stared at him in amazement. 'I've never heard anything so racist in my whole life! What century do you come from? Certainly not mine.'

'I think I'm going to enjoy our relationship,' Ceda added. He looked at his watch. 'We've got plenty of time to continue this discussion before our arrival.'

A look of doubt crossed her face. 'Our arrival where?'

'Didn't I tell you? Do forgive me. In Pakistan, of course.'

'Pakistan? What the hell are we going there for?' She rounded on him, making full use of the opportunity now that her gag was removed at last. 'And why have you kidnapped me anyway?'

'Yes, I'm sorry about that. It was all a bit of an accident.'

'Was the murder of my parents an accident?'

'We needed information.'

'What could they possibly have told you?' Tears burst from her and she broke into sobs. 'My father ran a restaurant, that's all. Are you from some protection racket?'

Ceda scowled. 'Please don't insult me.'

She was becoming desperate, hunting through her brain for any scrap of information that might give her a clue as to why she was being abducted to Pakistan. The clue was presented to her by Ceda Bandram's innocent-sounding request.

'Tell me about your grandfather.'

'My grandfather? Whatever for?'

Ceda shrugged noncommittally. 'Where was he?'

Eli paused before answering, wondering why on earth they would want to know about him? 'He was out.'

'Obviously. We're not complete fools. Does he still live with you in Bramley Road?'

'Why do you want to know?' she asked, becoming bolder now that she saw her captor wasn't going to treat her as they had treated her parents.

Ceda wagged a finger at her. 'I'm the one who asks the questions. So tell me, does he still live in Bramley Road or has he got some other address?'

She stared at him suspiciously. 'It was him you were after, wasn't it? That was why you killed my father. He wouldn't tell you where my grandfather was.'

'Not at all. He was only too willing to help my associate. He told us every possible location that came into his head. He'd have sold your grandfather down the river if he had been able. We eventually came to the conclusion that he simply didn't know.'

Now it was Eli's turn to laugh. 'You fools. You had the right house all along. My father couldn't tell you because he didn't know. My grandfather has never been able to sleep well. Every morning he gets up before daylight and walks the streets for exercise. Had you waited a bit longer he would probably have walked straight into your hands.'

She saw Ceda blanch. His lips tightened and he turned away quickly. 'It doesn't matter. It's an inconvenience, that's all.' He faced her again. 'A big inconvenience for you, above all. I hope your grandfather is a reasonable man.'

'Let me guess. You're going to hold me to ransom, is that it?'

'Perhaps.' Ceda was beginning to enjoy his exchange with the girl. She had a keen mind and was courageous.

'How much do you intend to ask for me? My family owns a chain of restaurants, but they don't have any disposable cash, if that's what you're after.'

'There are more things to swap a hostage for than just money,' Ceda answered enigmatically.

Down below Eli could see the countryside disappearing below a sea of thickening cloud. The dense whiteness blurred past the window until the plane had been completely enveloped in it and a moment later it burst through into a dazzling blue sky.

'OK,' Eli said at last. 'So you want my grandfather, is that it?'

'Bright, aren't you?'

'Why do you want him?'

Ceda didn't reply. Instead he stared out of the window, signalling by his silence that the conversation was over for now.

Don had only a relatively short stay in the local police station. Not surprisingly he had been ordered to surrender his gun the moment the police had arrived at the copse and seen the array of bodies.

'I'll tell you straight, Mr Headley,' the inspector said as he stirred his mug of instant coffee in the interview room, 'I take a dim view of cowboys holding their gunfights on my patch as if it's the OK Corral. What the hell did you think you were up to anyway, giving chase like that?'

Don sighed in exasperation. He had been over the story a dozen times already and was becoming impatient. He hadn't slept properly for several nights and had just taken part in a life-or-death struggle with a gang of armed terrorists.

'I've given you the name and phone number of someone who can verify my story,' he said, stifling an immense yawn.

'I'm sorry if I'm boring you, Mr . . .'

'And it's Captain Headley,' Don snapped. 'I've told you that as well.'

'Oh yes, of course,' the inspector sneered. 'You spun my sergeant that SAS crap.' He leaned closer across the table. 'Personally I don't give a shit if you're fucking Superman. I'm going to nail you for your little performance this morning.'

'You'd be better off trying to apprehend the rest of the gang.'

'My patrolmen only reported one car, the one you destroyed.'

'Then who do you think smashed the barrier at the service station?'

'We're checking that out now. I don't intend jumping to conclusions.'

Don shook his head. 'By the time you do the terrorists will be out of the country.' Suddenly he couldn't stand the stupidity any longer. He got to his feet and, planting his fists on the table, leaned towards the inspector, who flinched.

'Look here, pal. Have you rung that sodding number or haven't you?'

Realizing that he wasn't going to get anything more out of Don, the inspector got up and left the room, muttering a brief 'Stay here' as he went.

Don sank into the chair again and crossed his legs. The four walls were completely bare, and apart from the table and the two chairs it was unfurnished. A police constable stood by the door, his hands behind his back, watching Don steadily as if they expected him to make a break for it.

If I was going to, Don thought, *that fat git certainly couldn't stop me.*

It was a good half hour before there was the sound of footsteps in the corridor and the door opened on the inspector.

'You've got a visitor,' he announced sullenly.

Rod Chiltern stepped through the door-frame. 'Hear you've been busy?'

Don heaved a sigh of relief. 'Rod, thank fuck you're here. These guys have been giving me the third degree.'

'That's not really too surprising considering you've broken almost every rule in the Highway Code, and killed four men as well.'

He stood to one side. 'Come on. Let's get back to London.'

'London? I was hoping to be in Hereford this afternoon.'

Chiltern guffawed. 'How I love that SAS sense of humour.' He glared at Don. 'Get your arse in gear, Headley. We haven't finished with you. I always knew the SAS were soft at heart. It isn't Endex yet.'

As they walked out of the station Don asked, 'What about my pistol?'

'We're keeping it as evidence,' the inspector replied, barely concealing his frustration at losing his prisoner.

'Well, take good care of it. That's army property.'

Leaving his own car in the police pound, Don collapsed into the back of Chiltern's Rover. 'Mind if I get some kip?'

'Please yourself,' Chiltern replied, and a moment later Don was snoring lightly. His sleep was deep but troubled, images of the chase tumbling through his brain. An hour later he awoke with a start to find that they had arrived at their destination. He sat up and rubbed his eyes, peering blearily through the windows. But instead of the police station he had expected to see, he found himself looking at an impressive country house.

The car was parked on a gravel driveway and on either side of the house smooth green lawns stretched away to low-hanging cedars and beeches. Ivy crept up the sides of the house in great enthusiastic swathes, clipped and trimmed around the windows, like a well-kept beard. Don looked behind him.

There was no sign of the road. The driveway swept out of sight round a corner, the screen of trees obscuring his view of whatever lay beyond.

'Where's this then? Butlins?'

'Shut it, Don,' Chiltern growled. He switched off the engine and got out, opening the rear door. 'Out.'

Don stepped on to gravel, feeling it crunch beneath his sodden shoes. For one brief moment he considered punching Chiltern in the guts and making a dash for it. But why should he? Surely his instincts were out of place here? He had known Chiltern since the beginning of the exercise and as far as he could tell he was just another regular cop.

'The police officers' rest home?' he said.

'Ha, ha. Very funny. Inside,' Chiltern shot back, jerking his head towards the front door, which was being held open by two anonymous-looking men in grey suits.

Don sized them up. Both were well built but undoubtedly capable of fast movement. Their hair was as trim as the creeper and their eyes narrowed as they followed him inside.

He had seen their kind before. They belonged to the Intelligence service – not the brain section, but the brawn. They were the enforcers and the bodyguards, and Don knew from experience that within their limits they were good. But as regards their broader adaptability, they were much like any other hood – less capable than they thought. They allowed themselves to be flattered by the title 'Intelligence', assuming erroneously that their employers' mental gifts had rubbed off on them. They hadn't, and if push came to shove, Don thought, he could use their self-delusion against them.

The entrance hall was dark and gloomy. Old paintings hung on the walls and two suits of armour flanked the foot of the staircase. Don couldn't help smiling at them, wondering if there were other guards disguised inside. He turned round to face Chiltern.

'Well, what's the game?'

Instead of answering, Chiltern pointed to an open door. 'Wait in there.'

'Listen . . .' Don began.

But Chiltern was already on his way up the stairs.

The room that Chiltern had indicated was a well-stocked library. Books covered the walls and a large leather-topped desk sat in front of a bay window that looked out on to the extensive lawns. There was a phone on the desk and for a moment Don considered trying to call his CO in Hereford. He went across to it and lifted the receiver to check for a dialling tone. There was one.

He was just putting his finger to the first number when there were footsteps in the hall and muffled voices. Quickly he replaced the receiver and moved a yard or two away and stood with arms folded, ready to receive whoever was about to enter.

Only one man came in, his colleague dawdling outside the door for a moment out of Don's vision before moving away to another room and closing the door noisily behind him. The man who confronted Don was every inch the civil servant. His suit was smart but off-the-peg and he wore a shirt that no self-respecting officer would have been seen dead in, the pale blue stripes respectable enough but compromised by the vulgarity of a plain white collar and cuffs.

'Good afternoon,' he said briskly, advancing on Don with one slim white hand outstretched. 'I'm so sorry to have kept you waiting.'

Taken aback by his manner, Don said that it was no trouble. After all, what else had he been planning? Only a couple of days' rest to catch up on sleep and relaxation.

'Now then, about this terrible business,' the man continued, ushering Don to a chair on the subservient side of the desk. 'I hope you don't mind but I'd like to run through it once again.'

'What? But I've already been debriefed by the police.'

'Exactly,' the civil servant said. 'But not by us.'

'And suppose you tell me exactly who you are.'

The man resisted a smile, steepling his fingers in front of him and gazing into the middle distance to present Don with his three-quarters profile. Don presumed that someone had probably once told the fellow that it was his best angle.

'We are part of Intelligence. That is all you need to know. As an officer of the SAS I'm sure you can appreciate our need for discretion.'

'Not particularly,' Don stated bluntly, his hackles rising. 'As an officer of the SAS I would have hoped that I could be taken into your confidence. I mean, we're supposed to be on the same side.'

'Indeed we are,' the man agreed, nodding vigorously. 'But if you don't mind I'd rather not tell you at this point who I represent.'

'OK. We'll play it your way then.' And he began to repeat the details of everything that had happened since the discovery of the bodies at Bramley Road that morning. As he spoke the door opened again and another man brought in a tray of coffee. Don continued with his account as the civil servant poured, sliding Don's cup and saucer over to him with a precise hand.

'You say you gained the impression that the men in the Ford Orion were professionals. What exactly do you mean by that?'

He had been taking copious notes, slipping into shorthand whenever unable to keep up.

Don shrugged. 'Special forces of some kind. Fuck knows whose.'

The man winced at the crudity and scrubbed out his last set of squiggles. Don leaned forward, curious to see what the shorthand for 'Fuck knows' looked like.

'At a pinch I'd say Pakistani.'

'What's that?' the man asked with the air of an innocent. He was a bad actor and Don guessed that he already knew full well the identity of the terrorists.

'It just seemed to all add up. The cartridge case at the house, the method of interrogation and the slickness of the executions, the blokes in the cars . . .'

'What about them?' the man interrupted eagerly.

'Asians,' Don said simply. 'Big buggers, most of them with moustaches.'

'They could have been Iranians or Iraqis.'

'No they couldn't. They weren't scruffy, fat and ugly enough to be Iraqis, and if they'd been Iranians they'd have had a good two days' growth of stubble. They reckon it makes them look macho.'

'And these men?'

'Clean-shaven, well-disciplined military types. At a guess I'd say ex-Pakistani Army.'

'Why ex?'

'If they were still serving we'd have an international incident on our hands instead of this hideaway, hush-hush crap.'

'Maybe we have got an international incident on our hands,' the man said, attempting an air of mystery.

Don smiled cruelly. 'In that case – forgive me for saying so – I wouldn't be being interviewed by a flunkey.'

The man flushed scarlet and Don felt a bolt of satisfaction at having ruffled his feathers at last.

'Right then, Captain Headley,' the man said hurriedly, masking his hurt pride, 'you've been most co-operative.' He shuffled his papers together and slid them into his briefcase.

'Is that all?'

The voice that replied came from behind Don.

'Not quite, I'm afraid.'

Don turned in his chair. A tall, grey-haired, patrician-looking man in his early sixties had silently appeared. 'Thank you, David, that'll be all for now,' he said, addressing the civil servant, who scurried obsequiously from the room.

He gestured to Don to remain in his seat, but instead of sitting down himself he strolled to the window and gazed out at the bleak gardens.

'My name is Sir Anthony Briggs,' he announced as if Don should shiver and quake at the very mention.

'I'm pleased to meet you.'

'If you are then you're a bigger fool than I thought.'

I see, Don thought. First the soft guy and now the hard one. What the fuck's going on here?

As if it was the most natural thing in the world, Sir Anthony said, 'How do you fancy being assigned under my command for a while?'

Don stared at him. He might as well have made some comment about the weather. 'Excuse me?'

'A rather interesting job has cropped up and I believe you're the man to handle it. In fact, you've already thrown yourself in at the deep end by undertaking that heroic chase of yours.' Sir Anthony turned from the window. 'Well?'

Don rubbed his tired eyes, feeling them smart. 'Why is it that somehow I get the feeling that's not a request?'

When Sir Anthony smiled it was like a shark at a feeding frenzy. 'I am glad. You're not so stupid after all. Thank God for small mercies.'

5

High on the glacier the wind cut through the layers of clothing of Ramesh Bandram like a knife. There were a good few miles to go yet before he could count himself out of danger, and on the glacier the threat came not just from natural sources but from human as well. Although it was impossible for anyone to remain in such conditions for any length of time, he well knew that the Indian Army maintained patrols that criss-crossed that part of the frontier with regularity. He had been unfortunate enough to encounter one on his last gun-running trip through the mountains and had narrowly escaped with his life. He had lost the complete shipment of weapons that the Kashmiri rebels so desired and in addition a number of his men had been either killed or captured.

A voice called out from behind and he turned to see that one of the mules had sunk into a drift of soft snow. For once he was glad of the wind, whose howling drowned out the cries of the stricken animal and the encouragement of her handler.

'Get a move on!' he called back, plunging his ice axe into the snow for purchase. He leaned on it heavily, gasping for the air that was pitifully thin at such a high altitude. Other men rushed to the muleteer's aid, the whole cluster thrashing around in the flurries of powdery snow until the mule staggered free of the pure white quagmire and tottered onwards, pulling its handler after it.

Ramesh was almost reluctant to get moving again, but he knew that such a reluctance was the first sign of hypothermia. Pulling his ice axe free, he plunged on up the slope. The crest was invisible, great drifts of snow swirling in the ferocious air currents that had risen all the way from the deep valleys, whipping into a frenzy the higher and thinner they became. He adjusted his goggles. Without them, snow-blindness would set in within minutes. Then the whole landscape would blur into a brilliant haze, and unless treated his sight would be gone for good.

Beyond that cloud of white he knew that the mighty ranges of the Karakoram mountains stretched seemingly into infinity, their towering, snow-capped peaks reaching for the heavens as surely as their few hostile passes reached northwards into China. It was one of the most inhospitable regions on earth, and yet it was where he and his family had carved out their lucrative trade. Ever since the Kashmiri secessionists had embarked upon their armed struggle against the forces of India, Ramesh and his family had made it their business to support them in every way possible. Of course there had always been the struggle, even as far back as the granting of Independence from Britain in 1947. That had been when the seeds of the current trouble had been sown.

It was supposed to have been a time of great joy, the winning of freedom after centuries of occupation and domination by foreign powers. Instead, Independence had ushered in one of the darkest periods in the history of the whole subcontinent. By dividing the country in two, India and

Pakistan, Britain had unwittingly laid the foundations of a struggle that was to cost millions of lives. Before 1947 Ramesh's family had lived in Delhi, owning property throughout the country but especially in Kashmir. At one stroke the British had wiped out years of tradition, and along with millions of other Muslims the Bandrams had been forced to trek north into the nascent state of Pakistan to rebuild their lives as best they could. Their properties in Kashmir had been confiscated by the new Indian state and from a position of wealth they had been driven into penury.

Ramesh bent into the howling wind and laboured up the slope. With every step he pounded out his hatred of all that had happened to his family. He appreciated that comparable tales of misfortune could be told about the millions of Hindus who had been forced to trek in the opposite direction, but it didn't ease the misery of his family's own state to know that others suffered similar torments.

The climb back to prosperity had been as hard and bitterly fought as this very mountain expedition. It had taken its toll on the family, Ramesh's own father dying along the way. It had been his uncle who had pulled the disparate group of blood relatives together and forged the links in the chain that now bound them. The more suitable of the sons had been sent into the army and there had been ample fighting to turn them from refugees into warriors. In the wars with India they had fought with distinction and when the two mighty states had been at peace the regiments had found plenty to occupy them in the frequent skirmishes with tribesmen on the North-West Frontier.

But always at the back of everything Uncle Gilma had been preparing an alternative route to wealth. At first Ramesh had been perturbed when he had discovered the illicit nature of the new family's business interests. The gun-running was excusable. After all, it was directed against the hated state of India. Less easy to come to terms with was the trade in drugs, smuggling and gambling. Nevertheless, for a family thrown into poverty, alternative options were severely limited and Ramesh had soon realized that fact. He had never been particularly religious and so there was little problem of conscience. His brother Ceda had been the one finally to persuade him to leave the army, as he himself had done after a distinguished though short career, and lend his considerable abilities to the furtherance of the family fortunes.

A number of times the family had come dangerously close to conflict with the government, but on each occasion Uncle Gilma had steered a steady course, avoiding exposure of his business interests and even ingratiating himself with those in power. Ramesh had never known whether anyone in the government fully appreciated the extent of the family's activities and was sure that if they ever did they would surely clamp down on them. For now, however, they were left alone to carry on at will, and so it was that Uncle's most daring scheme was shortly due to come to fruition.

Ramesh knew few of the details. Ceda had been chosen as the one to carry out the core mission. But Ramesh was aware of his own duties and was determined that the family would not find him lacking. Uncle had briefed him on the facts that were necessary for him to complete his own part of the plan and had stated mysteriously that when all the pieces were in place the prize would be greater than any the family had yet won. Indeed, he had said, the whole nation would thank them and reward them for what they had done.

A flurry of snow lashed his face and filled his mouth. He turned his head away and spat to clear it, and that was when he heard the cry from up ahead. Instantly he dropped to his knees, signalling those behind to do likewise. For the journey he had worn ex-army white camouflage overalls on top of his padded jacket and trousers, and as he lowered himself on to his stomach he was grateful for their protection. The driving snow blew over him and blended well with the thick waxed cloth.

'What is it?'

Murap had crawled to his side and peered into the haze to see what had caused the boss to call the halt.

Ramesh shook his head, not taking his eyes off the direction of the crest. 'I don't know, but I heard something.'

'Patrol?'

'Possibly. No one else would be dumb enough to be up here in weather like this.'

For a second the wind dropped and in the pause he again caught the sound of voices, this time louder than before. He scanned around and saw a line of boulders protruding from the snow about a hundred yards away further up the slope.

'Get the men behind those,' he ordered quickly. 'See if there's somewhere you can hide the mules.'

'Right,' Murap answered. 'Are we going to ambush them or let them pass?'

'That's up to them. Be prepared for a contact.'

Without waiting for further instructions Murap dashed away, waving a series of silent hand signals to the men. The majority of them were ex-forces, and those who weren't had been trained by Ramesh and Ceda themselves until their battle drills were probably better than those of the regular army.

Reaction was instantaneous. The muleteers led their charges as fast as they could in search of downwind cover in the hope that, should any of them bray, the noise would be carried away from the enemy by the wind. Meanwhile the rest of the force headed for the boulders Ramesh had indicated, preparing their weapons as they went. Because of the weather conditions every rifle barrel was covered to prevent moisture getting inside. As they ran the men drew off the sheaths and cocked their weapons. Once at the boulders they sought out the best positions, checking their arcs of fire to ensure they had a clear view of the ground where the enemy was most likely to appear.

Ramesh joined them a moment later. 'No one fire unless I give the order,' he said, keeping his voice low enough for secrecy but pitching it so that it carried along the line.

For himself he selected a gap between two boulders that faced directly into the killing area. Murap crawled to his elbow and said, 'Everyone in position.' He chuckled. 'You know, I think you'd be disappointed if we never had a contact.'

'It keeps us on our toes.'

'Sometimes it puts one or two of us on our backs.'

'Losses in battle are to be expected,' Ramesh replied stoically. 'The trick is to minimize your own while maximizing the enemy's.'

'I'll tell that to the widows. It'll be a great comfort to them.'

Ramesh shrugged. 'The trade keeps them fed while their husbands are alive, and we look after them if their menfolk fail to come back. What more could they ask?'

Murap slapped him on the shoulder. 'That's what I love about you, Ramesh. You're all heart.'

It was some time before they saw the Indian patrol, so much so that Ramesh was starting to wonder if either he'd been mistaken or they had taken another route. Eventually, however, a vague shape materialized out of the white mist and became the figure of a man, leaning into the wind, and behind him, a line of others.

Ramesh tapped Murap, who was busy fiddling with his self-loading rifle. 'Our guests have arrived. Prepare the welcoming committee.'

Murap grinned and slithered on his belly down the line of boulders to ensure that the others were ready. Everyone knew that if it was possible Ramesh would allow the Indian patrol to pass unhindered. The last thing he needed on his back was a follow-up operation. The patrol would undoubtedly be equipped with radios and the moment Ramesh's men opened fire the Indians would send a contact report to their nearest headquarters. Then, as soon as the weather permitted, there would be helicopters in the air searching for them, and on the exposed mountain faces it was often impossible to find cover at short notice. Once they were spotted, other patrols could be guided towards them, entrapping them in a pincer of steel and lead. It had happened only once before and it was not a trap that Ramesh wished to find himself in again.

He hugged the snow, loosening his face mask around his mouth in case he needed to shout out orders and control his men's fire. Fifty yards below him the patrol snaked into the open, traversing the slope with painful care. He estimated it to be of platoon strength, about twenty-five to thirty men in all. The commander was moving close to the front and beside him Ramesh could see two signallers, the long, waving antennas of their radios announcing to all the world that here were priority targets. He glanced sideways and saw that Murap was already on to it, directing the machine-gunner to lay on to the little group and prepare, at Ramesh's signal, to mow them down.

Everything seemed to be going perfectly. At their present speed and direction Ramesh estimated that the patrol would pass out of his way within a further three minutes and that they would head down into the valley he had just left. But the next moment he was cursing softly into his face mask.

With a dramatic motion, the lieutenant held up his hand for a halt. The patrol stopped and Ramesh bit his lip in frustration as he saw that they intended to take a short break. The men gathered in three section groups, and started to spread out groundsheets to sit on while they drank from their vacuum flasks and had a bite to eat.

'Of all the shitty luck,' he growled.

Murap looked at him and shrugged. 'Can't be helped,' he whispered.

Ramesh edged back from the gap in the boulders lest an inquisitive Indian soldier spot him. The snow was still being driven across the slope in flurries, but breaks were appearing in it as the wind lessened. To his horror Ramesh saw one of the Indians get up and start to walk straight towards him.

He can't have seen me, he thought. If that was the case he'd have been running in the opposite direction, or else shooting.

It seemed as though the man intended walking all the way to the boulders, but luckily for Ramesh, halfway there he felt tired, for the snow was deep and at each step he was sinking almost to his knees. So, instead of carrying on, he looked sheepishly back over his shoulder, undid his flies, fumbled through the layers of clothing and began to urinate. The relief on his face could be seen even by the men in the rocks and Ramesh thought it would be a shame to shoot a man caught in such an act. It had somehow converted him from a potential target into a fellow-human.

His task completed, the man refastened his trousers and turned to rejoin his companions, who had been jeering at him all the while. He hadn't gone more than four labouring paces when the unmistakable bray of a mule carried across the slope from the nearby shallow ravine where the muleteers had taken temporary refuge.

Ramesh stiffened, his eyes fixed on the man's retreating back to see if he had noticed. For a moment it seemed as if he might not have caught it, but then he stopped, cocked his head on one side and listened again. As if in answer the mule brayed again.

'I'll slit that beast's throat myself,' Ramesh murmured. 'And then I'll castrate its handler.'

The man turned to face the boulders, and by now the others in the patrol had heard it too. Ramesh tightened the butt of his SLR into his shoulder, thumb-flicked the safety-catch to the fire setting, and pulled the trigger. In front of him the man jumped in the snow and was flung backwards. As the round hit him in the centre of his chest it looked as if a giant hand had plucked him out of the snow and tossed him casually away. He fell soundlessly, the soft whiteness absorbing his body, but staining a second later with his spreading blood.

The rest of the patrol were on their feet and running. From further down the line of boulders the machine-gun started up. Murap was controlling it well and its fire fell with deadly accuracy to the lieutenant, his signallers and the protection party who were close about him. He had chosen a lousy place for his tea break, Ramesh reflected. Anyone worth their salt would instantly have seen that the boulders provided not only cover from fire but, more importantly – given the circumstances – cover from the all-pervading blizzard.

Realizing that they were caught in the open, the Indian patrol flung themselves into the snow and started to return fire at their attackers. On either flank some of them tried to work around the edges to see if they could outmanoeuvre

Ramesh's party, but Ramesh and Murap had prepared for this and their own flank guards cut them down before they had gone a dozen paces.

It seemed that the lieutenant had been killed by the opening machine-gun burst because the next thing Ramesh heard was the voice of the platoon sergeant rallying his men and trying to instil some sense of order in them once more.

'That's it,' Ramesh found himself saying admiringly. 'Get them sorted out. Return fire and either pull out or counter-attack.'

He remembered an old sergeant in a platoon that he had once commanded on a very similar operation. In that instance they had been caught much as the Indian patrol was now trapped. 'Whatever you do,' the sergeant had shouted afterwards at the young subaltern Ramesh had then been, 'you've got to get out of the killing area. So long as you stay there the enemy calls the shots.'

The strong voice of the Indian sergeant now rose above the noise of battle and Ramesh almost felt like calling off the attack. But not quite.

'Murap! Can you see him? If you can, get the machine-gun on him and shut him up!'

'Wilco!'

A handful of the Indians under the command of a foolhardy corporal attempted a frontal assault with fixed bayonets. It was brave but doomed to failure. Not one of them covered more than half a dozen yards before being scythed down by rifle and machine-gun fire.

More difficult to counter was a section machine-gun group that managed to withdraw away from the killing area and reach the relative cover of a cluster of snow-covered rocks. At first Ramesh had thought the rocks were just mounds of snow but as soon as his own machine-gun tried to fire at the men, the bullets blasted the snow away, revealing the solid cover beneath.

'What the hell do we do now?' Murap shouted when he saw that the Indians had found a temporary haven.

Ramesh didn't know. As he watched, the Indian machine-gun came into action, laying down an accurate fire on the ambushers. The wind shifted for a moment and on the sudden gust Ramesh heard the voice of the sergeant rallying his men.

'So you made it to the rocks, did you?' he said with a slight, reluctant smile.

Elsewhere across the snow, bodies lay in the limp poses of death, fresh white drifts covering the bloodstains and settling on the uniforms and discarded equipment. Ramesh hunted around for an answer to the problem. So long as the Indian machine-gun remained in action there was no way that he and his men could move. Of course he could always just sit tight and allow the contest to become a waiting game. He had had the time to choose his positions carefully, whereas the sergeant and his surviving soldiers had scrambled into the only sparse cover available. The wind would be considerably worse for him, added to which they had been forced to abandon their packs in the killing area. With the packs had gone their spare clothing and shelters. In such conditions they wouldn't be able to survive for long without them and any attempt to retrieve them would be met with certain death from Ramesh's machine-gun and rifles.

Nevertheless, Ramesh wondered how long he could afford to sit tight waiting for the Indians to freeze to death. If they knew what they were about they would burrow shallow snow-holes and use whatever kit they had to improvise a wind-break. Once out of the wind they could perhaps survive into the night. Could he wait that long? He doubted it. While he didn't think that they had managed to get a message to their headquarters before the signallers had been killed, it was likely that they would have regular reporting times. It was normal practice, especially in such dangerous conditions where an avalanche or crevasse could swallow a complete patrol in a second. All they had to do was miss one such reporting time and their base would send someone out to look for them. Then perhaps the dreaded helicopters would come.

He bit his lip in frustration. He had to act now. He couldn't wait, however much he might want to. Away to the left he could just see that the ground dipped away. If he could make it round there he might be able to creep up on the sergeant's party and surprise them. But what would he do when he got there?

'Hey, Murap,' he called softly. 'Have you got any grenades?'

Murap thought for a second before frowning and saying, 'Yes, but they're on the mules.'

He pointed over his shoulder and Ramesh saw that to reach them he would have to cross a stretch of open ground, at least twenty yards wide, which was swept by the Indian machine-gun. As he was thinking of a solution Murap called back to him.

'We might not have any, but he has.' Ramesh looked to where Murap was pointing and saw the body of the man who had first heard the mule. The snow had almost covered him by now, but hooked on to his belt Ramesh saw the familiar shape of two hand-grenades.

'Brilliant. How the fuck am I supposed to get them?'

'We can cover you from here.'

'I might as well try for the mules.'

Murap shook his head. 'I don't think they can see you from their rocks. Not if you keep close to the ground.'

88

Ramesh looked and saw that Murap was right. From his position further down the line Murap was able to see that the ground between the Indian sergeant and the body of the dead man rose into a gentle, convex slope. So long as Ramesh crawled in a perfectly straight line and hugged the snow it was unlikely that he would be seen.

He rolled on to one side and undid his belt, then stripped off his harness and shoulder straps. From one of his pouches he took two spare magazines and stuffed them in his pocket. Without the extra encumbrance of the webbing he judged that he had a better chance of making it out and back in one piece.

On the far side of his boulder there was a gap large enough for him to crawl through, and when he had shouldered his way between the two rocks he slithered forward out of cover. Once out on the virgin snow he felt unpleasantly vulnerable. To left and right there was nothing except the bare white expanse, and behind him he could feel the eyes of his men following his progress. He knew that Murap would keep up a steady fire on the Indian position, not increasing the volume as that might alert the sergeant to the fact that something was happening. Then, if he had grenades of his own, he might start to throw them in Ramesh's direction.

Keeping as close to the ground as he could, Ramesh eased slowly forward. His eyes were fixed on the dead body in front of him and on the slight rise behind it that masked him from the Indian machine-gun. Bullets from both sides stung the air inches above his head and at one point he glanced back with a scowl at Murap to warn him and the others to be careful. The last thing he wanted was to have his brains blown out by his own men.

Yard by yard the distance to the body lessened until Ramesh edged himself across the last small stretch of snow and drew level with the man's boots. Pulling himself alongside the body, he got his face alongside the man's belt and was just reaching across for the first of the two grenades when the head tipped his way and the eyes rolled open, fixing him with a deathly stare. Ramesh felt his heart miss a beat with the shock and he only just managed to stop himself crying out. As he stared back in horror the eyes blinked and the man's hand started to move.

Ramesh fumbled desperately for his knife, his fingers, numb with the cold, making hard work of it.

'Damn you,' he rasped, half to himself and half to the Indian. 'You're supposed to be dead.'

He got his knife free and was bringing it up when the man saw the blade and realized that, far from having come to rescue him, Ramesh intended to finish him off. With his last burst of strength he raised his head and cried out, the cry carrying back to his comrades behind the rocks. The next instant it was cut short by Ramesh's knife slamming down into his chest, the blade penetrating all the way to the hilt. His head fell back and the eyes rolled again – this time in death.

But the damage had been done, and the sergeant was alerted to the new threat. Bullets spat in the ground all around Ramesh and he wriggled backwards until protected by the rise in the ground. Even so, the fire was shaving dangerously close.

'If they keep this up they'll cut the bloody top off the hill,' Ramesh thought.

The grenades still hung tantalizingly close on the dead man's belt. As carefully as he could, he stretched up his hand, sliding it alongside the body, and then inched his fingers towards the first of the grenades. It was well fastened to the webbing strap but after a second it came loose and he was able to slip it in his pocket. The other grenade was more difficult as it was obscured by the man's body and Ramesh had to feel for it. At one point as he felt for the touch of the metal his fingers entered the wound that his earlier bullet had caused and he flinched in surprise. He steeled himself to try again and this time he retrieved the grenade.

He moved away from the body, feeling a flood of relief as the ground dropped steadily beneath him, increasing the degree of cover from the machine-gun that was still hunting for him around the dead body. There was an almost overwhelming temptation to break and run for the safety of the boulders but he knew the urge resulted from fear, and that it was illusory. The moment he showed his head it would be blown wide open by the 7.62mm bullets cracking all about him. So, keeping his nerves on a short rein, he continued back to the boulders, moving as stealthily as on the outward stalk.

Murap was waiting to greet him.

'Well done. I can see you've been a sniper in your day.'

Ramesh rolled on to his back and mopped his brow. Despite the freezing conditions he found that he was sweating, the beads stinging on his face as the wind discovered the rare moisture and stunned it into ice.

'Let's finish this,' he said stonily. 'It's time that machine-gun was silenced.'

'Do you want me or one of the lads to go?' Murap asked.

But Ramesh was already on his way. 'No. This one's mine.'

He resisted the urge to pause for a moment and rest, knowing that were he to do so his muscles would stiffen and the wind would chill him still further. He had to get the business done and get them all off the mountain. It had been bad enough for him, but in some respects it was worse for his men. At least he had been able to keep warm by moving. But they had been forced to lie stationary for some time now and Ramesh could imagine that the weakest and least experienced of them would already be well on the way to frostbite.

The line of boulders petered out some fifty yards to the right in dead ground. Unwilling to risk compromising his position, Ramesh crawled the full distance, arriving at the snow-filled hollow exhausted and gasping. His lungs sucked in the air and he felt the sharp stabs of pain as its dry iciness stung his chest like needles. His throat felt raw and he tightened his mask around his mouth. However, looking about him he judged it safe to run at a crouch for the next bit of the way, before the final crawl, which would take him to within throwing distance of the enemy machine-gun position.

Instead of his cumbersome rifle he had taken a Sterling sub-machine-gun from one of his men. Should anything go wrong with the grenade throw, he would rather rely on the Sterling's rapid rate of fire than on the single-shot capability of his SLR. The SMG's accuracy was poor by comparison but at close quarters a good spread of shot was more important.

Holding it close to his stomach, he ran bent almost double. He had folded the stock, and the weapon sat snugly against him, the curved thirty-round magazine resting on his left forearm as he cradled the underside of the barrel in his left hand and clutched the handgrip and trigger in his right. The safety-catch was off and he had pulled back the cocking handle so that the slightest pressure on the trigger would set it firing.

The ground fell away into a re-entrant and he decided to follow it to its end, which he estimated would bring him to a point roughly in the rear of the Indian position. However, as he moved, he became aware that the sound of the firing had dropped and that the only shots appeared to be coming from his own men. He slowed his pace, trying to figure out what had happened, when suddenly, round the bend not ten yards in front of him, the whole group of five Indian soldiers appeared at a jog. They had chosen that exact moment to bug out, selecting the same route for their escape that Ramesh had picked for his grenade stalk.

Ramesh swore and dropped to one knee, hugging the SMG firmly. Firing in short, controlled bursts, he directed his jets of 9mm bullets into the oncoming enemy. Taken by surprise, they began to fall as Ramesh raked the re-entrant from side to side with his fire.

Suddenly the hammer clicked mutely on an empty chamber. The man he had borrowed it from had failed to tell him that the magazine was already half expended. One of the Indians saw his chance and hurled himself at Ramesh, who swung with the short, stubby weapon, catching him on the jaw and laying him out flat. But it was the last remaining opponent who presented the real threat. The sergeant had been moving at the rear of his group and, seeing the others fall, had managed to take cover out of Ramesh's line of fire. As Ramesh threw aside the useless SMG and fumbled for his knife, the sergeant dived at him, knocking him to the ground and coming up on top, his own knife raised for the kill.

But Ramesh was no novice at hand-to-hand fighting and brought his knee into the sergeant's side, shouting out to focus the power of his blow. The wind went out of the sergeant and Ramesh thrust him to the side, finding his knife as he did so. There was a clash of steel as he drove down only to meet the sergeant's parrying blow. Both men were on their feet in an instant, circling, each gauging the other, looking for an opening in his opponent's guard.

The sergeant was the first to move, first aiming high and slashing at Ramesh's face and then lunging deeply towards the midriff. But Ramesh had read his intention, seen the desperation in the man's eyes. He knew that his combat subtlety would only extend to a simple feint and thrust, and the moment he was proved correct, he was already halfway into his own spoiling attack, sidestepping, parrying with the heel of one gloved palm and slicing straight into the sergeant's throat. His blade struck home, finding flesh and gristle. The sergeant slumped to his knees, his weapon forgotten as both hands scrabbled at his throat as if he would hold in the air and blood that rushed to escape. It was useless. Ramesh stood back gasping for breath as he watched the sergeant die, toppling over into the snow, dead before his face cushioned itself in the enveloping white softness.

There were voices from behind. Ramesh whirled but it was only Murap and two of the men. Murap whistled in admiration.

'You could have left some for us.'

But Ramesh wasn't in any mood for idle chat. Too many good men had died that day, and they had been delayed in the completion of their task.

'Let's get off this fucking mountain,' he said hoarsely, thrusting his knife into its sheath. 'We've got work to do.'

'What about the bodies?'

'Leave them,' he answered as he strode back towards the rocks. 'The snow will bury them for us.'

6

Jerry Patel had never ached so much in his whole life. His legs throbbed, his back was a sheet of fire, his arms felt as if they were about to snap, his eyes stung from lack of sleep and his head pounded. Every muscle in his body had been pulled and stretched and tasked beyond the limit of endurance, and yet somehow he was still enduring, still pressing on, still heading for home. The whole decrepit package that was himself was held together by one thing and one thing alone – his will. It was like a determined sea captain, steering his storm-blasted vessel the last miles to harbour, the hold awash, the crew mutinied and gone, the cargo lost. But Jerry was going to make it, or die trying.

The hillside before him went on and on, one false crest after another. As he rounded each supposed summit it was only to realize it had been a mere fold in the ground, with another higher, further, steeper one a few hundred yards beyond. He cursed the land, the weather, himself, goading himself on as if talking to someone else.

'Get your arse in gear, you idle bastard. You lousy wanker, you useless sod, you stupid, pig-ignorant git.'

Anyone listening to him might have been forgiven for thinking he was a hopeless mental case had they not understood that he always goaded himself like that, driving himself on as if his will marched alongside, integral yet separate, observing, criticizing, urging. It had driven him through the Parachute Regiment's gruelling P Company three years before, and the previous month it had dragged and kicked him successfully through the last hurdle of SAS selection. He had been a little disappointed to learn that, far from being allowed to rest on his laurels, he was expected to go straight out again on an extended exercise with his new squadron, but he supposed that it was all part of the deal. In the SAS, he was fast learning, there never would be any laurels to rest on, not until the Regiment had finished with you and you were back in the mainstream army or pushing up daisies in the cemetery; for Jerry the two amounted to the same thing.

As he struggled over yet another crest a strong wind hit him full in the face, carrying with it a freezing rain that had already soaked him. With the wind, the temperature dropped, and the rain began to turn to ice. It froze up his ammunition pouches and formed icicles on the shoulder straps, adding to the overall weight of his load. The one relief to greet him, however, was the sight of the valley beyond. He had reached the real summit at last and from here on would be able to descend.

He jogged over to a rock and eased down out of the wind to catch his breath and survey the lie of the land. The Brecon Beacons stretched away in every direction, bleak and rugged, their gently flowing contours belying the severity of the climb. Leaning back against the moss-covered rock, he slid to the ground, feeling the weight lift off his shoulders as the rock took the pack. He put back his head and sighed, pulling the straps away from his bruised flesh. A thin coating of ice covered his webbing and the hem of his jacket was stiff with it. He grasped a fistful of the material, feeling it crackle as the ice powdered. Undoing a pocket flap, he took out a tube of boiled sweets and popped one in his mouth, feeling the instantaneous rush of sugar on his tongue, sugar that would soon convert into much-needed energy. Once out of the wind it was surprisingly quiet on the hilltop, the only sound being the patter of driving rain on his pack and on his sodden combats. He took out his waterproofed map and compared it with the landscape below. His Silva compass was in his top-right breast pocket, secured to his jacket by a lanyard looped through the pocket flap's buttonhole. He laid it on the map and aligned the markings on its face with the map's north-south grid lines, twisting the dial until he was able to obtain a bearing from his present position to his destination. When he had it he ascertained his direction to travel for the next leg of the journey, sighting along the body of the compass to see where it pointed. The corner of a forestry block in the far distance marked the approximate spot and he judged that from there he should be able to see the final leg. This would take him to the rendezvous with the transport that would take him back to camp.

Camp. He closed his eyes for a moment and permitted himself the luxury of anticipation. In the corridor outside his room he would drop his pack and webbing, and strip off his wet, filthy combats. Then there would be a long soak in a hot bath, relaxing away the aching muscles and sprains. Afterwards, dressed in clean, warm, dry clothes he would go for a hot meal, perhaps out of camp to a local pub where he could also enjoy a pint or two, finally returning to sleep in a soft, deep bed under an enormous duvet, cocooned until late the next morning, a Sunday, when nothing would be expected of him except attendance at the bar for a few beers with the lads before a huge roast lunch.

The cold rain lashed against his cheeks, startling him awake.

'Fucking idiot,' he muttered bitterly. 'Nearly dozed off, didn't you? You useless piece of trash.' He began to stagger to his feet. 'Where would that have got you? The easiest death in the whole fucking world. They'd have found you in a day or two, frozen solid, so pale they wouldn't know you were a bloody Tandoori until they saw your ID discs and the name Patel.'

He slipped his map away and buttoned up his compass in his top pocket. Tandoori. Some of the guys had called him that during selection and it had stuck. That and other names. Funnily enough he didn't mind them here. In the Paras it had been different. There he'd met the biggest bunch of racists since school and it had been a long time before he had been accepted. In some ways he never had been, but here it was different. The lads were different – everything was. That was why for most of them there could never be any other kind of soldiering after Hereford. When his tour was over he hoped to be able to stay on. If not, he wasn't sure what he would do. He certainly wouldn't want to go back to the Paras and the dreary wasteland of Aldershot and Normandy Barracks.

The downhill going wasn't quite as easy as he had hoped. The ground was largely tussock grass, soft, spongy clumps with bog in between. The options were either to tread from clump to clump or weave around them. The former was fine when you had plentiful reserves of energy but in his present condition all Jerry could do was to slog on blindly, sometimes finding a firm footing on top of the tussocks, but more often than not stumbling into the brown morass that ringed and fed them.

In some respects walking on such difficult terrain demanded greater concentration than ploughing uphill and Jerry found that he had less time for his own thoughts, which was no bad thing. So long as he was busy watching where to put his feet he couldn't moan about how shattered he was. However, once down on the valley floor, the tussocks gave way to firmer ground and he was able to make up some of the lost time.

He came to a broad stream, the water a rich transparent brown from the surrounding peat. It was far from ideal but it would have to do. Down on one knee, he took out his water bottle and refilled it, dropping in a couple of sterilizing tablets. It would taste disgusting, a mixture of peat and chlorine, probably with a hint of sheep's piss to heighten the flavour, but it was all there was. Perhaps if he was lucky he might find a better source near the forestry block, but it was unlikely on the higher ground. For now, this would have to do and it was better to have foul water in your canteen than none at all.

Walking on the level came as an unusual respite from the more customary ascents and descents. For a while he almost began to enjoy himself. The rain continued, though it was not as ferocious as on the summits, but after all, according to one of the earliest pearls of army wisdom he had heard, 'If it's not raining, it's not training.'

God how the army loved its catch-phrases! There was one for every occasion and some folks Jerry had met seemed to be able to go through life uttering little else. They were 'army-barmy'. He could think of other descriptions for them.

His stride had lengthened and he was happy to note that he was covering the ground rapidly. Nevertheless, as soon as he began to climb again he slowed, leaning into the slope and slipping into the old familiar rhythm of the laden hill-walker. One of the unfortunate consequences of being on low ground again was that his destination had disappeared from view. It wasn't a problem as far as keeping direction was concerned; he had his compass bearing for that. But its effect on morale was less than beneficial. Seen from the opposing ridgeline where he had halted, the forestry block didn't look quite so far away, but as he laboured up the hillside he was confronted once again with false crest after false crest, the deceptive folds of marsh and bog that had not been visible from his resting place, now rippling upwards with sadistic inevitability.

Time blurred into a continuum of misery. He tried to switch off his brain and for a while it worked, but always it was the niggling little thoughts that intruded. Would he watch the skiing on TV on Sunday afternoon? Why were there no black Olympic swimmers and no white heavyweight boxers? Who went round nicking the badges off Volkswagens and what the fuck did they do with them? Did men with pony-tails have a higher or lower IQ than men who wore their baseball caps back to front? When would Cilla chuck the pretence on *Blind Date* and ask the only question everyone wanted answered: 'Did you get laid?'

He was so busy pondering the last question, head bent into his stride, that he almost walked straight into the wire fence bordering the forestry plantation.

'Thank buggery for that,' he wheezed, skirting around the edge until he came to the crown of the hill.

Sure enough, down below on the far side he could just make out the thin, grey ribbon of road and the slight indentation that signified the parking place where the lorry was due in a couple of hours. He leaned on the wire and studied the layout. The area surrounding the road looked barren and empty and if the rain and wind strengthened there would be nowhere there for him to shelter. But the forestry plantation was another matter. So, deciding to take a longer break, he clambered over the fence and pushed through the trees until he found a sheltered hollow beneath some low-hanging branches. It was cosy inside and he slipped off his pack, feeling as if, with the sudden weight loss, he was in danger of floating away like an untethered balloon.

It would probably take him half an hour to reach the pick-up point, so he estimated that he could relax for a good hour. The greatest feat would be not falling asleep and missing the RV altogether. The Regiment would definitely not be impressed. He might have passed selection but he felt as if he was still on probation. He had been particularly depressed when someone had told him that it was a feeling that never passed. The guy had said that you only really relaxed and felt you were 'SAS' when you were out. But when Jerry had passed this on to one of the training sergeants, the man had grunted 'Bollocks'. So what was a new boy supposed to do? Keep his head down and work hard, Jerry had concluded.

He rummaged in the side pouch of his pack and came up with a miniature camping stove. With his knife he dug out a small hole in the soft, needle-covered turf, sufficient to hold the burner, and settled it in. Then, placing a tin mug of water on the tiny blue gas flame, he set about making a brew. The shelter he had chosen kept out the worst of the wind and nearly all of the rain, but the air temperature was still low enough for the water to take an age to boil. When it did, he dropped in a tea bag and stirred the mixture, adding plenty of sugar and a little powdered milk, scrupulously returning the used sachets to his pack for later disposal in camp. The drill had nothing to do with keeping Britain tidy, but everything to do with basic field discipline, since a carelessly discarded piece of litter could lead to the compromise of a patrol.

When the brew was ready he packed away every item of kit and fastened all the loose flaps before settling down with his back against a tree to enjoy his drink. As always he kept his webbing on, his pack close beside him, and his rifle instantly to hand. The first sip of tea sent shock waves of pleasure rippling through him. It was better than alcohol, better than dry clothes, better than sex. Given the circumstances, that is.

The heat penetrated the metal sides of the mug and seeped into his dirt-ingrained hands. The skin was wrinkled from the rain water and it felt wonderful to touch heat, even in such limited quantities. Another sip, and he felt as if he was ready to do the tab all over again. Well, perhaps that was taking things too far. He remembered one of the wartime Chindits saying that whenever you find yourself confronting an insuperable problem, sit down and make a brew, and the problem will miraculously resolve itself. It certainly worked as far as morale problems were concerned. A whole new perspective was put on life and you could set out again on your mission, as if from a new and much more logical starting-point.

All too soon he had drained the mug, and only a grainy residue remained in the bottom. He tipped it out and clapped the mug on to the top of his water bottle, fastening the securing flap over it. The temptation was great just to lean back against the tree and close his eyes for a moment, but he knew that the moment would extend rapidly into a prolonged sleep. In the shelter of the trees it would probably not be fatal, unlike on the exposed hillside, but he would miss his transport, and in some respects that would be just as serious.

He hummed softly to himself for a while, thinking of nothing in particular until he remembered what one of his relatives had said when they heard he had passed the selection for the SAS. They had thought he had chucked in the army to join the Scandinavian airline with the same initials.

'I'm so glad you're out of that bunch,' one uncle had commented with obvious relief, little realizing the hole he was digging for himself. 'I can tell you now that the family has never really been happy with your choice of career.'

There had been an embarrassed silence as the other family members present had signalled frantic warnings behind Jerry's back.

'Yes,' the oblivious relative had continued. 'Both your father and mother have said to me on many an occasion that they felt you could do better for yourself. What with your education and family connections, there could have been a career for you in any number of areas. Accountancy, engineering, law.' He shrugged. 'But the airline business is fine, I am sure. At least it's out of the military! There's an old Chinese saying: You don't use good iron to make nails,' he concluded with a condescending smile.

In the ensuing leaden silence Jerry had looked from his mother to his father and around the room. No one had had the courage to meet his eyes and he had left the house soon afterwards, making the excuse that he was required back at camp.

So that was what they all thought of his chosen path. Wasted potential. They would rather see him sitting behind some desk. Of course, sometimes he felt that way himself, but always he came back to the same conclusion: that he was cut out for something more adventurous. He didn't know where the urge came from, but it was there, and he had to give it expression. The SAS was the perfect means for doing just that and he intended to see it through, wherever it led him.

He looked out through the thick screen of branches and saw that the rain had stopped. A thin winter sunlight was trying without much success to penetrate the heavy clouds. In the tops of the surrounding firs the wind softened from its previous howl to a friendlier if agitated whisper. Jerry stretched out his legs and massaged the muscles through his sodden trousers, kneading the flesh with numb hands. A shudder ran through his body and he checked his watch to see if it was time to press on. The hot bath and change of clothes were beckoning.

He slipped his arms through his pack's straps and eased the load on to his shoulders, juggling the weight until it sat as comfortably as possible. Crawling out from under his cover on hands and knees, he felt the breeze eddying between the tree trunks chill him as it touched his wet clothing. All he wanted now was to be on the transport and bouncing the last miles back to camp.

Once over the wire fence he set off down the far side of the hill, heading for the lay-by, carefully watching his step over the difficult ground yet glancing up every few paces to look at it as if he half expected it to fade from view like the unearthly Welsh equivalent of some desert mirage. But there it was, as hard and real as the tarmac that composed it. Yard by yard the ground separating him from his goal fell away. His pace quickened until he was jogging the final distance. Panting from the exertion, he arrived at last and for the first time in what seemed like an eternity set foot on a metalled road. After the spongy quagmire of the hill country it was as welcoming as a bed with crisp, clean sheets. Right on time, the sound of an engine groaned in the distance and a moment later a Bedford lorry appeared over the rise, gathering speed as it headed down the gentle gradient towards the lay-by. For one horrific second the thought crossed Jerry's mind that perhaps it might continue on past. But no. That only happened on selection. It was the final straw that separated those with unshakeable morale from those without. After a harrowing series of tabs the candidates would arrive at the final RV to be told there was one more to go.

With a squeal of brakes the lorry stopped, the driver peering out of the window as he reversed into the lay-by.

'Sorry about that, mate,' he shouted. 'I almost forgot you'd be here.'

'No problem,' Jerry replied, smiling with relief. Selection was over. He had passed. He was in the SAS now. There would be no more 'sickeners'. 'Don't bother to let down the tailboard. I can climb in over the top,' he said with genuine gratitude in his voice.

A familiar face popped out of the back of the lorry, rubbing sleep from his eyes. 'We here already?'

Jerry looked up to see Sergeant Gavin Steward of the training wing. Steward's eyes lit up when he saw the sodden figure standing at the roadside. 'Tandoori! Good of you to make it.'

Jerry returned the smile a little less certainly. 'Hi, Sarge. Room in there for me?'

'Are you pissed? You didn't really think the crap all stopped with selection, did you?'

Jerry steeled himself for a shock, forcing a smile. 'Fair enough. How many more miles to the PUP?'

'What do you mean, pick-up point? I'll see you back in camp.'

Jerry felt as if his heart had just stopped. 'But that's two days' tabbing, right back the way I've just come!'

'Smart lad,' the sergeant winked. 'You'll go far. Say, about forty miles.'

Jerry waited for Steward to tell him it was just a joke but instead the sergeant rummaged in the lorry and re-emerged with a holdall jammed with radio batteries.

'Oh and by the way, be a good lad and take these for me. You see, I've got my sleeping bag stretched out in here and when we go over a bump they rattle around and wake me up.'

He smiled disarmingly and banged on the side of the lorry to attract the driver's attention. 'Home, James, and don't spare the horses.'

As the lorry started to pull away he shouted back, 'How you doing for rations?'

'They're all gone.'

'Well, there's another lesson for you. Always maintain a reserve. Cheerio.'

The lorry drew out on to the road and accelerated away, a cloud of blue diesel smoke belching from the exhaust. Jerry stood in the lay-by looking after it until it bumped over a rise, rounded a bend and vanished, leaving him feeling suddenly terribly alone. He turned and walked to the edge of the tarmac, and with a heart as heavy as granite he took the first step back on to the spongy grass. He hardly dared raise his eyes to confront the mounting slope that he knew lay before him, the first of many, and as he trudged agonizingly away from the road he felt the clouds close over him and the patter of the cold rain.

7

The old man sat morosely by the window looking out at the bare winter garden. Wherever it was it looked like a hundred other anonymous gardens that sprouted the length and breadth of England. There were the neat flower-beds, now consisting of little more than wet black earth, a paved path winding down to a tool shed just visible between three or four tall firs, a ragged lawn and a plastic washing line strung with dangling beads of rainwater. Where the hell had the police found it?

He had been in the safe house for a week now and the only people he had seen were the two plain-clothes policemen and the one woman who had been assigned to guard him. All three were armed but Mr Sanji knew that if another attempt was made on his life their pathetic array of police revolvers would be of little use against the massed fire-power of his enemies. His only hope lay in the secrecy of his hideaway. He had made several requests for information but for some reason each had been met with polite ignorance. Then he had asked for a solicitor and even this, although noted, had not been acted upon. He was beginning to wonder if he was a fugitive under police protection or a prisoner.

He got up and went through to the kitchen to make himself a cup of coffee. Seated at the kitchen table, two of his minders were playing chess, while the third was in the adjacent room watching television. The senior one of the three looked up as he entered.

'Making a coffee?'

What the fuck does it look like? Mr Sanji thought to himself. 'Yes, do you want one?'

Alec leaned back in his chair and scratched his belly. 'That would be just the job. Dave?'

His companion grunted, his eyes remaining fixed on the board. Mr Sanji noted that most of Dave's chess pieces had been removed from the board and were now arrayed next to Alec's plump white elbow. Alec, on the other hand, appeared to have lost only two pawns and one of his bishops. It wasn't that he was particularly smart – more that Dave was a mental midget when it came to anything more complicated than filling out a parking ticket. Mr Sanji shuddered at the thought of such a man being entrusted with a firearm and, more importantly, Sanji's own life.

The kettle took a few minutes to boil and while he waited Mr Sanji leaned against the worktop and watched the chess game.

'What kind of guns are those?' he asked out of idle curiosity.

'Smith & Wessons. I'd offer to show it to you but it's against regulations.'

Mr Sanji waved his hand. 'I'm not much interested in guns. Never had any cause to learn about them. Is it difficult to use?'

Alec was clearly unhappy about being distracted from completing the defeat of his companion but shrugged and said, 'Not once you've done the training package. It's a close-range weapon anyway, so all you've really got to do is point it in roughly the right direction and keep pulling the trigger until your man goes down.'

The cursory explanation did little to increase Mr Sanji's confidence in his guards.

When the coffee was made he handed the two policemen their mugs and took his own through to the sitting room. Deep in an armchair, Anne Baron stared mesmerized at the afternoon chat show. Sanji lowered himself on to the sofa.

'Anything interesting?'

He knew the answer before she even opened her mouth. A television addict, Anne seemed to fear that she was missing out on life whenever she was obliged to leave the screen.

'They're talking about the Cones Hotline,' she replied without taking her eyes off the garishly decorated studio set. Two mannequin presenters were conducting a phone-in, their faces concentrated in sincerity as one simpleton after another aired his or her opinion to the nation. Technology had given them the capability of addressing their fellow-man, but no one had stopped to consider whether they had anything worth saying. It was entertainment by reduction to the lowest common denominator, the most primeval semi-human grunt given equal credence and air time alongside the most erudite latterday Socrates. Sanji looked across at Anne, at the dull glaze on her limp face as the images and sounds rotted her from the inside out.

He managed to stand the spectacle for a further three and a half minutes before surrendering all hope of conversation and climbing the stairs dejectedly to his bedroom. A small desk stood under the window and, set in the centre of it, a silver-framed photograph of his granddaughter smiled radiantly into the room. He put down his coffee, sank on to the bed and took the picture in his hands.

'Oh, Eli, why did I ever bring your mother to this terrible country? If only I had gone to Africa or Australia, anywhere but here.' He replaced the photograph, realizing that had he done so then the likelihood was that Eli would not even exist. His daughter wouldn't have married that ridiculous man but someone else instead, and although Sanji might not be in his present predicament, he would never had known the sweet laugh and gentle care of Eli. Life was a strange business, virtually all of it resting on complete chance, and yet no sooner had every random event occurred than it somehow acquired the feeling of destiny. It was deceptive, of course. Seductive even. But quite illusory.

He fluffed up his pillow and lay back on the bed, feeling his head sink back into the soft down. The bed at least was a success story. The house might be drab, his daughter and son-in-law dead, his dear, sweet Eli kidnapped, but the bed was wonderful and, in spite of all his worries, every night he was sleeping like a log.

When he opened his eyes he was startled to find the room in darkness. For one brief moment he was scared, but when he looked at the luminous hands of his watch he saw that it was some four hours since he had gone up to his bedroom. He obviously hadn't realized how tired he was and had slept the afternoon away.

'What a waste,' he thought bitterly, swinging his legs off the bed and struggling to sit up. But then this whole wretched business was a terrible waste, locked up in the house with three idiots as his only company.

He rubbed his eyes and it was only then that he felt a shiver run down his spine. There was something wrong. It was normal for it to get dark so early at that time of year but the house was fitted with spotlights, ostensibly as part

110

of a normal burglar alarm system although in reality they had more to do with the house's classification as a safe haven. The garden was pitch-dark, however. Ever since he had been there the lights had come on at dusk, and certainly long before their illumination was really needed. But now, as he peered cautiously out of the window, he couldn't even see as far as the fir trees at the bottom of the garden.

He opened his door as silently as he could, went out on to the landing and leaned over the banisters to listen. Through the closed glass-panel door of the sitting room he could hear the noise of the television. Anne was watching cartoons but the room light was off, only the glow from the TV screen flickering through the frosted glass on to the bottom of the stairs.

Sanji was really scared now. He opened his mouth to call out but thought better of it. If there was an intruder in the house the last thing he wanted to do was to alert him to his presence upstairs. But what was he thinking of? This was a safe house. He was under police protection and there were three armed officers downstairs whose sole present purpose in life was to keep him alive. One thought of Alec, Dave and Anne, however, was sufficient to cure him of such a misplaced confidence in his minders.

He crept back into his room and unplugged the bedside lamp, removing the shade and bulb and then, holding it like a club, he started down the stairs. One by one he crept down them, shifting his weight as delicately as a man of his age could. When he reached the bottom he paused to listen, straining his ears to pick up any unnatural sound. But his efforts were thwarted by the blaring racket of the cartoons.

The door knob turned softly in his hand and as the frame inched open he received the full blast of the TV. Tom and

Jerry had chosen that precise instant to batter each other and Sanji flinched as if he had been hit himself, almost dropping his lamp. Realizing his error, he cursed himself for being such a coward and went into the room. The armchair where Anne had been sitting was empty except for her gun lying in the middle of the cushion. Sanji stared at it for a moment, wondering whether to pick it up.

It was then that he heard the noise from the kitchen, the scraping of a table leg and a grunt as if someone was shifting something heavy. Like a body, Sanji thought, the goose-pimples rising all over him. After placing his lamp carefully on the floor he retrieved Anne's revolver from the armchair and studied it in the light from the television until he had located the safety-catch and flicked it to the fire position. Then, cranking back the hammer and clutching the grip in both hands as he had seen in the movies, he stepped silently towards the kitchen door. It was ajar and the slightest pressure from the toe of his running shoe swung it soundlessly wide. The glow from the TV screen shone into the darkened room.

Spread face down across the kitchen table, Anne Baron panted, her eyes tightly shut. Her skirt was up over her back and her knickers were gathered around one of her fat splayed ankles. Behind her, and looking equally ridiculous, Dave's fleshy white buttocks convulsed rhythmically against her rump, the business side of him mercifully concealed from view. His trousers had crumpled at his knees and he looked to Sanji like a small boy enjoying a rather unusual piss.

Sanji lowered his revolver, although the thought fleetingly crossed his mind of shooting the pair of them and robbing them of the critical moment. He was just wondering whether he should back away and leave them to their rutting when

Anne's eyes half opened and found themselves focusing with difficulty on Sanji's bemused gaze.

'Oh fuck!'

Dave moaned in response, mistaking her exclamation for one of ecstasy caused by his efforts. 'Yes, yes.'

'No, you git. Get off me.'

She bucked her hips to try and shake him off but he was no longer on the same planet. Seeing her dilemma, Sanji tactfully withdrew, pulling the door quietly closed behind him. He went across to the light switch and flicked it on as male cries sounded in the kitchen, followed, embarrassingly rapidly, by the hushed mutter of conferring voices, the one somewhat more breathless than the other.

Sanji gently eased forward the hammer on the revolver lest he fire off his own negligent discharge, and sat down to watch the news which had just begun. As a newscaster recited the day's triumphs, catastrophes and anecdotes, his face shifting gear with each take, ranging through boredom, concern and indulgent mirth respectively, the neon strip-light flickered on in the kitchen. Sanji could imagine the ugliness of its cold mortuary glare shining on the pale, guilty flesh of the two lovers as they rearranged their dress. Sure enough, when the door opened and they filed into the sitting room, it might as well have been the emergence of the living dead.

Without looking at them he asked merrily, 'Anyone making coffee?'

His question went unanswered. Instead Anne mumbled something about make-up and disappeared up to the bathroom while Dave perched on the edge of the armchair and pretended to watch the news. Sanji knew full well that he wasn't the least bit interested in it and it was barely half a minute before he said sheepishly, 'You won't tell Alec, will you?'

Sanji smiled at him, liking the fellow for the first time. 'What's there to tell?'

The relief on Dave's face could have been bottled and sold for a fortune.

'After all,' Sanji continued, 'I'm a man of the world.' But he was unable to suppress the devil in himself. 'You must love her very much?'

Dave blushed, inspecting his hands as he wrung them and, as Sanji had suspected, he didn't have the balls to deny it.

'Yeah, course. She's a great woman.'

Sanji sighed theatrically, not having had so much fun for ages. 'Ah, the antics of the young. It makes me feel like a youth myself to see such a tender pair of lovebirds.' He leaned forward earnestly, the bit now well and truly between his teeth. 'When do you plan to marry her?'

It was unfortunate that Dave had perched quite so close to the edge of his chair because only the most obvious effort managed to keep him from falling off it. However, deciding that he had been tormented enough, and appreciating that because of the interruption his passion had been rudely accelerated, Sanji relented and drew the baiting to a close by casually mentioning the absence of the spotlights.

For a moment, from the look of consternation that came over Dave, Sanji wondered whether the policeman was trying to get his revenge by unsettling his Indian guest. He spun in his chair, his earlier embarrassment entirely forgotten.

'I assumed you'd turned them off to get a bit of privacy,' Sanji said falteringly.

'No way. I might screw the WPC but I wouldn't tamper with the security system.'

He got quickly out of his chair and drew his revolver from its holster.

'Where is Alec, by the way?' Sanji asked.

'He went out for a pizza.'

'Of course. I forgot it's pizza night tonight.'

Sanji had no sooner finished his sentence than he realized what he had said. The blundering idiots had set a pattern. With only three takeaways nearby it was fish and chips one night, curry the second and pizza the third, in strict rotation, on Alec's insistence. Sanji had suspected that he had never really taken the task seriously, his overriding concern being with the contents of his stomach. The poor fools had no idea who they were dealing with.

Dave made for the light switch and turned it off.

'Where's the remote for the TV?'

'I've got it,' Sanji replied.

'Kill it, will you?'

The picture disappeared, and Sanji sat frozen on the sofa waiting for his eyes to become accustomed to the darkness. After a couple of minutes he was able to make out the figure of Dave standing by the curtain, holding it open a crack and peering out to the front of the house. But the police had chosen the place for its seclusion and it was at the end of an isolated cul-de-sac.

'Shit.' Dave's voice was cold and matter-of-fact.

'What is it?'

'Street lights are all out.'

Sanji's heart was suddenly chilled. He felt his gut heave and for a second he thought he was going to be sick. They had found him again, and this time he knew they would ensure the job was properly done.

'What about Alec?' he tried. 'He should be back at any moment, shouldn't he?'

He could almost hear Dave's mind racing.

'Yes. That's right.'

Neither of them dared voice the thought that entered their minds simultaneously. If they were indeed out there, then Alec would never be returning.

'Couldn't it just be a simple power failure?' Sanji asked.

'It could be. The street light could go out without it affecting the internal power source, but the spots should still be working.'

'Might Alec have turned them off for some reason?'

'No way. At least not without telling us first.'

There was the sound of footsteps padding down the stairs. 'What are you doing standing in the darkness?' Anne said, reaching for the light switch.

'Don't touch that!'

'Why ever not?'

'The external lights are all out.'

'But Alec . . .'

Dave was about to explain their fears when there was a knock at the kitchen door. All three of them stood as stiff as rods. The knock came again, more urgent than before.

'Get down, Mr Sanji,' Anne commanded coolly. 'Keep down until we've sorted this out.'

She and Dave moved through to the kitchen, leaving the door open behind them. In spite of her instructions, Sanji stepped after them, partly from inquisitiveness and partly from fear of being left alone in the darkness.

'Who is it?'

'Who do you think? Open the door.' And then, after a pause, 'It's me, Alec. The pizza's getting cold.'

Dave swapped looks with Anne and glanced accusingly at Sanji as if blaming him for getting them all riled. But as he moved to unbolt the solid back door Sanji hissed, 'Just a moment.'

'What now?'

Sanji wasn't sure. The voice certainly sounded like Alec but there was something not quite right although he couldn't pin it down.

'Ask him about the spotlights.'

Anne gave a long-suffering sigh. 'Do as he says, Dave.'

'Did you turn off the lights?'

Alec's reply came back fast and furious. 'Look, I'm freezing my bollocks off out here. Are you going to open the fucking door or aren't you?'

'That's Alec all right,' Dave grinned.

He started to unfasten the bolts, locks and chains that secured the kitchen door.

'For God's sake hurry, will you?'

Something in the tone of Alec's voice warned Sanji that he had been right to be suspicious. There was a poorly disguised desperation there. It was the voice of a frightened man trying very hard to be brave. Sanji remembered that he still had Anne's revolver and he raised it, bringing it up into an unprofessional aim and pointing it at the two police officers.

'Get away from that door.'

They turned and looked at him, their initial bewilderment swiftly turning to anger. 'What the hell are you playing at? Where did you get that?'

'It's mine,' Anne said guiltily.

Dave scowled at her. 'Great. That's just great.'

'Slide the bolts shut again,' Sanji commanded.

Reluctantly Dave did as he was told. For a moment the door had been secured only by a single lock but as each second passed Sanji watched with satisfaction the defences being put back in place.

'What's up?' Alec's voice again.

Dave coughed in embarrassment. 'We've got a slight problem here. Won't take a minute.'

To his surprise Alec screamed back, 'Open the door now! If you don't they'll kill me!'

Dave reacted faster than Sanji would have thought possible, dropping instantly to the floor and pulling Anne down after him. A second later rounds from a high-velocity rifle pumped through the reinforced door, shaving straight through the empty space where the two police officers had been standing.

Sanji was the last to react, only saved from being hit by being out of the line of fire. But the bullets were now zipping across the kitchen. A shotgun blasted from outside but failed to penetrate the door's solid metal core. There were voices in the garden and Sanji saw Dave mentally counting them.

'Get to the panic button,' he whispered to Anne. She scuttled away on hands and knees to press the button in the sitting room. In the nearest police station an alarm would ring and, recognizing the identity of the safe house, the duty officer would task armed officers to attend immediately.

'How long have we got before help comes?' Sanji called across softly.

Dave shrugged. 'Ten minutes? Fifteen maybe.'

Sanji shook his head. It was hopeless. They could never hold out that long. Their only chance was that the terrorists would realize an alarm had been raised and would want to get clear before reinforcements arrived. But a thought crossed his mind.

'The panic button. How's it connected to the station?'

'It's OK,' Dave reassured him, guessing his fear. 'It can't be cut like a telephone line. It's a radio signal.'

'Radio signals can be jammed.'

'Not this one. It's a special piece of kit. If its frequency's being jammed it automatically scans for another until it gets

118

through and is acknowledged. There's no way they could jam the full spectrum.'

As if to prove his point Anne's head popped round the door and she gave the thumbs up. 'They're on their way.'

'Then all we've go to do is hang on.'

'Easier said than done.'

Dave crawled towards the sitting-room door, and once he was well out of the line of fire he called out for Alec. There was no reply.

'We've got to try and help him,' Anne said.

'He's beyond help now, believe me,' Sanji replied.

To his surprise Dave backed him up. 'He's right. There's nothing we can do for him.'

The front-door bell rang and the three of them jumped. Keeping low, Dave crawled towards the hall, directing Anne to stay and cover the kitchen entrance. Sanji followed him, returning the revolver to Anne before he went. The front door was as solid as the back. There was a fireproof letter-box but it was made of solid metal, the outer face being the weakest so that any letter bomb would blow harmlessly outwards. To a casual eye the leaded windows were of dimpled glass in mock-Tudor style, but Sanji had been told that only a high-velocity bullet could penetrate them. Hand-grenades would bounce off and all low-velocity rounds would disintegrate on contact.

From outside the front door a voice hailed them.

'David, we want Mr Sanji. We don't want to harm either you or Anne. Just open the door and send him out to us. You have my word that you'll come to no harm.'

Dave looked at Sanji and grinned mischievously. 'Tempting offer, you've got to admit.' But he raised his voice and shouted back, 'You know I can't do that. Why don't you lay down your weapons and give yourself up?'

There was a hoot of laughter from the other side of the door.
'I won't give you another chance . . .'

'Then sod off and don't bother,' Dave snapped back.

Sanji was about to thank him when through the curtained dining-room windows he saw fleeting shapes darting round the side of the house.

'They're trying to attack from another angle,' he warned.

'They can try any bloody angle they like.'

For a while everything went silent. Sanji looked at his watch and saw that at least five minutes had elapsed since Anne had sounded the alarm. He was puzzled. Surely the terrorists must know that help would be on the way. Even if they reckoned they had sufficient fire-power to shoot their way out, they would know that once contact had been made the police would pour men in until the situation was under control. It would be extremely difficult for the terrorists to break contact and effect a clean getaway.

His questions were answered by a shout from the back garden, followed immediately by the ear-splitting roar of a rocket launcher and the deafening explosion of the munition impacting through the kitchen door.

'Anne!' Dave screamed, forgetting his own safety and getting to his feet. Instantly a hail of high-velocity bullets tore through the front door, threatening to cut him down. Sanji kicked out and hit him behind the knees, knocking him to the floor.

'Stay down!'

Together they scrambled back through the sitting room towards the kitchen. Bullets were now punching through every window, the firers standing as close as they could and aiming down into the rooms, hoping to catch the invisible fugitives on the inside.

'Why don't you shoot back?' Sanji hissed.

'Wouldn't do any bloody good. My bullets would just ricochet off the inside of the windows.'

The inside of the kitchen was an appalling mess. The cupboards had been blown off the walls and every piece of crockery was smashed, splinters littering the debris-strewn floor. The table on which Anne had so recently been splayed had broken in half and the mixer tap at the sink had been torn off so that cold water fountained into the air and spattered in a cascade on to the floor.

Under a layer of dust and debris, Anne lay motionless next to the shattered table. Dave and Sanji crawled to her side and carefully rolled her over to check for a pulse.

'She's still alive.'

'God knows how.'

Sanji glanced up at the door and saw a large, round hole in the centre where the shaped charge of the rocket had driven through. They had only seconds before the terrorists completed the destruction and gained entry to the house.

'Get her into the sitting room. Upstairs if you can,' he said.

He located her revolver and snatched it up. 'Go!'

'You take her. I'll have to stay here to hold them off,' Dave protested.

'I couldn't lift her.'

'But you don't know how to fire that.'

Sanji waved him away. 'It can't be that hard. Now go.'

As Dave half dragged and half carried Anne from the room towards the stairs, Sanji looked up to see a hand-grenade bouncing through the hole and on to the kitchen floor. The handle had gone and as it hit the surface and came to a stop it was spinning like a top. He threw himself into the sitting room and slammed the door the moment it exploded. The door shredded, blown off its hinges by the force of the blast.

But it had served its purpose, taking the full force of the explosion and saving Sanji on the other side.

He stuck his head back into the kitchen, gagging on the fumes, to see through the smog a hand sticking through the hole and feeling for the door locks which still held. Bringing his revolver into a wobbly aim, he closed one eye to sight the weapon, then squeezed the trigger. The recoil was not as great as he had expected but the noise was worse, leaving his ears ringing. He had missed, the mark of his bullet a good six inches from the hole, although it had done its job. The hand had gone, its owner not knowing that the gun was being fired by an amateur.

That should give us a few precious seconds, Sanji thought. And every second counted now.

There was a shout from upstairs as Dave called down that they had made it to the top unscathed. Sanji scuttled after them, crouching into a corner as a hail of rounds powered through the front door and fired the length of the hall. But the moment they ceased he was on his feet and pumping up the stairs with the speed of a man thirty years younger.

'Help me with these,' Dave shouted when he reached the landing.

He was manhandling every item of furniture he could find to the top of the stairs and stacking it to form a barricade.

'It might delay them a bit longer.'

Sanji was panting furiously, his heart pounding as he stuffed the revolver in his belt and laid hands on chairs, mattresses, chests of drawers, bedside tables – everything that could be carried by two men.

Suddenly from the kitchen there was a second explosion, different from the first. Dave automatically dropped to the floor in reaction. 'Plastic explosive. They've blown the locks. They'll be inside now.'

As if in confirmation, they heard the sound of booted feet pounding through the downstairs rooms and into the hall.

'At least I can fire back now,' Dave said, and putting the barrel of his revolver through a gap in the barricade he pulled the trigger. There was an answering cry of pain and someone fell heavily. Shouts rang through the ground floor of the house as instructions were barked out.

'What's he saying?'

Sanji strained to listen, but his ears were still ringing with the cacophony of noise. 'Something about going into every room.'

Dave looked puzzled. 'What good will that do? They must know we're all up here.'

They got their answer à moment later when the intruders started to fire up through the ceilings. Although the exterior openings of the house had been reinforced, the internal floors were like those of any other suburban dwelling, a thin mixture of concrete, plaster and wood. To high-velocity bullets they presented little obstacle. In every upstairs room and all along the landing, bullets started to burst through, their lethal potential magnified by the fragments of concrete and wood that they took with them.

'Quick! Into the bedroom!' Dave shouted. It was the largest of the upstairs rooms and therefore the one which would be hardest for the terrorists to cover with fire from below.

Once inside, they flattened themselves against the walls, watching in terror as hole after hole appeared in the floor, the bullets continuing up through the ceiling. Sanji started to say something but Dave waved him to be quiet, whispering, 'Don't let them hear you. If they get a fix on your position they'll drill the area around you with lead.'

To his horror, as he was pinned against the bedroom wall, Sanji heard the sound of someone coming up the stairs and laying hands on the far side of the barricade to tear it down. His eyes met Dave's, both men acknowledging that if the terrorists got through they were done for.

Dave gripped his revolver in both hands, smiled at Sanji and started towards the door. His steps must have been heard from below because he hadn't gone three paces when a long, unbroken burst of fire shot up through the floorboards at his feet and bracketed him. He spun on the spot and as his face came round Sanji saw that one of the bullets had removed his jaw. The revolver fell to the floor, clattering all the way to the door-frame and his hands came up to the horrific wound. But there was nothing to be done. He sank to his knees and as he toppled forward a second burst found him again, pumping into his chest.

Sanji stared transfixed at the jerking body. So this is it, he thought bitterly. This is how I am to end my days, cornered like some rat. He sank into a ball in the corner, gripped his revolver and aimed it at the bedroom door. The firing from below had stopped now that the terrorists had gained the upper floor. Out on the landing Sanji heard the approach of footsteps. There was a crash as the door to the next room was kicked in, followed by prolonged bursts of firing. Voices, and then more steps, coming closer, approaching, bringing with them death.

8

Anne felt as if she was floating, dimly aware that she had to fight to regain consciousness if she was not to lose it for ever. Above her she could see something whirling. It was slightly out of focus but, try as she might, she couldn't make it any clearer. Then, with one momentous effort, she screwed up her eyes and when she opened them again she saw that she was staring at circular patterns in the plasterwork of a bedroom ceiling.

For a moment she was confused. How had she come to be there? The last thing she remembered was . . . what? The past was a blank, at least the recent past was. Further back she could remember an interview. She was enlisting in the police force. She could remember small-arms training, a run, a passing-out parade. Yes, things were starting to return. She could remember a building, a police station, she thought, and then a briefing, the details of a close-protection job.

With sudden embarrassment she remembered Dave and the kitchen table, and flinched away from the recollection as if there was someone else with her inside her mind who might see her being screwed that way. But she had liked Dave. It wasn't the first time they had had sex. She couldn't call it lovemaking; she was too truthful for that. The first time had been in a patrol car on a stake-out, the tenseness of the situation adding to the thrill of the act. Then there had been the second morning of the present assignment. Alec had been out and the Indian gentleman had been asleep. It had been early morning and she was in the shower. Dave had been on watch throughout the night and had come in to shave. They had done it there, on the bathroom floor. She had had to bite her lip to keep from making a sound, but it had been great. The best.

She tried to move and winced with sudden pain. What the hell had happened? For an instant she thought it might have been the sex, but this was a very different ache and far less pleasant. With a shock she remembered seeing the Indian staring at her from the kitchen door. It had been terrible. Until then it had been terrific. She saw again the stairs as she padded up them to wash. Dave had laddered her stockings but she hadn't bothered to change them. Who the hell was there to notice in the safe house?

Image by image the past swam back into view. She had gone downstairs and then . . . yes, there had been the question of the lights, Alec's voice, the Indian's caution, and then . . .

She turned her head and a bolt of pain rocketed down the length of her back and legs, reaching to the very soles of her feet. With the vision, however, came the noise, drifting in as if from a far distance. She became aware of the sound of shooting and then of the air around her being alive with fragments of wood, concrete and plaster.

'My God,' she murmured, her syllables slurred so that even she was unable to recognize them. 'They're in the house.'

She realized at once what must have happened and tilted her head towards the door. Someone had carried her into one of the bedrooms. She remembered that there were four bedrooms and she recognized her present location as the smallest one, at the very end of the corridor. Bullets were tearing through the floor, fired from below and someone was coming up the stairs. Anne clenched and unclenched her fingers, relieved to find she could. Slowly she moved them across her body, searching for the wounds. There seemed to be cuts and bruises all over her, but nothing too serious. The shock waves from the rocket exploding in such a confined space must have caused severe concussion. She felt her ears and sure enough there was dried blood there.

She struggled to sit up but it was hopeless, so instead she rolled first on to her side and then her stomach. She knew it would be no use trying to push her body up as all her limbs felt drained of strength, but when she attempted to crawl she found it was just possible to move. Seeing the fire still coming sporadically through the floorboards, she skirted the edge of the room until she reached the door and then eased it open. Peering through the crack, she saw the back of a man disappear into the first of the bedrooms. There was a hail of gunfire and then the crash of furniture and slamming doors as he ransacked the room and cupboards in search of his prey. She ducked out of sight as the man re-emerged but luckily he was looking down at the M16 rifle in his hands, too busy clearing a stoppage and reloading with a fresh magazine, to notice her.

It was then that she heard a noise in the next-door bedroom and instantly guessed that it must be Mr Sanji. If Dave was still alive, she reasoned, she would have heard him firing or at least shouting to try to reason with the terrorists. But there was nothing – only the noise that sounded like someone crawling along the other side of the wall.

Desperately Anne thought whether there was anything she could do. There were several options. She could lie on the floor and play dead. After all, the terrorist would see ample blood on her. But no. His most likely reaction would be to fire a couple of shots into her head at point-blank range to make quite certain.

She could try to hide under the bed or in a cupboard, but she had no sooner thought of it than she rejected the whole idea. This was a terrorist house-clearance operation, not a theatrical farce with the comedians dashing from room to room to avoid being detected. She had already heard him firing into every possible piece of cover in the other room, following it up with a visual search. He would obviously do the same to her room, but she'd rather die in the open than stuffed away in some claustrophobic cupboard.

For a moment she toyed with the idea of trying to escape. Perhaps it would be possible to force one of the security windows open. She smiled sardonically. And what the devil would she do then? Knot the bedsheets together and climb down like an eloping schoolgirl? She couldn't even get to her feet, so jumping down was out of the question, and there was no way she could make it downstairs, where the other terrorists were guarding the exits, waiting for their comrade to complete his mission and rejoin them.

The only other thing she could think of was to tackle the man in some way. She couldn't possibly do it head-on. She would have to catch him completely by surprise and even then she would only get one shot at it.

One shot! With cold dread she realized that she was unarmed. Her revolver was nowhere to be seen. She would have to improvise a weapon from something.

But what if she was successful? There was an unknown number of people downstairs. Nevertheless, her surprise attack on the lone terrorist might just buy enough time for the reinforcements to arrive. They could not be far away now.

She hunted around the room until her eyes fell upon an iron standing inoffensively on a shelf, its flex wrapped tightly round the handle.

'Come here, my beauty,' she whispered. 'Time for a bit of housework.'

Even with the iron firmly in her grasp she still felt little better than defenceless. How was she going to achieve surprise? In her present condition she wasn't capable of any great speed or stealth. The best moment, she reasoned, would be when the terrorist himself was off his guard, and that would be the moment he thought he had got what he wanted. So what was she to do? Wait until he had shot Mr Sanji? Perhaps. But she was uncomfortable with the idea of saving her own skin by sacrificing the life of the man she was supposed to be guarding. However, what if she was able to catch the terrorist at the moment he detected Mr Sanji? He might just pause for a second and perhaps even question him. Yes, that was it.

Taking care not to reveal her presence, she peered through the crack in the door and saw that the terrorist had cleared his weapon and reloaded and was approaching the neighbouring bedroom. Its door was closed and as he reached it he braced himself back against the banisters and prepared to kick it open. Anne shuffled to her knees in readiness. Her head swam and for a couple of seconds her vision blurred, but as she heard the thump of his boot and the splintering of wood, she moved.

The half-dozen paces to the adjoining bedroom were the longest distance she had ever covered, not just because of her injuries, but because she had never killed anyone before.

And although she tried to suppress the thought of what she was about to try to do, it chilled her to the bone.

The man's back came slowly into view. He was standing just inside the doorway, his rifle pointing into the room ready to fire from the hip. He was saying something, and with a feeling of triumph Anne realized she had been right. His complete attention was on Sanji's quaking response. The terrorist was ordering him to drop his revolver and as Anne closed the last couple of feet behind him she saw the old man about to comply.

The iron felt surprisingly light in her hand as she swung it up and brought it down with all her remaining might on the crown of the terrorist's head. She had angled it point down and with a sickening crunch she felt it drive into the man's skull. It was as if an unseen puppeteer had cut the strings holding him in play and his body crumpled to the floor, where it lay twitching spasmodically. The thought crossed Anne's mind that perhaps she should wield her terrible weapon again but the tell-tale pool of blood signalled that her immediate task was done, and in any case she doubted she would have been able to muster the strength for a second decisive blow.

A voice called up the stairs.

'He's asking his comrade why it's taking such a long time,' Sanji translated in a whisper.

Anne sank to her knees and retrieved the M16. She had never fired one before but had once used a Heckler & Koch on the indoor range and figured that the mechanism couldn't be all that dissimilar.

'Let them try and get us now,' she threatened weakly, leaning back against the door-frame, the rifle across her lap and pointing down the landing.

Sanji crawled across to her. 'Let me take that. You haven't got the strength.'

But she clung to it doggedly. 'If they come again, use your revolver.' She reached across and picked up Dave's, which was lying nearby. 'Hold this in the other hand and fire them both at once. It doesn't matter if you can't aim properly. They won't know that.'

The voice sounded again, this time more urgent. Sanji paled when he heard another terrorist start up the stairs but now there was another sound, farther away and fainter, but growing louder with every second. It was a police siren.

'About bloody time the cavalry got here,' Anne wheezed.

There was one last shout up the stairs and then they caught sight of a head poking round the corner. Anne squeezed the trigger and to her shock and relief the M16 sprang into life, jarring back in her loose grasp but nevertheless spraying its 5.56mm high-velocity rounds in the right direction. The terrorist cursed and ducked back out of sight. A stream of abuse poured at them from their unseen attackers but the siren was louder than ever now and Sanji and Anne could hear others close by.

A final volley of bullets pocked through the floorboards, but wild and random, venting the defeated terrorists' frustration rather than claiming the victims they so desired. And then they were gone.

Out in the road there was the sound of a car engine, spinning tyres and a powerful engine accelerating away. A few moments later the sirens were wailing at the end of the street, car doors were slamming and there were footsteps pounding down the driveway. Hearing them, Anne closed her eyes and the rifle slipped from her bloodied hands. The last thing she had seen was Dave's lifeless body in the middle of the bedroom floor. So that was that, Dave and Alec were dead and she herself had escaped the same fate by the narrowest of margins.

And what for? The strange little Indian man kneeling concernedly next to her, about whom she had been told virtually nothing.

The officer in command of the police firearms unit went through the house as the bodies were being taken away and stared in amazement at the damage. He had never seen anything like it.

'It looks like a bloody war zone.'

He turned at the remark from the young constable next to him, and said, 'Did you see what the bastards did to Alec?'

'No?' the youngster queried with morbid interest.

'Well, take my advice and don't.'

'What about Anne?'

'What about her?'

'Will she live?'

The police officer shrugged. 'I only had a quick word with the doc but he seemed to think so. She's a tough one.'

He made his way back to the sitting room, where Mr Sanji was sitting in the armchair, his head in his hands.

'It's all right now, sir. We've got the situation under control,' he told the old man.

Sanji looked up at him doubtfully. 'Did you catch them?'

The officer quickly busied himself with his holster. 'Erm, not yet.'

'Then how can you say you have the situation under control?'

'We'll get them all right. It's only a matter of time.'

'And so long as they remain at large it's only a matter of time before they get me,' Sanji replied sourly.

The policeman opened his mouth to reassure him but decided to remain silent. He could well be correct after all. There had clearly been a security breach and investigations were already underway to discover the leak.

There were voices in the hall and Chief Inspector Chiltern came in. 'Hello, Ted. Everything OK?'

'Could be better. I was just trying to put Mr Sanji's mind at rest, saying he was safe in our hands.'

Chiltern stared back stony-faced. 'He isn't in our hands any more. There's a car waiting for him outside.' He turned to Sanji. 'Ted will take you to it.'

Sanji looked from one to the other in bewilderment. 'What's going on?'

'Everything will be explained outside, Mr Sanji,' Chiltern replied, not without a trace of bitterness.

Getting the impression that further questioning would prove fruitless, Sanji got shakily to his feet and hobbled after the police officer. As he exited through the front door, he took one last look at the supposed safe house and then went out into the night.

Unlike before, the house was now in a blaze of light. The spotlights had been switched on and in the driveway and road the headlights of cars, vans and ambulances criss-crossed the lawns, while blues and reds flashed on every vehicle roof. However, much to Sanji's surprise, he was led in the other direction, towards the only remaining area of gloom. As he left the glare behind and his eyes became adjusted to the dark, he was able to make out the shapes of three nondescript cars. They were parked in a row, the front and rear cars each appearing to contain four men, and as Sanji walked past the rear car he glanced at the men sitting in it. Even that one restricted view showed him that they were a very different bunch from the Alecs and Daves of the world. All four were lean and could even be described as slight, but from their wiriness he could guess that they were physically very fit. Their eyes were the most noticeable thing about them, alert and wide awake, taking in everything at a glance. Although they were seated in the car, they seemed somehow to be full of energy and Sanji was struck by the impression of an unexploded bomb.

'Who are they?' he asked the police officer.

The man grunted an unintelligible reply from which Sanji deduced that he was none too happy about being required to hand over his charge to someone else. In effect he and his men had been relieved of duty.

The door to the centre car swung open as he approached. Sanji turned to thank the policeman but he was already walking back towards the house.

'Mr Sanji, welcome. Do get in out of the cold.'

The voice was warm and hospitable, but underneath was a formality that signalled a new professionalism. He stooped and lowered himself into the back seat of the car, the driver closing the door after him. All he wanted to do was sleep but he looked to his side to identify his host. The man was well dressed and trim, his greying hair neatly cut but too long to be military. He extended a hand towards Sanji.

'Tony Briggs. We're going to be looking after you from now on. You needn't worry about a thing.'

From the confidence in his voice and from the evidence of the men in the cars with them Sanji felt that for once he could believe this man.

'That's very kind,' he answered, taking the offered hand and wincing at the hearty grip. 'Forgive my curiosity, but who exactly are you?'

'I represent the Intelligence services and the gentlemen in front and behind are members of the Special Air Service. I expect you've heard of them?'

'The SAS? Yes, of course I have.' He had picked up a book on the famous 22 Regiment after its relief of the Iranian

Embassy siege, but had discarded it as propaganda, refusing to believe that any organization could be peopled by such characters. It was so obviously a ruse. However, now that he had glimpsed a handful of men belonging to it he began to wonder whether he had been too hasty in that assumption.

'How is it that you are involved? I mean, wouldn't an increased police guard suffice?'

Sir Anthony smiled indulgently. 'I'm no longer prepared to take that chance. Believe me, you'll be far safer in our hands.'

He reached over the seat and tapped the driver on the shoulder to signal that they should leave. The driver flashed his headlights at the front car and the procession pulled away. Sanji turned to have a last look at the house.

'I'd like to know how Anne Baron progresses, if that's possible.'

'Of course it is.'

'She saved my life, you see. She's a remarkable woman,' Sanji concluded, suppressing the image of her bent over the kitchen table, but only after he had dwelt on it for a few moments.

The little convoy shot away from the district in a very different manner to the police convoy that had taken him there. Unlike the stolid, steady police procession, the SAS cars sped along, none of them seeming particularly concerned to keep the other cars close by. Now and again Sanji turned to look behind him. On most occasions the rear car was nowhere to be seen, but always, just when he was about to enquire whether they had perhaps become lost, he would glimpse its distant headlights in his driver's rear-view mirror. The lead car was similarly independent, shooting ahead and only once or twice coming into view. Yet even so, Sanji couldn't help feeling more secure than he had done in a very long time. There was no ponderous radio communication, no close tailing, and he began to wonder if contact was maintained telepathically.

He suddenly remembered that one of his questions remained unanswered. 'You haven't told me why British Intelligence is now involved.'

Sir Anthony smiled. 'Why shouldn't we be?'

'Well, after all, I'm a retired restaurant owner whose granddaughter's been kidnapped. What's it got to do with the British government?'

'Look, Mr Sanji. We can play these games if you like, but you and I both know who you are.' He paused. 'Or should I say, who you were.'

Sanji felt himself go cold. 'And who do you think I am?'

'Well, now you are exactly who you say you are, the founder and owner of the excellent Mogul chain of restaurants spread across south London. However, in 1947 – correct me if I'm wrong – you were an Indian government minister in Delhi responsible for the refugee resettlement programme. A minor one, I'll grant you, but nonetheless influential.'

Sanji quickly looked away, staring out of the car window into the dark. The car was streaming along a country road, the trees flashing past in a blur. So it wasn't only the Pakistanis who had found him.

'So what if I was?' he conceded at last.

'Perhaps you should put that to the men chasing you.'

'They never gave me the opportunity.'

Sir Anthony recrossed his long legs with difficulty in the confined space of the car, his hand tapping on his lap. 'We have traced the men who carried out the attack on your house in Southall. They were . . .'

'I know who they were.'

136

'Then why didn't you tell the police in the first place?'

Sanji closed his eyes and sighed heavily. 'I should have done. I'm sorry. I hoped to be able to avoid all this. I hoped . . .'

'What?'

'Oh, I don't know.' He turned to face Sir Anthony. 'Look, I'm a tired old man who just wants to be left alone. I thought I'd managed it, and then . . . all of this happens. My whole world gets torn apart.'

'Why do you think that is?'

'I don't know.'

Sir Anthony stared at him hard. 'Why do I get the feeling you're not levelling with me? Why would someone in Pakistan want you dead or a prisoner? I can only assume it has something to do with 1947 and the Independence troubles.'

'I don't know, I don't know, I don't know?' Sanji's head was pounding and he felt at the very edge of exhaustion.

He felt a hand patting his. 'All right. I'm sorry, old chap. We'll leave it until tomorrow.'

A thought suddenly crossed Sanji's mind as he watched the countryside speeding past. 'Where are we going?'

'Somewhere that really is safe. Somewhere we can talk and sort all this mess out. I'm no more prepared to have armed terrorists running around the country than you are.'

For a while Sanji dozed, sinking deeper into the seat until a bump in the road woke him. He glanced sideways at Sir Anthony but saw that he was looking out of the window. In the driver's rear-view mirror there was nothing to be seen but a black expanse of night. It surrounded them like some vast land of the dead. And then Sanji heard them, the voices of the countless dead, and he knew that he had to speak. He had kept quiet for too long. He had to unburden himself to someone, and the man next to him seemed as good as anyone.

'Mr Briggs?' he said at last.

Sir Anthony turned. 'Oh, I thought you were asleep.'

Sanji drew in his breath and began. 'I have something to tell you.'

By the time they arrived at Sir Anthony's country retreat, Don was more curious than ever about Mr Sanji. From his first meeting with Sir Anthony he had guessed that the wily old agent knew far more about the case than he was willing to admit to, certainly to Don. He had concluded their meeting by saying that all would soon be revealed.

After that the rest of the team had been assembled and he had been pleasantly surprised to recognize many old friends from Hereford. Once complete, they numbered eight in all, including Don, whom Sir Anthony placed in command. Their first sight of the mysterious Mr Sanji had been when they had gone to the police safe house with Sir Anthony to collect him. He had narrowly escaped death and Sir Anthony was concerned to remove him into their own far safer custody at the earliest opportunity.

The journey went smoothly, Don riding in the front car. His only other brief glimpse of Sanji was when they arrived at the country house and Don went to escort him inside while the other members of the team did a quick scan of the grounds.

Sanji was polite but visibly very tired from his recent ordeal. Don saw him to his room on the second floor, and noticed that Sir Anthony slipped away the moment the cars arrived. Before he disappeared, however, making for his own study, he drew Don aside for a moment and told him that his own CO would be briefing him the next morning.

'Will you be attending as well, sir?'

'No. I have to get back to Whitehall to do some checking. I'll be confirming details for the next phase of the operation with your CO, who will pass them on to you tomorrow. Right now I suggest you get some sleep. Any questions?'

Don had a thousand of them but recognized from Sir Anthony's tone that he had asked Don only out of form, and that he had not the slightest intention of providing him with any answers, at least not there and then. In any case, Don reflected as he watched Sir Anthony march away down the hall, he would prefer to tackle his CO with them. He would be more likely to get a reasonable response from him.

His own room was directly next to Sanji's and the two were linked by a door. A change of clothes for Sanji had been provided by a police team that had brought them from Bramley Road. Don was tempted to have a chat with the old fellow before he went to sleep but no sooner had he knocked on the door and peered round than he heard the sound of snores. Sanji was lying on the bed, still fully dressed, and fast asleep.

Before turning in himself, Don checked with every member of the team that they were all in position. The house was sealed tighter than a drum, with the police providing both an outer cordon and other guards closer in. The role of the SAS troopers was to concentrate on the close protection. If anyone got through the armed police this time, they'd be in for a very nasty surprise. Don had taken the team round every inch of the building and they had spent the day conducting rehearsals in the event of an attack, running through their reactions to every possible combination of assault techniques, so that by the time Mr Sanji was safely in bed they each knew exactly how to react whatever happened.

However, the night passed without incident, as Don had expected. He knew that the terrorist organization would be unlikely to make another attempt on Sanji's life and liberty at such short notice so soon after their last operation. It was also to be hoped that the leak had been discovered and cut, so that no more information would be passed to the terrorists.

The following morning Don was up before first light, having slept for only a few hours. He started by touring the house and when he was satisfied that it was secure he went around the garden and grounds with two of his men.

'What time's the boss coming?' Rob Lindsay asked.

'Nine. He'll be briefing me first and then once I'm happy with the mission I'll sketch out a rough outline plan and then call you all in. I've got a feeling I'm going to need every brain working on this one.'

Rob scratched his head. 'Er, shit, boss. You didn't say I needed to bring it with me.'

'Ha bloody ha.'

When they had completed the clearing patrol, they returned inside and Don went quietly to Sanji's room. The old man was still asleep and Don thought it best to leave him in peace. He could get all the information that he needed from him later.

A cooked breakfast had been laid on in the dining room, and as soon as it was over Don made his way to the library, where he had been told to expect his boss. Sure enough, shortly before nine, a car drew up in the driveway by the front door and a moment later the library door opened and the CO walked in.

'Morning, Don.' Colonel Clive Barrett went briskly to the desk, slapped down his briefcase and opened it, taking out a wad of printed paper, files and maps. 'We've got a lot of ground to cover, so let's get cracking. I ordered coffee on the way in. We're going to need it.'

Don pulled up a chair opposite Barrett. 'I hope you're going to be able to tell me what all this is about, boss.'

'I'll tell you all I know. That Tony Briggs is a tight-lipped bastard. He's hardly given me much background information.' With his papers arrayed in front of him he sat down and paused to catch his breath. 'Right. Here's the mission. You're to go to Pakistan, locate the girl who was kidnapped from Bramley Road, rescue her and bring her back to Britain. Any problems?'

Don felt his mouth drop open. 'Just a few, sir.'

Barrett sat back and smiled. 'It's all right. I've got a bit of information for you.' He pushed a file across the table. 'Read this. It will give you everything we know about the organization we're up against.'

'Is it Pakistani secret service?'

'Good Lord, no. Their government's got nothing at all to do with it. That much we do know. This organization is strictly freelance, though a lot of them are ex-special forces.'

'I gathered as much from the way they handled themselves. What's the op going to be called?'

Barrett grinned. 'How about Operation Takeaway? It seems kind of fitting, given Sanji's business interests and the kidnap of his granddaughter.'

Don groaned. 'If you insist.'

'Thank you for humouring me. Now then, here's what I propose, although of course the details of the plan will be completely up to you.'

Naturally, Don thought. And when the whole thing turns to rat shit, guess who'll take the rap?

9

For Eli the journey seemed to drag on interminably. Several times the plane landed to refuel, each time at anonymous-looking airstrips. It had obviously all been planned well in advance because people were waiting and the whole procedure was carried out with the minimum of fuss. Although the others on board took each opportunity to walk up and down the tarmac to stretch their legs, she was ordered to stay on the aircraft, closely watched by one of the guards.

After one of the halts, Ceda Bandram handed her a drink that had been included in the pack of supplies and from the writing on the can she saw that they had stopped in Libya. He saw her looking at the Arabic script.

'As you see, we have influential friends,' he told her.

'Influential with whom? Libya's hardly everyone's favourite country, is it?' she answered.

'Only for now. Tomorrow or the next day they'll be back in the fold. Western politicians are the most fickle in the world. The second they see an advantage to be gained from it, they will be wooing even their worst enemies. The only reason they dislike Gaddafi is because he dared to stand up to them. In the Americans' view that is the worst crime of all.'

Eli decided against pursuing the point. So far Ceda had treated her reasonably and she didn't want to antagonize him. She was certain that she would soon be needing all the help she could get. Far better to appease him, lull him into a feeling that she was just a docile victim. Then, if an opportunity to escape presented itself, she would be ready to seize it. Hopefully, that would be the last thing Ceda and his colleagues would be expecting.

The plane flew on and now that Eli had got her bearings she speculated on its route. From Libya it passed over the southern regions of Egypt before crossing the Red Sea. Then there was a seemingly endless expanse of desert which she was certain must be Saudi Arabia. There was another stop at a desert airstrip and this time she guessed from the dress and features of the people that they were in the Yemen. After that they took off and flew out to sea and for the next few hours she could see that they were over water, the Arabian Sea.

It was the attitude of her fellow-passengers that finally told her that they were nearing the Pakistani coast. Long before land was sighted they were peering through the small, oval windows, and then someone shouted out and pointed eagerly. Ceda leaned over to look and Eli saw a smile crease his lips.

'Who said we wouldn't make it?' he asked triumphantly.

'The game's not over yet.'

'Oh this is no game, my dear. It's far too serious for that.'

Eli resisted the temptation to rise to the bait a second time.

'Anyway who's going to come after you?' Ceda went on. 'The Indian government won't be interested and even if they were there's nothing they could do to help you. They wouldn't dare send troops over the border and risk starting another

Indo-Pakistan war. And if the Indian government can't help then the British certainly won't. What are you expecting? The SAS to come storming after us?'

He laughed and added, 'They'd hardly be interested in a single kidnap victim. And even if they did come we'd have a surprise waiting for them when they arrived. As you will see.'

Eli couldn't help wondering what he meant by that. He didn't seem to be afraid of anything.

Down below she could see the brown flatlands and waterways of a river estuary and as if in answer to her enquiry Ceda turned to her and said, 'The Indus. One of the great rivers of the world.'

He stared down at it as the plane followed its course. 'It was along the Indus valley that the first human settlements were established, before Egypt and the Nile even. The Indus, the Tigris and the Euphrates. These were the cradles of civilization. People in the West look down on us now. Few of them realize that our ancestors were living in cities while theirs were still shivering in damp caves. We enjoyed art and culture while they were scratching at cave walls with crude stone implements. And it all began down there,' he said, pointing to the dark, meandering line.

The Indus seemed to go on for ever. Eli rested her head against the seat back and fell asleep, and when she awoke a couple of hours later she looked out of the window and saw that they were still flying along the river's course. Nor had the countryside around it changed. If anything, it was even more barren and when she asked Ceda the reason he answered, 'That's the Thal Desert down below. Pray that we don't have to crash-land here.'

She remembered from her knowledge of the region's geography that if they were crossing the Thal Desert then they were just to the east of the mountainous North-West Frontier Province and most likely en route for Rawalpindi. But when she at last noticed the outlying sprawl that heralded a city of such a size, the plane flew on, only beginning to descend when it was far to the north and the towering blue ranges of the Karakoram mountains were in sight.

'That's Muzaffarabad,' Ceda said, noticing her querying look. 'It's not far now.'

The plane started to lose height shortly afterwards and Eli caught sight of the thin line of a landing strip growing larger with every second. The pilot banked sharply as he dropped down towards it and she was able to get a good look at the surrounding countryside. Everywhere was brown and desolate, the land rising abruptly into bleak, barren hills.

Lining up on the runway, the plane swooped down on to the strip and sped to a halt, turning on the spot before the pilot cut the engines. On board everyone stretched and smiled happily. They were home.

From the edge of the makeshift airfield three old, battered Land Rovers headed out towards the plane as the crew opened the door and Ali and the others filed out on to firm ground. Ceda helped her out and steered her towards the newest of the vehicles.

'It's a bit of a rough ride from here. We're more likely to make it in one piece if we ride in this one,' he said, playing the charming host.

From the airstrip they drove in convoy into Muzaffarabad, Ceda explaining that they had to pick up supplies.

'Why? Where are we going?' Eli asked.

'Since it's not likely to do you any good to know, I can't see any harm in telling you,' Ceda conceded. 'My uncle owns some land north of here, up close to the Kashmiri border.'

'You mean the Indian border,' she corrected him.

He smiled sourly. 'Kashmir should always have been Pakistani. The British messed things up when they drew up the boundaries in 1947. The entire population is Muslim, after all.'

'It's still Indian territory,' Eli persisted.

'Not for long, if we have our way.'

'What do you mean? Is that why you want my grandfather?'

'Never you mind,' Ceda said abruptly. 'Perhaps my uncle will feel like telling you more.'

Eli was keen to keep the conversation going. Every scrap of information was potentially useful if she was going to get away somehow. 'So tell me about this land your uncle owns. Does he have a house there?'

'A house?' Ceda chuckled. 'You could say that. But why don't you wait and see for yourself?'

I will, Eli thought. But don't expect me to stick around. If you think I'm some helpless woman, then you've got another think coming. The first chance I get I'll be out of here.

The bazaar was a ramshackle affair, and after stacking sack upon sack of provisions in the back of each of the Land Rovers, the convoy set off again, heading north out of the town along the Neelam Road. Once more Eli recalled her knowledge of the region. The River Neelam wound parallel with the border. It was a wild area of thick woodland and mountain and if the Bandrams were involved in some sort of nefarious dealings with the Kashmiris, then it was an ideal location. Pakistani governmental control was far from secure and all manner of bandits and tribespeople carried on lives of smuggling unchanged for centuries.

As she had suspected, the road crossed over rivers and made its way steadily upwards, climbing into pine forests that stretched up the sheer mountainsides. The bridges were rickety affairs and the roads were almost entirely unmade, riddled with potholes and often cracked completely in two by landslides. Whenever they encountered any such obstacle the drivers simply engaged the vehicles' four-wheel drive and skirted around the edges until they were clear.

Even though she was tired beyond belief, Eli fought to keep her eyes open. The scenery was spectacular so it wasn't too hard, but the main reason was to try to lodge in her mind a picture of the ground over which she might have to travel should she be able to effect an escape. She realized that to attempt to cross into India would be all but impossible. The mountains were steep and swept with snow at this time of year. Her best hope was to make her way south and try to find a Pakistani army camp or a police station. Then she would simply have to hope that they were not in league with the Bandrams.

At one point they stopped for a short break beside a river. She was allowed to walk down to the edge and even considered making a break for it. She was confident that if she pretended she wanted to relieve herself they would let her go unaccompanied into the trees. But where would she go from there? No. Now was not the time or the place. She would have to prepare herself first, lay up a secret store of supplies somehow, lull them into a false sense of security, and then, at a time of her own choosing, make her bid for freedom.

She crouched down by the water's edge. It was crystal-clear and cold. The trees whispered in the light breeze and they were so high that the snow crept down almost to their level. Another mile or two and she guessed that they would have entered the snowline proper.

A voice from the Land Rovers hailed her, shouting that they were about to leave. She waved that she was on her way but wet her face first with the icy water. It brought her vividly awake and she gasped with the shock of it.

It was four hours later that the lead vehicle rounded a corner and drew to a halt.

'There we are,' Ceda announced. 'Our destination. Looks a bit like Shangri-La, doesn't it?'

Reluctantly, Eli felt she had to agree, and the prospect of spending some time there would have been almost pleasant had she not known that the place was to be her prison. But pushing to the fore of her emotions was a sinking dread, for the instant she set eyes on their destination she realized how absurd her notions of escape now were.

It was not so much a house as a hilltop fortress, with walls surrounded on three sides by sheer drops that fell into a tumbling river.

'Legend has it that it was built by Yashman, a brigand, over two centuries ago,' Ceda said proudly. 'Apparently he and later his ancestors held out against the forces of the British Raj until the very end of the nineteenth century, and even then it was only because of treachery that the citadel fell. Some slighted relative betrayed the family to the British and opened the gates one night. It was after a festival and the guards were all drunk. The British stormed in and massacred the lot. Only the leader was taken captive. There was some sort of show trial, after which he was thrown into jail, where he died several years later.'

'And what happened to the disgruntled relative?'

'I'm glad you asked that,' he replied with a sinister grin. 'Another family member caught up with him eventually and slipped a cobra into his bed. But before he did so he had milked most of the beast's poison so that when it bit the traitor it took him several days to die. By the end he was writhing in agony and begging for the release of death.'

Eli stared up at the fortress, watching it grow higher and higher before her as they approached. Her heart sank and for the first time since leaving England she felt truly lost and beyond the reach of help.

'Tell us another, Jerry.'

Jerry Patel paused from his telling of anecdotes from India and sat back in his seat, waiting for the air hostess to set down his meal. From beneath the tin-foil lid of the little tray an aroma was struggling to get out, and when it did Jerry thought it might have been for the better had it failed. He squinted across at Rod's menu.

'What's this supposed to be?'

Rod traced the name with his finger. 'Chicken Madras.' He grinned. 'Up your street, mate. Wog scoff.'

'The Army Catering Corps might think so, but take it from me, this has got nothing to do with what you so politely call wog scoff.'

Rod sniggered. He liked Jerry, even if the lad was the new boy in the team. He enjoyed ribbing him, as did all the lads, but then that was just the way of it. No one meant anything by the name-calling. Everyone had their tag. Rod was a cockney, Geoff a Geordie, Alan a Taff, Tom a West Country yokel, and Jimmie was naturally a Jock. Sergeant Gavin Steward, the archetypal Essex man, had been virtually dragged screaming out of retirement in the Training Wing and Captain Don Headley was the fly-boy in the ointment of the team, a nondescript Home Counties wallah, but good enough for an officer.

Jerry tested his food with the fork and lifted a morsel to his mouth. It wasn't quite as bad as it looked, although his mother would have had a fit at the thought of anyone daring to call it a curry. He looked about him. The British Airways flight to Delhi was about two-thirds full and all the passengers were busy tucking into their meals before the start of the film. It seemed strange to be going to India. Born in England, he had only been to India once, on holiday with his parents, and even that had been a number of years ago. He could remember visiting a string of relatives, all of whom he had heard of but none of whom he had ever met before. But the overriding memory of that trip had been a sense of dislocation. He felt that he didn't belong there, although in a deeper sense he felt that he did. It was difficult to explain. His cultural roots had become tangled by his parents' emigration to Britain, yet even though they had done everything in their power to integrate him into his adopted country they had at the same time ensured that he absorbed his cultural heritage. He had therefore been taught to speak both Hindi and Urdu, although he counted English as his native tongue, and in Britain he had attended the local Hindu temple with his parents, while learning about Christianity at school.

For a while he had been very confused by the mixture, but in time he had come to accept it. Now, however, he regarded his broad education as a source of strength. The SAS greatly valued language skills and it seemed that he was about to put his own to good use on an operation.

He had been intrigued, as had all the lads in the team, by Captain Headley's briefing. Although their final destination lay over the Pakistani border Captain Headley had decided to conduct the approach to it through India and in particular the province of Kashmir. Jerry had never been to Kashmir before and relished the opportunity to see it for himself. He had read so much about it and as part of his own preparation for the operation he had carried out a thorough map study. He had to admit that he was surprised at the SAS getting involved in such a rescue mission in the first place, but Captain Headley had said that the victim was no ordinary person. Apparently there were higher political reasons why she had to be brought home and for Jerry that was enough. Give me the task, he thought, and that's all I need to know.

He had been longing to tell his parents where he was going but in accordance with SAS security procedures he had kept quiet, even during the weekend visit he had made to his home after the last exercise in Wales. When he had finally staggered back into camp carrying Sergeant Steward's load of batteries he had flopped exhausted into bed and slept for twelve hours. But realizing that he was in danger of wasting his weekend he had driven home and spent a relaxing couple of days with his family. He had taken advantage of the trip home to question his parents surreptitiously about Kashmir and had been happy to glean a number of useful tips from his father.

Now, sitting back in his seat, he listened contentedly to the purring of the engines, consumed by the feeling that he had made it. Instantly he remembered yet again the old adage about not having made it until the Regiment was finished with you, but nevertheless there he was, sitting on the plane, a member of an SAS operational team on his way to a mission. He glanced around at the other passengers, wondering if any of them could possibly feel such happiness or fulfilment. Could any of them guess that he and the men with him were special? Marked out for great deeds? He smiled, pushing away his tray and taking up his coffee instead. Whatever might happen on the mission he knew in his heart that he had already attained an important goal. Even if he were to die in the mountains of Kashmir he had at least achieved something in life.

The airport in Delhi was chaotic and Don Headley almost missed the man from the British High Commission. As India was a member of the Commonwealth it didn't have an embassy, although the High Commission served much the same purpose.

Head bobbing above the crowd of taxi drivers and porters, all of whom were furiously vying for trade, the British official had dressed in the hope of appearing inconspicuous. In consequence he resembled a character from a Humphrey Bogart movie, dressed in a crumpled, sweat-stained linen suit that once upon a time might have been white.

'Captain Headley?' he whispered conspiratorially from behind his hand.

Don stared at him in disbelief. 'Who's asking?'

The man grinned knowingly, as if expecting an exchange of passwords. 'Knowles. Terence. British High Commission.'

He pronounced his identity with great seriousness.

'Headley. Donald. British Army,' Don responded in kind.

Knowles glanced theatrically to left and right, thrilling at the melodrama that had dragged him away from his in-tray. 'Follow me, Captain. Transport is waiting.'

Don looked round at his men, who stood behind him in an amused gaggle.

Prancing on tiptoes like a moorhen, Knowles stepped towards the exit.

'Anyone would think he's looking for trip-wires,' Gavin Steward whispered in Don's ear.

'He's a natural, isn't he? Nice mover.'

Transport consisted of two vans. At a signal from Knowles, the drivers pulled up at the kerb and the SAS team piled in, stacking their kit alongside them.

'Has the hardware arrived?' Don asked.

Knowles tapped the side of his nose with his forefinger. 'Diplomatic bag this morning.'

'That must be some bag,' Rod observed loudly.

'It's a figure of speech,' Knowles explained unnecessarily, missing Rod's exasperated sigh. 'I take it you've brought everything you need with you?'

'Yes,' Don replied. There had been some hasty last-minute packing but they had managed to lay their hands on everything he reckoned they were likely to need. Apart from their packs and equipment, radios, rations and standard kit, they had brought a selection of weapons that would give the team flexibility and fire-power while allowing it to move quickly across difficult terrain. It had been no easy task, but they were confident they had achieved a good balance.

For personal weapons they had a mix of British SA80s, American M16s and Colt Commandos, and German Heckler & Kochs, as well as a variety of pistols ranging from Brownings to Glocks. Then there were the claymore anti-personnel directional mines, plastic explosives and demolitions kit, hand-grenades, 40mm grenade launchers, M72 rocket launchers, and for the fire-support role an American-made light machine-gun. The ammunition for that modest little arsenal would take some carrying and Jerry had started to see the relevance of Sergeant Steward's insistence that the men carry batteries across the Welsh hills as part of the exercise.

The road away from the station was clogged with traffic, but once at their hotel the team entered a world of calm.

The men were shown to their rooms and Don called Gavin Steward to his for a chat about the next stage. Once they had managed to persuade Knowles to leave them in peace, they spread out maps on the bed and began. First they confirmed the times for their onward flight north to Srinagar, the capital of Indian Kashmir, and then they ran through the details for the mission thereafter.

Sir Anthony Briggs had obtained clearance from the Indian security forces in the region for the SAS team to be left alone to carry out its mission. They were to approach the border with Pakistan, cross, carry out the rescue mission and return by another route across the mountains. In the event that they were discovered by Pakistani border guards the Indian government would deny all knowledge of the operation and initially the SAS team would try to bluff their way out by saying that they were a British forces mountaineering expedition. But for that to work they would have to be able to dispose of their hardware beforehand. The whole plan was fraught with danger but it was the best that Sir Anthony could come up with.

'Beats me how he can even get the Indians to allow us near Kashmir. They're usually paranoid about security, especially in the border region,' Gavin said.

'It's all down to contacts, I suppose,' Don answered. 'I tried to ask him but he was pretty vague about the whole thing, saying he had dealt through an old friend who owed him a favour.'

'It gets better and better.'

'Yes, but it's not the Pakistani or Indian border guards that I'm worried about. I don't think we'll have too much trouble evading them. The real problem's going to be the break-in to the terrorists' strongpoint.'

Don laid out the satellite photographs that had been supplied of the Bandrams' fortress.

Gavin whistled. 'It's like something out of Kipling.'

'That's because it is.' Don told him the story of the fort's brigand founder and then produced a sketch-map plan of the layout. 'This is as much detail as the Int boys were able to come up with.'

'We'll have to do our own close recce then,' Gavin observed as he studied the sketches.

'Assuming we have time. The weather's worsening by the day. We have to get in, do the business and get back over the mountains before the snow clags in and traps us on the wrong side. If that happens we can expect some embarrassing questions from the Pakistani authorities.'

'If the Bandrams don't get to us first,' Gavin added.

Don slept badly that night, his head spinning with the plans and the dangers of the mission. So when the morning's first light cracked through the curtains he got up and went out to walk the streets before meeting the others for breakfast. The chill in the air surprised him. Somehow he had supposed that Delhi would be hot, but then he remembered Jerry Patel saying something about the cold in winter reaching down to the plains.

He hugged his coat about him and walked through the city, watching the stalls begin to open like the petals of some exotic flower after the iciness of the night. A couple of early beggars tried their luck and found Don an easy touch. One look at their rags was enough to coax a handful of coins out of him. A rickshaw pulled up alongside him and the youth trotting between the shafts tried to persuade him aboard but Don shook his head and lengthened his stride. The youth kept abreast of him, pleading to be allowed to pull Don wherever he chose.

'Look, pal, I'm just out for a walk. Taking the air, OK?'

The youth frowned, not understanding, until at last Don climbed on to the seat and told him in sign language to take him once around the park and then back to the hotel. After all, it was a pretty miserable way to have to earn your living and if he could pass a couple of coins the fellow's way then he would be better able to enjoy his breakfast with a clear conscience.

However, when the rickshaw eventually pulled up outside the hotel foyer Don was embarrassed to see the rest of the team staring at him from the restaurant windows, pointing and jeering.

'Morning, sahib,' Gavin said when Don had paid the youth and made his way inside to their table. 'Checking out the getaway transport?'

Fits of laughter erupted around the table.

'We could put a pintel mount on the back for a GPMG. Maybe the MOD equipment procurement branch would be interested in the design blueprint. Drop them by parachute behind enemy lines.'

Don helped himself to a bowl of cereal and smiled bravely throughout. 'Sticks and stones,' he muttered through a mouthful of cornflakes.

They didn't see Knowles again until they were at the airport and waiting for their onward flight to Srinagar. There had been a brief meeting with the Defence attaché at the High Commission, who had assured them that their weapons and other kit would be waiting for them on arrival in Kashmir. Then, after a briefing on the current sensitive political situation in the state, they had bundled into their vans and continued on to the airport.

As they were standing waiting for their flight to be called, the public-address system crackled into life and the next instant they were staring at one another thunderstruck.

'This is a call for the members of the SAS. Would the members of the SAS please report to the information centre.'

Don gaped at Gavin, who stared back with a mouth wide open. Around them the rest of the team looked as if they had just come under artillery fire, eyes searching for the nearest cover.

'Knowles,' Don and Gavin said together.

Feeling as though they could rip his head off, they strode rapidly towards the information desk.

'I believe you have a message for us,' Don said self-consciously.

The man behind the desk scrutinized him carefully. 'You are SAS?'

Don realized it was pointless to deny it. 'Yes,' he admitted glumly, feeling the mission crumble about him and wondering what Sir Anthony would have to say when they arrived back at Heathrow the next day. For surely there was no way the mission could go ahead now that it had been so clumsily compromised.

'A Mr Terence Knowles telephoned to wish you luck and say he was sorry he couldn't be here to see you off.'

Don nodded. 'Is that all?'

'That is all.' The man smiled. 'I didn't see your plane on the tarmac.'

'Our plane?' Don asked, puzzled.

Jerry Patel was the first to understand and was at his side instantly. 'No, we're a relief crew,' he stammered. He looked at Don meaningfully. 'Aren't we, Captain? It's an exchange arrangement with BA.'

'An exchange?' Don said, starting to understand. 'Oh yes, sure! An exchange flight crew. We're SAS all right. Scandinavian to a man.'

For the first time Jerry had cause to thank his family for having mistaken the title once before.

'Why, who did you think we were? Members of the Special Air Service?'

The man found this hilarious and shook his head vigorously. 'No, no, no. You could never be that.'

'Why not?' asked Rod, taken aback.

'I mean no offence, but none of you are smart enough to be soldiers of such an illustrious regiment.'

They looked themselves up and down and had to agree with him. Surely such a ragtag bunch of misfits would never have made it through the portals of Hereford.

10

When the time came for Ramesh, Murap and the party to leave for the return journey to Pakistan, the leader of the Kashmiri rebel group turned out his men in a semblance of an honour guard. Each of them was now carrying a brand-new Kalashnikov rifle thanks to Ramesh, and there were RPG7 rocket launchers and medium machine-guns in their secret stashes.

'It is always a pleasure doing business with the Bandrams,' the leader said.

'And it is always a pleasure helping our brothers from across the border,' Ramesh replied diplomatically. The real cause of his pleasure, however, lay in the saddle-bags slung across the mules, the payment for the arms he had supplied. Apart from the gold coinage, there were sacks of opium that would fetch a handsome price on the black market.

With a cheery wave Ramesh led the way out of the compound and up the hillside, aiming for the point where the treeline came nearest to the clutch of farm buildings that served as the rebels' hideaway. Pine forest extended up the hillside and would provide welcome cover for the march over the days to come. He was apprehensive about their extraction from Indian Kashmir as, after their clash with the border troops, they could expect a large number of Indian reinforcements to have flooded the whole area. On previous occasions they had been lucky to make it back at all, and the rumour was that the Indian forces had brought in a new batch of Soviet-made helicopters with a good troop-lift capability.

As they entered the line of the pine trees, he paused and looked back. Far below them the rebel leader had been reduced to a tiny matchstick figure. His arm rose in a farewell salute and then he turned and disappeared into his stronghold. Within days he would be putting his new weaponry to good use against the Indian forces in a series of ambushes and raids. But by then, Ramesh sincerely hoped, he himself and his men would be safely out of the country.

It felt good to be in the shade of the trees. The chilly gloom closed about them like a fist, but protective rather than claustrophobic. In there they would be shielded from the Indian reconnaissance helicopters and only thermal-imaging devices would be able to pinpoint them. Ramesh knew that the Indians had such equipment, but thankfully not in any great numbers.

The path wound upwards for mile after mile. Because of the closed nature of the country he pushed two of the men out in front to act as lead scouts. They trotted off, ready to give instant warning should they spy any elements of the security forces. Murap fell into step beside Ramesh.

'Which route do you intend to use this time?'

Ramesh pondered. He had given the matter considerable thought and although he had settled on one of the passes he was still far from convinced that he had made the correct decision.

'I thought we could try the Tartha Pass.'

Murap tilted his head on one side as he considered the implications. 'Fine. We haven't been that way for some months. It might still be free of snow.'

'It's not the snow I'm worried about. We're equipped to cope with pretty much any weather.'

'Of course,' Murap agreed readily.

'It's a question of gauging where the Indians will concentrate their patrols. Assuming they've found the bodies by now, they've probably deduced which way we were going, so they know we have to return at some time.'

'And you're gambling that they'll choose to put their patrols on the high ridges, thinking we'll take the hardest route back?'

'Exactly. With luck they'll write off the passes as too obvious. At best they might stick a couple of sentries there, and we can cope with those.'

They walked on in silence for a while before Murap said, 'I believe Ceda will be back by the time we get home?'

Ramesh smiled. 'I hope so. It'll be good to see him again. He's been out of the country for too long.'

There was a friendly rivalry between the two brothers but it was never allowed to spill over into hostility. Both excelled in their relevant fields, Ceda preferring political intrigue and Ramesh the nitty-gritty of combat, and over the years each had learned to respect the other. In the special forces they had served alongside each other and had become something of a legend throughout the army. At first it had been a disadvantage when they had left and entered a different kind of service under their uncle. Their fame had caused questions to be asked about their sudden disappearance from the busy social circles in which they had once mixed, but with time people had forgotten and only then had their uncle put them to work.

It was towards evening that they made the first contact with an Indian patrol. They rounded a bend in the track to find the two scouts waiting for them. One of the men put his finger to his lips and waved them into a corner.

'There,' he whispered, pointing ahead to where the trees tumbled down and eventually opened out into a valley. A stream ran along the bottom of it and beside the stream the flames of a small camp-fire could be seen leaping up amid a shower of sparks.

'How many?' Ramesh asked.

The man shrugged. 'I can only see two, but I think there are another two washing down by the river. The ground dips and we can't see them, but when I look through the binoculars I can count four packs around the fire.'

Ramesh looked for the sun. It had already disappeared below the line of peaks and within an hour it would be dark. The moon would not rise until several hours after that, so in sixty minutes they would have complete darkness to cover their crossing of the bare valley. He gave out instructions to the men and ordered Murap to have the mules taken well out of range, adding, 'We don't want to give ourselves away again like before.'

He withdrew into the trees to rest until it was dark enough for them to continue on their way without being seen. After slipping out of his shoulder straps, he settled down beside a rock and checked the magazine on his rifle. Despite the Kalashnikovs that he carried as contraband on almost every gun-running trip, he still preferred his old SLR. It might not be able to put down the volume of fire of the Kalashnikov, but for long-range accuracy it was unparalleled. In the mountains and valleys of Kashmir that was the quality he felt he most required. Fields of fire were wide open and it was often possible to see an enemy several kilometres away. As a smuggler his aim was to keep that enemy as far away as possible, and only the SLR had a real chance of either picking them off or of putting down an accurate harassing fire.

It was almost dark when he was brought fully alert by a familiar sound. Murap was at his side in an instant.

'Helicopter!' he hissed, his face a mask of alarm.

Ramesh's mind swam. Had they been spotted? Perhaps the men in the valley had seen them approaching and reported in to their HQ, requesting reinforcements that were now about to arrive and swamp the area. If so, they would need the darkness to effect an escape.

'Shall I prepare the men to open fire on it as it comes in to land?' Murap asked.

Ramesh hesitated. 'Get them in position but no one's to open fire unless I give the order.'

Murap darted away and within seconds the men had been deployed in a ragged line, their weapons trained on the valley to their front.

'Get the machine-gun to cover that flat patch to the left of the camp-fire,' Ramesh directed. 'It's an obvious LZ. But remember, no one is to fire except on my order.'

The sound of the approaching helicopter rolled around the valley, making it impossible to tell from which direction it was coming until the very last moment, when it appeared over the far treeline.

'There it is!' Murap said, pointing.

It was a Soviet-built Hip troop-transport helicopter. Ramesh scanned the sky for others. If the Indians had called in reinforcements then they would probably be flying in a company and that would require at least a further two Hips. However, as the seconds passed it seemed that only the one had come.

'What are they up to?' Murap asked. 'Perhaps they reckon they can make do with a platoon?'

'That assumption would be foolish in the extreme after the drubbing we gave them the last time.'

The helicopter swung along the line of the valley, hugging the ground until it was over the camp-fire and the landing zone that Ramesh had predicted.

'They were using the fire as a marker,' Murap said.

However, instead of more troops disembarking, the men by the fire and their two companions doubling up from the riverside, gathered up their packs, weapons and equipment and ran towards the Hip, ducking under the rotor blades and clambering hastily in through the side door. Helping them, an aircrewman hoisted them in, one by one, took a quick look around and then slid the door closed. The engines surged and the helicopter lifted, tilting forward and swinging away along the valley, lifting slowly over the trees and disappearing into the gathering night. The noise of the engine faded away and a moment later Ramesh, Murap and their men were left with the valley, the forest and the surrounding mountains to themselves.

Murap grinned. 'How's that? We've driven them off without a fight! Now we can just walk across.'

Ramesh stared after the helicopter, watching the spot where the darkness had closed about it, swallowing it from view.

'What's the matter?' Murap asked. 'Disappointed we aren't going to have to shoot our way out?'

Ramesh shook his head, smiling uncertainly. 'No, of course not. It's unusual, that's all.'

'What is?'

But Ramesh shook his head, unable to identify the cause of his concern.

'Get the men ready to move. We'll wait for ten minutes to ensure they're not coming back and then we'll be on our way.'

Murap darted away though the trees to collect the men and bring forward the mules, and a few moments later

166

Ramesh heard the familiar jingle of the bridles and harnesses as the animals stepped patiently over the fallen trunks and soft coatings of pine needles.

First Ramesh sent across the two lead scouts, detailing them to check on the area of the earlier fire and the riverbank where the two Indian soldiers had been washing. Their report came back over their walkie-talkies that the enemy had completely gone.

'Not even their usual piles of rubbish have been left. It looks as if they don't even want anyone to know they were here.'

That's exactly what it is, Ramesh thought suspiciously. But why? Normally they would want smugglers to avoid the passes, driving them into the more difficult terrain of the mountains, where they were more likely to fall victim to avalanches and frostbite. Yet now it was as if a door was being left purposefully open.

A powerful sense of unease filled him as the whole party crossed the valley and entered the forest on the far side, beginning to climb again as they headed for the border with Pakistan, on the other side of the ridge. There again they would have to be watchful, taking care to avoid the Pakistani army patrols. But the greatest danger always lay on the Indian side of the border, for the gun-running traffic was always one-way, feeding the Kashmiri rebels.

All the way up the hillside he wrestled with the fears and doubts, trying to work out why the way had been made easy for them. And if it had not been done for their benefit, then for whose?

Uncle Gilma Bandram sat in the bright room, feeling the fresh, cold air wash over him like a balm. It heightened the feeling of living in an eagle's eyrie, far above the concerns of the world, yet able to swoop down at will, returning with whatever plunder you chose.

He had watched the approach of the convoy from a distance, having already noted with pleasure how his nephew Ceda had turned an initial disaster into a possible future triumph. The loss of Sanji had come as a blow but the news that Ceda had secured his granddaughter brought swift relief. Perhaps they would be able to do a deal and get their hands on Sanji after all. It was him that Uncle Bandram wanted, him and no other. Anyone who got in the way would have to die.

In preparation for the guarding of his new and unwilling guest, Uncle Bandram had called in manpower from all parts of the family until, by the time the Land Rovers turned the last hairpin bend on the road up to the fortress, the stronghold was a hive of activity. Not since the days of Yashman the brigand had it been so well defended. Even the Pakistani army itself, if it chose, would be hard pushed to take it by storm.

He finished his cup of strong black coffee, throwing the dregs from his high window and watching them diffuse in the darkening air. Six bold strides took him out into the hall and to the top of the steps that ran down to the courtyard. He must be there to greet the young lady. For although she was his hostage and he would not hesitate to have her shot should circumstances dictate, he was a man who enjoyed playing the game of manners, and regularly entertained the very best of company in an ongoing effort to polish his already impeccable social skills.

The large, double front gates stood open on his orders and he placed himself at the foot of the steps as the first of the Land Rovers entered the compound. In the front seat,

Ceda sat in a relaxed pose, concealing the inner tension that kept him wound like a spring, ready to explode into action at the drop of a hat. Uncle Bandram smiled warmly at his nephew. It was hard to choose between Ramesh and him. Both had their considerable strengths and few weaknesses, and together they made a formidable pair.

'Welcome,' Uncle Bandram said effusively as one of the guards opened the rear door of the Land Rover and gave Eli a helping hand. 'I trust the journey wasn't too trying?'

In response she glared at him angrily. 'You have my parents killed and then kidnap me, and now you greet me as if I've come willingly!'

He bowed his head in playful acknowledgement of his guilt. 'All very regrettable, I assure you. But you have your grandfather to blame.'

'And how is that? An old man, that's all he is.'

'Only half true, I'm afraid. He might be old, but that most certainly is not all he is.' He sighed heavily, his smile as chill as the night air around them. 'I can see he has told you nothing of his past life, before he emigrated to Britain. Or should I say, before he fled to Britain?'

'You can say what you damned well like,' she spat at him. 'Whatever it is it'll be a pack of lies. He'd never harm a fly. My grandfather's a devout Hindu. He respects life, and always has.'

Ceda took a step forward, noticing the tell-tale twitch at the corner of his uncle's mouth. The girl should indeed be told the truth, but this was neither the place nor the time.

'Uncle, I owe you an apology. I have failed in my mission.'

Uncle Bandram waved aside his nephew's words. 'These things happen. But never fear, we might get Sanji yet.' He turned to Eli. 'In the meantime why don't you show our visitor to her quarters. We are forgetting our manners. She must be cold and tired after her journey.'

Ceda took her by the arm but Eli shook him off. From out of the shadows two old women appeared and moved to either flank of her.

'These ladies will attend to you,' Uncle Bandram said. 'You will find them kind and courteous.' He smiled. 'But don't try to give them the slip. They are local tribeswomen, tied to me by blood. They would kill you as soon as look at you if they had to. And they will if you try to escape.'

When she had gone, Uncle Bandram took Ceda into his study to hear a full account of the mission to Britain, his brow furrowing when Ceda spoke of Ali's lack of self-discipline.

'He was like that as a boy, I remember. I regret my promise to my sister to look after him, but he is family.' He shrugged. 'Still, you have my word I shall not impose him on you again. From now on I will keep him close to me.'

They talked of the second half of Ceda's team – of their deaths and of the backup team's failed attempt on the safe house.

'It seems that we are encountering a lot of bad luck,' Uncle Bandram concluded.

'You get it in every operation,' Ceda tried to console him. 'That man at the motorway service station for instance. I would dearly like to meet him again.' He stared icily out of the dark window. 'I have a score to settle with him.'

The room that Eli was shown into was more comfortable than she had expected. Rugs were scattered about the floor and the coverlet on the large bed was of pure silk. But the first thing she noticed was the window. As soon as the women had left her, locking the door noisily behind them, she ran across to the sill and leaned out to look for a way of escape. The precipitous drop that loomed beneath her almost made her head swim and she staggered back from it quickly lest she lose her balance.

A glance around the room revealed another two windows, but like the first one, neither opened on to anything but a sheer cliff whose base was invisible. She might as well have been locked in an inaccessible tower from a fairy tale.

True to his word, Uncle Bandram had provided sufficient clothes for her. There were trousers, blouses and sweaters, and a warm sheepskin jacket and hat should she venture outside. In the adjoining bathroom there were towels and pyjamas and, feeling suddenly overcome by the stresses of the journey, she decided to run herself a bath.

The water was wonderfully hot and when she had undressed she lay back and allowed it to soothe her aching muscles. It was only then that the despair she had held at bay for so long threatened to break out. Huge tears throbbed in her eyes and she bit her lip so as not to cry out loud. That wouldn't do, she told herself. She would only find a way out of there if she managed to keep her head. But how? The place seemed impregnable and even if she escaped from the fort she was still miles from any source of help.

When she had dried, she slipped into a skirt and a light cotton blouse and went to the door, being met by the smell of food as she went back into her bedroom. A small trestle table had been set by the bed and on it a tray bore several dishes, varieties of curry, with an accompanying basket of chapattis. She went across to inspect it.

'I doubt it'll be up to the standard of Grandpa's restaurants.'

She spun round at the sound of the man's voice. Ali was sitting on the window-sill, smiling at her coldly.

'How long have you been here?' she asked, glancing at the bathroom door, which she had left ajar.

He followed her eyes and his smile broadened. 'Long enough.'

A thought suddenly occurred to her. 'Does your uncle know you're here?'

'Of course,' he lied. 'It was him who told me to bring you some food.' He got up and sauntered across to her.

'I don't believe you. You took it from the women.' She pointed to the door. 'Get out of here.'

Instead he reached a hand to her hair, running a strand of it between his fingers.

'It's wet. You'll catch your death of cold. Let me dry it for you.'

She tossed her head, flicking away his hand, but as she tried to turn from him he caught her by the shoulder and spun her round. The next thing she knew his mouth was on hers, his lips pressing into hers, hands holding her by the throat. She writhed in his grasp until he was forced to draw back.

'Keep quiet,' he hissed in her face, 'or I'll . . .'

'Or you'll what? Kill me? I wonder what your uncle would think about that?'

'There are more ways of punishing a girl like you,' he said, his eyes narrowing.

Before she could react he had grabbed her by the arms and flung her on to the bed. She tried to scream but he clamped one hand across her mouth. With the other he tore at the neck of her blouse, the buttons exploding across the silk coverlet.

'I warned you,' he said, his breath coming in gasps. 'Don't struggle or you'll only make it worse for yourself.'

She felt his hand on her leg, caressing, as she thrashed at him with her fists, using her nails to gouge at his face. He cried out, taking his hand from her mouth. She opened it to scream but the next instant he slapped her hard, pinning both her wrists in one tight grasp while his free hand yanked at her skirt.

'Think yourself too good for me, do you? We'll see about that.'

He fumbled with his belt, loosening it as he pressed himself down between her knees. Eli's head was swimming from the force of the blow, but she desperately tried to shake him off her, fighting to retain consciousness and the will to resist.

Suddenly she was aware of a shadow on the periphery of her vision, fleeting and swift, and the next instant she felt Ali's weight being lifted off her. She struggled to sit up, pulling down the hem of her skirt to cover herself, and saw Ali being swung to his feet in the iron grip of Ceda Bandram.

'Thought you'd join her for a little supper, did you?' Ceda said through gritted teeth. His right hand drove into Ali's stomach immediately below the diaphragm, the fingers straight and rigid like a shaft of steel. Eli heard the air go out of Ali's lungs and saw the eyes bulge in his head. But Ceda hadn't finished with him yet.

With Ali's feet barely touching the floor, he held him out by the scruff of the neck with one hand and with the other delivered a short, sharp series of blows. Each blow was directed accurately at a vital point and after every shattering impact Ceda's hand curved or clenched into a new and deadly shape, each one fashioned precisely for its own special task. Forefinger and thumb widened to present the hand's web for a strike at the windpipe, then the hand became a fist, but with the middle knuckle of the middle finger extended for a punch to the solar plexus. Next the hand curled and stiffened into the semblance of an eagle's claw that slapped and clenched tight on Ali's testicles, Ceda using the grip to lift

Ali towards the window. Ali opened his mouth to scream but all that escaped was a shrill yelp of agony.

'If you'd wanted some excitement you should have asked me,' Ceda said. 'How's this for stimulation?'

He lowered Ali to the floor and allowed him to achieve a wobbly balance, but the next second he chopped hard down on the collar-bone with the edge of his open left hand. Lastly, with Ali lined up in front of the window that Eli had first seen on entering the room, he clenched his right fist and propelled it into Ali's nose in three ferocious jabs. Blood poured from the man's nostrils, the bone beneath shattered. Ali tottered backwards and sat heavily down on the sill. Ceda took a step forward, swept up his ankles and tipped him backwards out of the window, maintaining his grasp as Ali's last shred of consciousness woke in him the survival instinct. His limbs jerked and he squealed for mercy as Ceda levered him backwards, tipping him head first into the darkness above the sheer drop.

'Ceda!'

Ceda turned at the voice of his uncle.

'Enough!'

Without releasing his grip, Ceda glared out at Ali, enjoying the terror he saw there.

'He deserves to die, Uncle. He has dishonoured the family for the last time.'

'That is for me to decide.'

Uncle Bandram's voice was stern and unflinching and Ceda reluctantly understood that there was no room for negotiation. Slowly he hauled Ali back into the room and let his body slip from his grasp. As he hit the floor Ali retched, bringing up his most recent meal. Ceda glowered down at him in utter disgust.

'Get out of here.'

He placed the toe of his boot under Ali's rump and pushed, sending him sprawling across the floor. Ali scuttled away, flicking a frightened glance at his uncle. But as he reached the doorway he turned and said, 'I'll get even with you for this, Ceda. You think you're so damn clever, with your military bearing and proud ways. Don't think I don't know what's on your mind.' He glanced at Eli on the edge of the bed. 'I know you want her as much as I do. But you haven't got the balls to take what you want. You never have. That's why you'll always be someone else's lackey.'

'Ali,' Uncle Bandram said softly. 'I wouldn't push your cousin too far. Next time I won't call him off, I promise you. Disgrace me once more and I'll let Ceda have you.'

'Yes, Uncle. OK. We'll leave it for now. But don't expect me to forget.'

He glared at Eli as if lodging the sight of her in his mind for later use. Then he was gone. Uncle Bandram followed him out of the room, calling for the two tribeswomen and instructing them to remain outside Eli's room throughout the night.

Ceda wiped Ali's blood from his hands as he walked towards the door.

'Thank you, Mr Bandram,' Eli called after him.

He turned in surprise. 'I didn't do it for you. I don't like to disappoint a lady, but I was thinking of my family's honour.'

'Honour? But you've kidnapped me!' she said in astonishment.

'Exactly. But that doesn't mean I have to stand by and watch you raped as well. You might temporarily be my prisoner, but you're not going to come to any harm if it can be avoided. And Ali's assault on you could be avoided.'

He continued towards the door. 'I'll have one of the women clean up Ali's mess,' he said over his shoulder, indicating the vomit.

When he had gone and she was once more alone, Eli went to the bathroom and splashed cold water on her face and throat. She found that her hands were shaking, and looked at herself in the mirror.

'Oh Eli, whatever are you going to do now?'

The reflection didn't have an answer. It stared back at her blankly, admitting with the silent passing of each second that she was beyond hope.

11

'So that's about the size of it then.'

Sir Anthony Briggs waved the piece of notepaper at Sanji, who sat dejectedly on the bed.

'They offer the release of the girl if you take the first available plane to Pakistan and hand yourself over to them.'

He waited for Sanji's response but when the old man remained silent, staring morosely at the floor, he went on, 'You'd be committing suicide of course. You can't go.'

'Why not? There's nothing else I can do. I must go.' Sanji got unsteadily to his feet and ambled across to the window. Outside the lawn was being swept by a fine, cold rain. 'I've got nothing else left to lose.'

'Nothing to lose?'

'Don't sound so surprised. I'm an old man, Sir Anthony. My daughter's dead, my business means nothing to me any more, and the person who means more to me than anything or anyone else in the world is in the hands of madmen. If anything happened to my little Eli I could never live with myself. I have to do as they ask.'

Sir Anthony paced the carpet, rubbing his chin in thought. 'I'm afraid it's not as easy as all that.'

'What you do mean?'

'You must realize that if your story comes out it could inflame relations between Pakistan and India and they're tense enough as it is. We've known for a long time that they both possess nuclear weapons and if any conflict erupted into war we are certain they wouldn't hesitate to use them.'

Sanji smiled sadly. 'I think you overestimate my importance. It was all such a long time ago.'

'Not to those who remember.'

'Like Mr Bandram?'

'And there are probably many like him on both sides of the border.'

Sanji shrugged. 'It doesn't alter the fact that I'm at last prepared to offer myself up as a sacrificial lamb, if that's what they want. I've been hiding for long enough. It's time to end the charade.'

Sir Anthony's expression hardened. 'Then there's one other reason for preventing you from going.'

'Which is?' Sanji asked, becoming suspicious. There was a deviousness about the British Intelligence officer that Sanji disliked intensely. It reminded him of the many similar individuals he had been forced to deal with during the Independence movement in 1947.

'The embarrassment caused to my country.' He corrected himself quickly, 'To *our* country, that is. Since you're now a British passport holder.'

Sanji looked into his eyes but saw them only as ball-bearings, devoid of human warmth or feeling. 'We are talking about the life of my granddaughter, a young woman with her life ahead of her. You and I are old men.' He saw Sir Anthony blanch and added, 'Yes, even you, Sir Anthony. Our lives are behind us. These affairs are just the scrag-ends. We delude ourselves if we think that the world wants anything for us any more. Let us do all we can to help the young to their inheritance. Help me recover my granddaughter, even if it means a few red faces in Whitehall.'

Sir Anthony stalked to the door, coughing to hide his outrage. 'I'm afraid I can't, Mr Sanji. Not after what you've told me. My own research since has confirmed what you said. You may be willing to give up the ghost and throw away your life but I'm still responsible for the security and prestige of this nation. And as long as I am you will remain here and silent.'

He let himself out and although there was no sound of any key turning in the lock Sanji knew that to all intents and purposes he was Sir Anthony's prisoner. The winter rain was now lashing into the swaying trees and looking out at it he realized that he had come to hate the country of his adoption. He sank on to the bed and buried his head in his hands once again, but a new fire had been kindled in his heart. He would not remain silent any longer. Somehow he would confess the errors of the past, even if it was too late to save his beloved Eli. For her there might be no salvation, but at least he would set the record straight and dedicate the bitter truth to her memory.

On another continent, a file of men moved stealthily through the forest gloom. From their fieldcraft it was impossible to guess that none of them had ever operated in the country before. As far as they were concerned, the techniques of soldiering were an international language, adaptable to any land and any situation as required. The moment they were off the beaten track and submerged in the vast Kashmiri mountain forests, the SAS eight-man fighting patrol felt utterly at home. In their case, however, the feeling at home did not in any way herald relaxation. Rather the opposite.

It heightened their senses like those of the fox on its night stalk for prey.

The distance between each man was adjusted without thinking, to suit the terrain and the light, the single file expanding or contracting like an accordion so that each man was able to keep easy sight of the individuals in front and behind. Every member of the patrol had been allocated his arc to observe, which, in the event of a contact, would become his primary field of fire. The weapons were distributed throughout the patrol so as to ensure an even balance, the only exception being at the front of the file, where the two lead scouts carried between them enough fire-power to suppress an average infantry company.

Marching third in the patrol, Don surveyed the ground around him, mentally comparing it with the features he had memorized from his extensive map study before setting out. Every so often he slipped the compass from his breast pocket and checked their direction of travel. At each of the short halts, he would move forward to speak to the lead scout, indicating a noticeable feature for him to steer by for the next leg of the march. With such an obvious target to aim for, the scouts were freed from the task of navigation, their full attention being concentrated on their fieldcraft, alert to the slightest sign of another human presence which could mean trouble.

Don, on the other hand, apart from his responsibility for navigation, was constantly considering the options should such a contact occur. As the patrol crossed a valley he would decide what to do if a machine-gun opened up from any one of a number of potential enemy positions. Such mental contingency planning didn't take any particular time. It was ingrained in him and he was constantly slipping easily through the procedure as he marched.

Sergeant Gavin Steward, marching near the rear of the file, had been assigned as check navigator, confirming his boss's compass bearings and map reading and trying desperately to find a fault, but always without success.

Jerry Patel had been detailed to bring up the rear.

'Tail-end Tandoori,' Rod had joked, digging him in the ribs as he passed to take up his own position behind Don. 'We'll send you out for the takeaway when we harbour up for the night. You speak the lingo, after all.'

Jerry was aware, however, that the tail-end position was almost as important as the lead scout's. For if the patrol should pick up an enemy tail the results could be disastrous. An enemy patrol, if sufficiently skilled, could track the SAS team to their night harbour, allow them to start on their drills for establishing the night base and then catch them when they were at their most vulnerable. Don, as commander, would have gone forward with an escort of at least one man to close-recce the potential position, while the remainder of the patrol would cluster in all-round defence to await his return. An attack at such a time would catch the patrol split in two, the commander away from the bulk of his patrol, and no one knowing who was firing at whom. It all boiled down to Jerry's alertness to ensure that any such tracker was detected before he could close up and do the damage.

In such an event the patrol would either go into the contact-rear drill, if the enemy was so close that a fire-fight was imminent; or, if there was a little more time, they would establish a hasty ambush, circling back on their own track to lie in wait and fire on the unwitting enemy – the hunted hunting the hunter.

Jerry's pack was lighter than on his last Welsh exercise, and he derived a grim satisfaction from seeing Gavin Steward stopping every so often to mop his brow. At one point when they closed up for a slightly longer break, he couldn't resist saying, 'Having a spot of bother, Sarge?'

Gavin winked at him. 'Me? A spot of bother? On yer bike.'

It was after they had been moving for a couple of days that they made the first contact with anyone, but rather than a hostile patrol it was an old shepherd close to the border.

The patrol was in the middle of a bare, steep-sided valley and halfway across a slender bridge over a raging torrent, when Gavin raised the alarm. Instantly everyone went into the contact-front drill, closing up as fast as they could to form an extended fire line facing in the direction that Gavin had indicated in his shouted command. However, once they were all on the ground and safely in cover, it became clear that the old man was alone with his flock and presented no threat.

'What the fuck do we do now?' Taff rasped.

'Slot the old bugger, I say,' Geordie replied, only half joking.

'Shut it.' Don studied the ground. The shepherd had obviously seen them but didn't appear to be in any way concerned. He remained sitting on his rock, poking the earth with his gnarled stick.

'Do you reckon he's close enough to see we're not Indian army?' Don asked Gavin.

Gavin weighed it up. 'Doubt it. From his reaction I'd say he's used to seeing patrols in this area.'

'Agreed.' Don looked around for Jerry. 'Time for you to earn your keep. Go and sound him out. Stick to our cover story but don't let him ask too many questions. See what you can get out of him.'

'Wilco, boss.'

As Jerry got up and walked towards the old shepherd Rod asked, 'Shouldn't someone go with him as backup?'

Don grinned. 'You're sounding very caring all of a sudden. Jerry will be flattered to hear you care.'

Rod blushed. 'Just thinking about the drills, boss. Couldn't give a stuff about him myself.'

'Sure, sure,' Don said unconvinced.

Jerry felt suddenly very vulnerable with the thought of the whole battery of SAS weaponry at his back. The old man watched him approach, unimpressed. He was sitting cross-legged on the rock, and as Jerry walked towards him he put his hand inside his jacket. Behind him Jerry heard half a dozen rifle bolts click in readiness to drill the old fellow full of holes, but there was something peaceful about the man and Jerry held up his hand to restrain his comrades. Sure enough, a second later the old man's hand reappeared holding a battered pipe which he proceeded to fill with tobacco from a cloth pouch. He looked up and smiled as Jerry covered the last yards between them.

'Greetings,' Jerry said in Hindi.

'Greetings,' the man replied in Urdu. He was a Kashmiri Muslim but it was obvious from Jerry's appearance that he was Indian. Also, if Jerry was to pass himself off as a member of the security forces he would most likely be a Hindi speaker. However, in an effort to communicate with the local population the Indian forces used Urdu as well, so when he next spoke he used that language, though keeping it rough and ready as befitted an ordinary soldier.

'How many sheep have you got?' he asked pleasantly, looking around the valley.

The man jerked his chin at the flock. 'Just what you see. The grazing's not very good around here, so I'm taking them higher.'

Jerry nodded knowingly. He crouched down in front of the man, judging it to be less confrontational. It could also

183

be interpreted as deferential to the old man's greater age. To Jerry's delight the old man clearly took it as such, smiling at the youth before him like any grandfather upon his family.

'What brings you here?' he asked.

'You know how it is,' Jerry replied. 'Patrolling the frontier and looking for rebels.'

The old shepherd tut-tutted. 'Ah, the rebels. Must there always be men of violence?'

'Our thoughts exactly.'

'Of course,' the shepherd added mischievously, 'you could always go home and leave us alone.'

Jerry chuckled and wagged his finger. 'You know we can't do that. Kashmir is part of India. We love it and its people and want to keep it.'

'Even if its people don't love you? We are Muslim, after all. Wouldn't it make sense for us to join Pakistan?'

'There are many Muslims living happily in India. Why can't you?'

The old man laughed. 'Let us not argue. Will you have some milk?'

He hoisted a goatskin bottle off his shoulder, unplugged the stopper and passed it across. Jerry accepted it doubtfully and held it up, wincing as he tasted the gush of warm, sweet sheep's milk.

'I can see you are a city boy,' the shepherd said as he watched. 'Where do you come from?'

Careful, Jerry thought, ever on his guard. 'Delhi.' It was the one city he had visited with his parents and felt that he could bluff the old man if he had to.

'Ah, that was a Muslim city until 1947. But then all the Muslims were driven out. Many were massacred in the race riots.'

Jerry had heard about the massacres from his father. Countless thousands had died, millions perhaps. No one would ever know the true figure. 'Hindus were killed as well.'

'True,' the shepherd conceded. 'They were terrible times. Many of the perpetrators have never been brought to book.' He held up his hands to heaven. 'But one day they will stand before Allah to account for their evil deeds.'

Thinking it was time to get moving, Jerry said, 'Tell me, have you seen anyone else hereabouts?' He kept his voice as casual and unconcerned as he could.

'No one,' the man said a little too quickly. But then, Jerry thought, he wasn't likely to offer help or information to the Indian security forces voluntarily.

'No other patrols?'

The old man's eyes narrowed. 'Do you not keep track of your own men?'

'Of course. But we've been out for a long time. It's easy to wander into someone else's patch.'

The shepherd looked past Jerry at the prone figures of the SAS patrol. 'Why don't your friends come over here? They could have some milk as well.'

Jerry rolled his eyes conspiratorially, 'It's our commander. He's a real arsehole. Doesn't like to mix with the local population.'

The man nodded sympathetically. 'That's a funny uniform you're wearing,' he said reaching to touch Jerry's combat jacket.

'Yes, it's new. We're paratroopers. Only we've been issued with it so far. Smart, isn't it?'

The shepherd wobbled his head from side to side noncommittally. He looked past Jerry at the patrol. 'I think your commander wants you.'

Jerry turned to see Don waving him back.

'See what I mean? He obviously doesn't like me talking to you.'

'May Allah go with you,' the old man said as Jerry made to leave.

'And peace be with you too, old man,' Jerry replied.

Back at the patrol's fire line, he crouched down beside Don and reported on what the shepherd had said.

'I thought you were going to get a fucking brew on,' Don said.

'You have to show the correct respect for elders out here. He doesn't give a shit about our timetable. If I'd given him the brush-off he'd have known we weren't security forces. They're ordered to do everything they can to appease the locals.'

Giving the shepherd a wide berth, the patrol continued on its way. While Jerry had been talking to him, the members of the patrol had blacked up their faces with cam cream but even so Don didn't want to get too close and risk being recognized as Westerners.

'I still think we should have slotted him,' Geordie said with a backward glance at the lonely figure on the rock.

'That's a real hearts-and-minds philosophy,' Jerry said. 'Very subtle, O wise one.'

'When you've got 'em by the balls the hearts and minds follow,' Geordie countered.

The patrol followed the valley towards its mouth, the ground rising all the time until they were struggling up steep banks of shale.

'According to my calculations, the border should be just two miles on the other side of that ridge,' Don said as they approached the top of the valley. Gavin grunted his agreement and they pressed on.

'Sir Anthony might have been able to pull strings with old friends in the Indian army and have their patrols withdrawn from the area, but we'll still have to give the Pakistanis the slip.'

'I've heard their mountain troops are pretty hot stuff,' Gavin replied. 'Shouldn't we restrict our movement to darkness only?'

Don had already weighed the pros and cons. It was imperative that they get back across the border as soon as possible, spending the minimum amount of time in Pakistan necessary to achieve the mission. On the other hand, if they were compromised by the authorities before reaching the Bandrams' fort then the mission would fail anyway, and the chances of compromise were greatly increased if they moved by day as well as by night. It was unlikely that the Pakistani border patrols were well equipped with night-sights and image-intensifiers, so darkness offered the best chance for a successful infiltration.

He issued his instructions accordingly and when they topped the ridge at the head of the valley and began their descent towards the frontier, Don and Gavin started to look for an LUP where they could lie up until nightfall. They found it a couple of miles further on, in a small cave hidden among an old rockfall, and when sentries had been posted, the rest of the patrol unrolled their sleeping bags and tried to rest.

Before curling up himself, Don crept forward with his binoculars to spy out the lie of the land which they would have to cross later that night. Peering from behind a rock, he laid out his map and compared it with the ground itself, taking a series of bearings to pinpoint his own position. Gavin had already confirmed their location using the patrol's satellite navigational system, which gave them an accurate fix to within ten metres, but Don still liked to keep his old skills well honed. Technical kit could always go wrong or take a bullet through it, and then they would have to fall back on basic compass resection. It was as well to practise the skill while there wasn't the added pressure of necessity.

In this remote part of the mountains there was no form of physical barrier delineating the frontier, but from his map Don worked out that it lay approximately one mile in front of him. The Bandrams' fort was several miles beyond that, so he reckoned that they would be able to reach it that night without too much trouble. With luck there would be enough time left to do a close recce, and then they would have to lie up during the following day in an observation position to observe the various comings and goings of the occupants. That would give them a good chance to pinpoint the defences, locate any sentries and the times they changed stags, ate their meals, went to relieve themselves and so on. With luck he could also establish the whereabouts of Eli herself. He would then be in a position to make his plan of attack. The strike could take place the next night, the idea being that they would infiltrate the fort, effect the rescue and tab across into the relative safety of Indian Kashmir before first light.

Of course they would then have to make the RV with the transport that Sir Anthony had arranged, but so long as his contacts continued to play the game and keep the Indian patrols out of the way, Don couldn't foresee too many problems.

When he got back to the cave he noted down all he had learned from his brief recce and then tried to sleep. It was strange how relaxed he felt, lying among the rocks, staring up at the clear blue sky overhead. He could hardly believe that he was in Kashmir, about to cross the border into Pakistan. As far as he could tell by looking about him he might as well have been on exercise in Wales. But that was what it was all about. If you got the training right, then the actual operation should feel like an anticlimax. Of course, it never was. Once the lead started flying there was always the added excitement and adrenalin that only ever came with a real mission, but at times like this, on an approach march or in a lying-up or observation position, you should always have the confidence of having been through the drills a hundred times before, knowing them so thoroughly that they were in your very blood and bones.

Before he knew it he was being shaken awake and the blue sky above him had miraculously turned into a deep velvet studded with pinpricks of light.

'What time is it?' he asked, rolling out of his sleeping bag and coming fully alert.

'Nineteen hundred hours, boss.'

He recognized Jerry's gentle voice. He was a good lad, he reflected. He would do the Regiment proud, given time.

As Don rolled up his bag and packed it away, Gavin brought him a brew and some food. All around him the men were preparing to move, their actions disciplined and confident, stemming from thorough training and considerable experience. Each of them had had a distinguished career in a line infantry regiment or the Paras before selection for the SAS and their professionalism made Don almost pity the opponents they were shortly going to confront.

'All ready?' he asked quietly when they were in their patrol formation.

Each of them gave him the thumbs up.

'Move now,' he ordered softly.

For crossing the open ground they shook out into an arrowhead formation, but once at the border they would once again slip effortlessly into single file. As they pulled away from the LUP each man checked his arcs, feeling stiff muscles complain before settling into the rhythm of the march.

A short while later Don turned to the man next to him and whispered, 'The border,' giving the hand signal for single file. The man passed it back, and so on down the line until the patrol had glided effortlessly into the new formation.

They hadn't gone more than a couple of miles when the lead scout dropped soundlessly to the ground, waving the others into cover behind him with the thumbs-down signal for enemy. Don crawled forward. He had assigned Jerry as lead scout in case his language skills were needed. In the event of their running headlong into a Pakistani army patrol it just might be possible, in the confusion of darkness, to pass themselves off as another such patrol.

'Trouble up ahead,' Jerry said quietly as Don came up beside him. 'I think it's a listening post of half-section strength.'

Don stared into the darkness but could see and hear nothing. In answer to his doubting look, Jerry said, 'One of them just lit a cigarette and the post commander told him to put it out.' He grinned. 'Abuse sounds the same in any language, be it Urdu or Brit.'

'We'll have to skirt around them,' Don said, making a mental note of the position to avoid it on the return journey the next night.

There were two other such contacts before they were clear of the immediate border area and started to see the lights of distant villages and farmsteads. Then, towards the early hours, they entered a region of harsh, rocky landscapes where streams cascaded down from the heights and the skyline showed as a jagged relief of peaks and razor-backed ridges.

Gavin moved forward down the line of the patrol until he reached Don. The moon had risen and in its silvery light Don could see a sheen of perspiration beading the sergeant's face. 'By my reckoning we should be just about there,' he said softly.

'Mine too,' Don agreed. They called a halt, and while the members of the patrol waited in all-round defence, they went forward alone until they came over a slight rise and saw the distant silhouette of the fortress.

'Jesus Christ,' Gavin muttered. 'That nut's going to take some cracking.'

'Let's get a bit closer and look for an LUP. I'll do the close recce myself and take Jerry with me.'

Gavin checked his watch and looked at the eastern rim of the horizon for any sign of light. 'You haven't got long.'

'I know. If I can just get a look at the other side of it that'll have to do. We can check out the rest from an OP after sunrise.'

They found an LUP within fifteen minutes and once the men were established in it Don ordered Gavin to put out claymores to cover the approaches. 'If the Bandrams' men bump us by mistake I want to make sure we can give them a warm reception.'

He took Jerry to one side and briefed him on the close recce. Both men stripped down to the minimum kit necessary, setting out with little more than belt order and their personal weapons. For the recce, their belt order consisted of spare ammunition, water, emergency rations, sheath knife and survival kit. Maps and compasses were carried in their pockets and Don had a small notebook and pencil to jot down all he gleaned from the recce about the defences and layout of the fort. In a pouch on his belt he carried a Sopolem OB44 night-sight.

Aware that he was now racing against the approaching sun, Don set a ferocious pace. Relieved of the weight of their full packs and webbing, both men felt suddenly liberated and hopped over rocks and streams, covering the distance with ease. Jerry moved several paces behind Don, periodically checking the rear for tails. Every so often they stopped and crouched into cover, Don using his night-sight to scan the fort, jotting down every scrap of information before moving on to the next vantage point.

The view from the far side told him what he needed to know – that the fort was surrounded by sheer cliffs on three sides. The choices open to them appeared to be either to scale the cliffs the following night, or to attempt an approach along the only track leading in. However, the night-sight revealed a thick belt of mines and wire obstacles covering the slender peninsula that extended towards the fort's front entrance.

'Hope you brought your crampons,' he whispered to Jerry.

Jerry stared in awe at the cliff face and swallowed hard. It was going to be some climb.

They arrived back at the LUP as the sun was brightening the eastern horizon, spreading a heavy line of orange and crimson from rim to rim behind the mountains. As Don crawled in he was challenged quietly for the password, knowing that behind the low, controlled voice of the sentry lay the muzzle of the American M249 Squad Automatic Weapon, a 5.56mm round in the breech, the safety-catch set for automatic fire, and a box magazine packed to bursting clamped beneath.

'Welcome home, boss,' the sentry whispered as Don and Jerry crawled past him and into the LUP. Four of the team were asleep in their sacks while Gavin sat beside his stripped M16 dry-cleaning the working parts for the fire-fights to come.

Don quickly briefed him on all he had gleaned from the short recce. 'I wish we had had more time. I'd like to have been able to take a closer look at the road approach. I don't like ruling it out just because the goons have sown a few mines and strung a bit of wire across it.'

Gavin laughed soundlessly. 'You're just afraid of heights. Admit it.'

'Bollocks.'

When the sun finally appeared, Don crawled forward to the crack between two rocks where Gavin had set up the OP. Perfect, he thought as he looked out at the fort across the valley. Now all we have to do is sit back and watch and wait. With luck, he thought, the Bandrams' men would give away their routine and their positions, and then the next night all they had to do was walk across the valley floor, shin up the rockface, and rescue the princess from her tower. Piece of piss.

12

Ramesh had arrived back at the stronghold with his sense of unease magnified. The return journey had been too simple, without a single Indian patrol being encountered. Such a thing had never happened before and the initial pleasure of the surprise had rapidly turned into a grave suspicion. The military patrols and guards on the Pakistani side of the border appeared to be the same as ever, but it nevertheless left the inexplicable behaviour of the Indian authorities unaccounted for.

He was still puzzling about it when he entered the courtyard and saw Ceda and his uncle standing there to receive him. Ali stood behind them, a huge ripe black eye and a bandaged nose telling of yet another disagreement in his troublesome life. His uncle greeted him but it was Ceda who noticed his disquiet. When he explained the problem Ceda rubbed his chin and suggested that perhaps the Indians were simply changing over the divisions responsible for the sector. If such a hand-over went badly it could often result in a gap in the patrol programme as the outgoing and incoming units shuffled around the district. Ramesh agreed that that was probably what had happened, but all the same he recommended that the guards should be strengthened for the rest of the week.

'The Indians would never dare cross the border,' Ceda answered. 'Our gun-running gets under their skin, but if they were caught in Pakistani territory it could spark a war. They wouldn't dare risk it.'

'Perhaps not, but a small special forces unit might have a shot. A quick in and out.'

Ceda was unconvinced but agreed that there would be no harm in doubling the sentries for a few nights.

Ramesh was interested by the news of the kidnapping of Eli but disappointed that they had failed to get their hands on Sanji himself.

'Don't worry,' Uncle Bandram replied. 'He should know by now that we're prepared to do a swap, and if my information is correct, he'll sacrifice anything to safeguard his grand-daughter. Even his life.'

That evening they had a special dinner to celebrate the homecoming of both brothers, and throughout it Ali sat sullenly by himself nursing his swollen face. Murap tried to coax him out of his sulk, but Ali would have none of it.

'What's the matter with him?' Ramesh asked Ceda quietly when the plates were being cleared away and the next course was being laid before them.

Ceda recounted Ali's fit of passion over Eli.

'So she's attractive, this Eli?' Ramesh said, eyeing his brother playfully.

Ceda shrugged. 'For an Indian, I suppose she might be called that. But she's not my type. She's been corrupted by her upbringing in Britain. She has no idea how to behave in front of a man and from the way she dresses, it's not surprising that Ali thought she'd let him have his way.'

Ramesh laughed. 'That's not very enlightened of you.'

'I think I become less enlightened the older I get. Give me a good traditional Pakistani girl any day.'

The next dish arrived, a huge brass platter piled high with rice, mutton and chicken. Ramesh wiped his moustache, happy to be back and enjoying a decent meal instead of facing the hardships of the mountains. But as he ate he relaxed, and as he relaxed, his thoughts went back to the journey over the mountains. Something continued to worry at his peace of mind until he sat back, his appetite gone. He shook his head in dismay and got to his feet.

'Still worrying?' Ceda asked.

'It's no good,' he replied. 'I'm going to have to take a look around.'

Uncle Bandram sat with his face buried in his food, taking little interest in the concerns of his nephew, but Ceda nodded.

'Do you want me to come too?'

He had worked alongside his brother on numerous operations and exercises and knew enough to respect Ramesh's intuitions.

'No, it's OK. You stay here and enjoy your dinner. I won't be long. I'm sure it's nothing, but there's no harm in making sure.'

Don was immensely relieved when he reached the foot of the cliff to find that it was not as sheer and smooth as it had appeared through his binoculars. Lying in his OP earlier in the day he wondered whether they would be physically able to scale it or whether they would be forced to gain access to the stronghold by some other means. However, as he eased into his harness and sought out the first hand and footholds above him, he saw that an ascent would indeed be possible.

Before leaving the OP and moving across the valley floor, the SAS fighting patrol had established a cache for their bergens and extra equipment, each man taking with him only his weapons, ammunition and sufficient kit to carry out the mission. The cache would also serve as an RV after the raid, a place where they would assemble before the tab back to and across the border. Don knew that it would be essential to gather their wits and take stock before starting on the exfiltration phase of the patrol, forcing themselves to ignore whatever hornets' nest their attack had stirred up, so as to retain the initiative and not simply end up fleeing in panic from the surviving enemy.

Don started to climb, the rope around his waist playing out behind him. To left and right of him, the other members of the team started upwards, the patrol climbing in four pairs. His own partner for the ascent was Jerry, and at each leg of the climb Don anchored himself to the rockface and waited for Jerry to come up beside him. So, in a series of caterpillar movements, they made their way painstakingly towards the battlements high above.

It was hard going but the rock itself was firm and dry, providing a wealth of solid holds. Don had often climbed in Wales, as had every member of the team, and for all of them it was second nature. Little by little the ground fell away below, until, looking down, Don could no longer see it in the darkness. The moon had risen and shone on him, lending its welcome light to his efforts. Before setting out he had been careful to secure every item of kit so that his movements were soundless. The slightest noise could betray his presence to the terrorists above and the last place he would want to be caught was splayed out against the rockface. If they were spotted while still climbing they would be completely vulnerable to attack.

When he had been climbing for nearly fifteen minutes he came to a narrow ledge and, checking his position, he saw that he was only a few yards short of the top. He signalled for Jerry to join him and then looked to left and right for the other teams. All of them were visible and he signalled to them that they should gather there in preparation for the final push up to the battlements.

Jerry scaled the rocks quickly and heaved himself up on to the ledge beside Don. Their faces were blackened with cam cream but Don could see the perspiration shining through. Jerry grinned with excitement and gave the thumbs up. Next, Gavin arrived with Rod in tow, and off to the left Taff and Geordie, and Tom and Jimmie.

Pair by pair, Don checked that everyone was set. They were. Steadying his breathing, he was just about to launch himself up the final stretch when directly above them he heard footsteps and the sound of muffled voices. Instantly he reached for the Browning pistol at his belt, leaving his Colt Commando automatic assault rifle slung over his shoulder. He looked at Jerry, who strained to catch what was being said above.

'. . . watch . . . report instantly . . . shoot on sight . . .'

Jerry's eyes widened and he put his mouth to Don's ear to repeat the terse message he had heard.

My impressions from the UK were correct, Don thought as a chill ran through him. These guys know how to handle themselves. It's going to be no pushover.

He holstered his Browning again as the footsteps passed on, and signalled to the team to use knives for as long as possible. They would try to conduct the necessary killing in silence until the alarm was raised and only then resort to the full use of their fire-power. With luck, stealth would get them part of the way through their mission and even when the first shots were exchanged he hoped that surprise would carry them a bit further.

Hand by hand and foot by boot, he edged his way upwards, moving with agonizing slowness. His instincts screamed at him to power up the rockface, leap over the battlements and blaze away at anything that moved, but his training and self-discipline kept them on a tight rein. Doubtless there would be ample opportunity for his instincts to have their way later that night. For now caution was the watchword.

A foot below the battlements, he stopped and listened, trying to locate the nearest sentry. There was nothing. Only the gentle sounds of the night answered him, and somewhere deep inside the fortress the noise of a banquet. He reached up and curled his fingers over the stonework, pulling himself up and vaulting over the top. He landed on a walkway on the other side, his leg muscles taking the impact like springs, cushioning his landing as quietly as if he had come down on sand. His head shot to left and right. There was no one to be seen. Whoever had been speaking earlier had passed on. Two light tugs on the rope brought Jerry up behind him and within the next thirty seconds all the other members of the team hopped over the battlements on to the walkway around him.

Before setting off into the fortress they anchored their ropes to the rockface in readiness for a quick getaway, ensuring that nothing could be seen by anyone walking past the spot. To detect the ropes a sentry would have to lean right over the battlements and stare directly at them.

Don was confident that during the time spent in the OP in the preceding daylight hours he had located the part of the stronghold where Eli was most likely being held captive, and the moment the team was complete he directed Tom and Jimmie to lead off. Behind them he placed himself and Jerry, with Gavin and Rod behind him, and Taff and Geordie bringing up the rear. As they moved, each man traced his assigned arc, the pattern ensuring that every angle could be instantly covered by automatic fire if required. Each man now carried his primary weapon system, the squad light machine-gun being manhandled by Rod in the centre of the formation and therefore able to switch its heavier weight of fire in any direction, forwards or backwards, to right or left.

There was an M206 at both front and rear, the one at the point being carried by Tom and the one at the rear being carried by Geordie. The variant of the basic M16 rifle with a 40mm grenade launcher fitted under the rifle barrel, the M206 was able to provide a fearsome weight and variety of fire, the most flexible weapon system carried by the team. Jimmie carried his Heckler & Koch MP5 sub-machine-gun, the fire selection catch set to automatic, ready to spray anyone who got in his way with its lethal 9mm bullets at a rate of 800 rounds a minute. Taff had opted for the standard British Army-issue SA80 with its automatic capability and 5.56mm rounds. Gavin and Jerry both hefted orthodox M16s, while Don carried his Colt Commando, the shortened version of the M16 that fired the identical 5.56mm bullet but was especially suited to close quarter battle. It was much favoured by commanders who needed a compact weapon to enable them to use radios, maps and compasses with ease while still being able to contribute to the fire-fight when required.

In addition, everyone carried a pistol, but once again the makes varied from man to man as each opted for his own particular favourite, while maintaining a commonality of ammunition wherever possible.

The walkway skirted the outer walls, but within twenty yards of their entry point the patrol encountered the first sentry. Tom was nearing a door when he heard the man clear his throat. Instantly Tom froze, hand-signalling for those behind him to halt. Moving without sound, he handed his M206 to his partner, drew his killing knife and edged forward. When he was right up against the corner of the doorway, he went swiftly into action, swivelling round and grabbing the man, clamping his left hand over the mouth to prevent any warning cry, and at the same time yanking the head back and to the left side, exposing the right side of the neck. Tom arched the sentry back, tipping him off balance and as the man started to go down, he thrust the point of his knife into the gap behind the collar-bone, driving down to sever the artery there.

The sentry convulsed, his arms thrashing wildly, but Tom had him firmly in his grasp and there was nothing the man could do to save himself. When his motions had stopped, Tom lowered the lifeless body silently to the floor, looking around for somewhere to conceal it. Doubtless it would not be long before the man was missed, but if they could make it seem that he had simply strayed from his post rather than been killed, then the patrol would buy valuable extra minutes.

Jimmie now took over the lead, heading down a staircase that led into a courtyard. Three Land Rovers stood in a row and Don inspected them one by one. For a moment he considered the possibility of using them to make their escape, but then rejected the idea. There were limited tracks navigable by vehicle towards the border and to use any one of them would be to telegraph their intentions to the enemy. It would be no difficult task for the terrorists to track and follow them, whereas if the patrol remained on foot they might be moving slower but they would be able to choose any one of dozens of different routes.

'Disable them,' he whispered to Gavin.

While the patrol fanned out to cover him, Gavin worked through each of the three vehicles, opening the bonnet and cutting through every wire in sight. Lastly he removed all three rotary arms and hurled them over the wall. When he had finished he silently closed the bonnets so that to a casual observer they would look as if nothing had been touched.

Several covered alleyways led off the courtyard and, checking his sketch plan, Don indicated to Jimmie the one he thought would take them towards Eli. Jimmie couched the black plastic stock of his MP5 lovingly in the cupped palm of his left hand with his right firmly around the pistol grip. His forefinger was on the trigger and as he moved forward he swept the barrel to left and right in perfect alignment with the direction of his eyesight. It was a technique that he had perfected on the urban CQB ranges at Hereford, where he excelled at snap-shooting – firing by instinct at opportunity targets.

It was a skill he was thankful to have mastered, because suddenly, out of nowhere, two large men came briskly round the corner thirty yards ahead of him. They were deep in conversation, gesticulating with sweeping hand movements, their weapons slung over their shoulders and quite out of reach. The moment they saw the man to their front they froze, mouths wide in astonishment. Jimmie cursed. For a split second he considered rushing them with Tom to silence them with knives, but it was no use. Already they were reacting, hands fumbling for their Kalashnikovs as if in slow motion. Jimmie shook his head, trying to signal them to surrender, but then one of them started to shout a warning, turning to make it carry down the corridor behind him.

Jimmie fired two short, ferocious bursts, switching in between them from one man to the other. Each burst found its target, the clutch of 9mm bullets impacting in a tight group in low centre chest.

'That's done it,' Don said firmly. 'Cat's out of the bag. Move it!'

In a strange way every one of the SAS men felt as though a great weight had been lifted from his shoulders. The need for silence and stealth had now passed and the operation had shifted, in seconds, into a new and higher gear. It was a gear for which they were all well prepared.

Jimmie and Tom darted down the corridor, stepping over the two dead men. Behind them, Jerry quickly stooped and unfastened the top covers of the two Kalashnikovs, thereby disabling them. They were made of thin metal, and after leaning them in the corner of the floor and wall he stamped down on them hard, bending them beyond immediate repair.

'Nice work,' Don said.

'At least that's two weapons in the fort that aren't going to be shooting at us,' Jerry replied, warming to his commander's praise.

Gavin came up behind him. 'Shall I booby them, boss?'

'Why not?'

Gavin grinned and stooped beside the dead men. 'Watch and learn, lad,' he said to Jerry. 'You might have fucked up their weapons, but this is the way to take out a few of their mates as well.'

He took a couple of hand-grenades from his webbing and laid them on the floor. Then, after rolling both bodies on to their stomachs, he placed one grenade under each, gingerly removing the pin but ensuring that the dead man's weight on top of it prevented the handle from flying off.

'There we go. When their mates roll them over to check if they're dead, the handles fly off and the grenades explode, taking another couple of guys with them. Simple but effective.'

The patrol moved away from the courtyard fast, each man sweeping his arc in readiness for another contact. They could hear shouts now, echoing through the rooms and corridors of the stronghold as word spread that something was up and that intruders had breached the defences.

Suddenly there was a cry from the rear and Geordie let rip with his M206, firing the grenade launcher into the middle of a pack of men who appeared in pursuit. The 40mm grenade struck the lead man and exploded, cutting him open but showering the rest of the group with shards of white-hot metal. Geordie switched his finger from the grenade launcher to the automatic rifle's trigger and squeezed off a long burst, raking the falling men as Taff added a burst of his own from the SA80.

As they ran on, Geordie popped open the launcher and dropped out the empty case, slipping in a replacement and clapping the barrel shut.

'Reloaded!' he shouted back to Taff, who had been covering him and now backed away, skipping backwards after the retreating patrol.

They were now running, spinning down seemingly endless corridors and crossing rooms and courtyards.

'Eli!' Don shouted. 'Eli!'

If she could only let them know where she was, he thought, it would save valuable time. Then they could grab her and get the hell out of there. With each passing minute the odds were stacking up against them. For now there was undoubtedly confusion among the enemy. They wouldn't have any idea of the strength or exact whereabouts of the intruders, but that would soon pass as the shock of the assault wore off. Gradually they would establish which areas were still safe, and with that narrowing down would come a picture of the battle. Control would be re-established and blocking positions could be put in, restricting the movement of the SAS patrol and starting to hem it in. Unless they could achieve their aim and get out quickly they would end up boxed in and involved in a battle of attrition – and such a fight they couldn't possibly hope to win.

As they came to every doorway, one of the team would kick it open, searching for any clue as to the girl's whereabouts, but time after time there was nothing but disappointment.

'This place is a sodding rabbit warren,' Gavin barked angrily as he turned back from yet another empty room.

They emerged into another courtyard, larger than the one where they had found and disabled the three Land Rovers, but they hadn't gone half a dozen paces when a burst of machine-gun fire stitched the ground in front of them.

'Take cover!' Tom bellowed, throwing himself into a forward roll and coming up in a kneeling position, firing off the rifle part of his M206 as he sought out the target.

The second he located it, he flicked his finger to the trigger of the grenade launcher, braced himself and fired. The incoming fire had been from a man with a Kalashnikov in a window one floor above the courtyard. Overlooking the space below, it gave him a good view of the SAS patrol, and unless he was taken out Tom knew that he would be able to pin them down until help arrived. But the 40mm grenade was about to do its job.

It popped from the barrel of the M206 and shot through the air, slicing upwards in a neat little arc and in through the window itself. The startled look on the man's face was plain to see, turning halfway to blind panic in the instant before the grenade exploded behind him. His body was catapulted out of the window by the blast, somersaulting with the beautiful grace of an Olympic diver before ploughing head first into the unforgiving paving stones of the courtyard.

'Nice shooting, Tom,' Jerry called.

But Tom was too busy reloading to hear. His full attention was on the drills. For praise might give you a momentary warm glow of pride, but fast and accurate drills kept you alive. Praise was for the new boys.

A flight of steps led up to a platform, on the other side of which Don could see a doorway that seemed to give access to the main living quarters he had spied from the OP.

'That looks like it,' he shouted to Jimmie. 'Take the lead and go for it!'

'Right, boss,' Jimmie acknowledged, darting past Tom, who had completed his reloading drills and was refastening his ammunition pouch.

Jimmie sprang at the steps and hurled himself up them, but halfway up, the stairway darkened and he looked up to see a man blocking his path. Instantly he blazed away with the MP5, but unlike his first victims this man was ready. Pulling back out of the line of fire, the man managed to get clear just in time to avoid being cut down. Armed with a Soviet-made AKR sub-machine-gun, he held the compact little weapon in a pistol grip over the top of the stairs, and squeezed the trigger. The gun shuddered from the savage recoil, spraying the 5.45mm bullets inaccurately in every direction. Jimmie flinched and hugged the sides of the wall, making himself as small as possible so as to reduce his target area.

Seeing him pinned down, Tom took careful aim with his M206 rifle from down below and fired at the blazing AKR. His fourth round struck the wooden stock, shattering and jarring the firer's wrist. There was a cry of pain and the man dropped the weapon and clutched his aching hand.

Jimmie reacted immediately, powering up the steps and throwing himself over the top, spinning as he landed, seeking out the man. He found him shrinking back against the wall and drilled him with a burst from the MP5.

'Clear!' he yelled down the steps, crouching ready to provide covering fire to the others as they pounded up to join him.

But even he couldn't prevent the inevitable first casualty that the patrol then suffered. As Taff closed up, the last man up the staircase, a single shot rang out and he staggered and dropped to one knee.

'I'm hit!' he cried.

Jimmie desperately sought out the sniper but whoever he was he had chosen his position well. Then a second shot rang out and Jimmie saw Taff's head jerk forward as if hit with a baseball bat. He toppled to the floor and rolled back down the steps, coming to rest in a heap at the bottom. His eyes were open, dead.

Before the sniper could conceal himself, Jimmie caught sight of the rifle's muzzle.

'Dragunov,' he muttered, reciting the name of the dreaded Soviet 7.62mm sniper rifle. Equipped with a detachable non-variable ×4 scope, it had an effective range of at least 600 metres. Firing from a tower that dominated the courtyard, it had been required to cover barely a third of that distance. Taff hadn't stood a chance.

Jimmie slid out the retractable butt-stock to give himself a more stable shot and tucked it into his shoulder and cheek, before taking quick aim and firing off a double tap at the sniper's location. But the MP5 was a short-range weapon and although as accurate as a rifle up to 100 metres, at anything over that distance its accuracy deteriorated. Jimmie saw his rounds impact on the plaster and brickwork around the muzzle of the Dragunov but the firer was already sighting on a second target, the rest of the patrol on the platform above the Scot.

'Get that fucker someone!' Jimmie shouted as he tried again. 'Line of water barrels, twelve o'clock, fifty yards, Dragunov sniper,' he barked out.

'Got 'im,' Rod's voice rang out.

Jimmie flung himself on his belly and tucked in behind the M249 light machine-gun. The next instant a stream of accurate 5.56mm bullets was pasting the area of the water barrels, snaking closer to the sniper. Suddenly the barrel of the Dragunov twitched and the whole rifle tumbled into view, falling from the wounded man's hands and down into the square.

'Good shooting,' Don shouted.

Instead of staying in cover and nursing his wound, the sniper stupidly broke out and tried to make a run for it. Rod's M249 followed him all the way, finally cutting him down within sight of his escape.

'That's for Taff,' Rod said bitterly.

There were shouts from behind them and as the patrol sprinted across the platform towards the doorway on the far side, a group of men appeared in the courtyard. However, having learnt that the SAS were not to be messed with, they held back, taking cover and trying to pin the patrol down with longer-range fire rather than closing with them in CQB.

'We can't afford to let them delay us,' Gavin said to Don, crawling up beside him as Rod and the others returned fire. 'If we get bogged down in a fire-fight it'll give their mates time to surround us and then we're done for.'

Don thought for a second. 'We'll split in two, each fire team covering the other by bounds. Fire and manoeuvre.'

'Roger.'

In accordance with pre-arranged drills, Gavin took command of the second fire team, which consisted of Rod with the M249 LMG, Geordie with the M206 rifle and grenade launcher, and himself with his M16. Don continued forward with the lead fire team of himself, Jerry, Jimmie and his MP5 and Tom with the second of the M206s. Both teams were as balanced as possible, each able to provide effective covering fire for the other in the deadly game of leapfrog that now ensued.

While Don led the way off the platform and into the next warren of rooms and corridors, Gavin kept up a steady fire on their pursuers, watching for the moment to order the break-clean from cover. There were at least half a dozen men in the courtyard now and others were joining them by the minute. What was more serious was that they were starting to work their way around the edges. Some form of command was being imposed upon them and, unlike the initial chaotic response, they were becoming a cohesive force instead of a frightened rabble. The clock was ticking and unless the SAS were able to extricate themselves within the next ten to fifteen minutes from the stronghold, the chances were that they would all die there.

It was the thought that was uppermost in Don's mind as he pounded up the steps leading into the new block.

'Go firm here. Prepare to give covering fire.'

His men toppled into cover around him, each settling into position and readying his weapon.

'Jerry, make ready an M72,' Don ordered.

'Wilco, boss.'

Jerry unslung the slender khaki tube from over his shoulder and tore off the end covers. Then, holding the tube in a firm overhand grasp, he snapped it open, and as it telescoped out, almost doubling in length, an eyepiece popped out from the body. Next, with thumb and forefinger he pulled back a small catch to arm the rocket couched inside the disposable fibre-glass tubing.

'Ready,' he shouted.

'Try to get that doorway,' he ordered, indicating the main entrance into the courtyard from which yet more men were appearing.

Jerry crawled forward until he could get a bead on it, and, with the tube over his shoulder, he checked that its backblast area was clear and then sighted on his target.

'Firing now,' he said.

The tube was over his right shoulder, his left hand holding the front part of the body, while his right curled over the middle, its fingers on the rubber-capped firing lever. He pressed this down firmly and the rocket exploded into life, firing out of the tube and shooting down towards the door. Jerry looked behind him and saw the black scorch mark of the backblast on the stonework, but the real damage erupted in the court-yard, where the 66mm rocket powered into the concrete above the door-frame and exploded in a shower of falling masonry and metal fragments.

'Now, Gavin!' Don shouted out, ordering the break-clean.

As Gavin's fire team broke from cover, zigzagging back to Don's position, Don's men poured a ferocious stream of lead into the enemy positions, raking them from end to end and keeping their heads down while Gavin, Rod and Geordie sprinted back.

'Last man,' Gavin shouted as he backed past Don, shooting from the hip in short, controlled bursts.

Once through the doorway, Gavin led his team up the stairs, taking the steps three at a time until he found himself in a corridor with only one closed door leading off it.

Without pausing he stood back, bracing himself against the opposite wall, and kicked at the lock with the sole of his boot. The wooden frame shattered and the door fell inwards, landing with a crash on the floor. On the other side of it he saw a bedroom, comfortably appointed, and, from behind the bed's bright coverlet, a frightened pair of eyes peeked out at him. He stared in disbelief.

'Eli?'

The girl rose into view. 'That's me. But who the devil are you?'

'I'm the man with the box of chocolates, love. Time to go.'

13

The moment he heard the firing, Ceda was on his feet.

'Murap, go to the girl. Take two of the men with you. Whatever happens we mustn't let her go.'

At the head of the table Uncle Bandram looked up. 'Who would come all this way for her? Who is it?'

'I don't know, but whoever they are they won't get away with it,' Ceda replied.

He went briskly to his room nearby, buckled on his ammunition belt and took a Kalashnikov from the rack by the door. Ali came in after him, fingering a pistol.

'What about me? Shouldn't I stay here with Uncle?'

Ceda glanced at him with contempt. He picked up another Kalashnikov and tossed it at him. 'You're coming with me. You've wanted to join the family and be accepted for years. Well, now's your chance. Welcome to the heart and hearth of the Bandrams.'

Another burst of gunfire sounded deep in the stronghold, followed by screams.

'Just one thing,' Ceda added cruelly. 'Don't expect these men to be as compliant as the trucker you murdered in Britain.'

To Ceda's delight Ali went pale. Ceda grabbed him by the

scruff of the neck and propelled him out of the room. 'Come on, cousin. You can have the honour of leading the way.'

'But . . . but . . . I . . .'

'No buts. Move!'

He planted his hand in the small of Ali's back and shoved him towards the sound of the firing.

Murap jogged past with his selected men, two large tribesmen armed to the teeth.

'If you see Ramesh, tell him to seal all the exits,' Ceda shouted. 'I'll hunt down the dogs and kill them.'

The first thing he came upon were the bodies of the two men that Jimmie had shot. He was just rounding the corner when he saw another of his men stooping to check them. Something stopped Ceda in his tracks and as he hauled Ali back around the safety of the corner he shouted, 'Don't touch them!'

But it was too late. The man had grabbed the nearest corpse and was rolling it over. Even from his position Ceda heard the metallic click of the grenade lever flying free. His instincts had been right. Neither body had been lying in a natural pose of death, no wounds were visible on their backs and the bloodstains on the ground had been smeared by movement. They had clearly been moved, and an enemy only moved a corpse for one of two reasons – to search it or to booby-trap it. Infiltrators would have little cause to search a dead guard, so the second solution was all that was left.

Ceda winced at the sound of the explosion, magnified in the confined space of the corridor. Dust and debris spiralled along to him and he covered his mouth and nose with one great hand. When he looked there was a third body added to the previous two, only this latest one was lacerated from head to foot by the grenade fragments. Ceda moved cautiously towards it. The second body had not been harmed by the explosion, whose blast had been driven upwards, but Ceda guessed that there would probably be a second grenade under him as well.

'Stand back,' he ordered Ali. 'Over there around the corner. Watch and learn.'

With that, he lay himself carefully along the top of the second corpse, grasped it around the shoulders and rolled backwards, pulling the body on to its side into a position where it fully shielded him from the grenade that he had known would be there. Once again there was the ping of the lever followed by the detonation. When the dust cleared, he got to his feet and surveyed the damage. Ali reappeared sheepishly from around the corner.

'Nice,' Ceda said to himself.

Ali, thinking that the compliment had been intended for him, grinned, but Ceda disabused him of it the next second.

'Nice work, by whoever planted those.' He crouched down and inspected the wounds on the corpses. They were peppered with tiny fragments from a metal coil instead of the larger splinters that an older make of grenade would have inflicted.

'Could be British,' he said thoughtfully.

The bullet wounds in each of the two original corpses were tightly grouped, and clearly 9mm. Ceda nodded knowingly. 'I see,' he said to himself, and his thoughts darted back to the man he remembered from the service station in Britain, the one who had so nearly prevented his escape.

'What is it?' Ali asked, becoming concerned.

Ceda smiled. 'It is a worthy opponent at last.'

They left the scene of the carnage and went in pursuit of the infiltrators, gathering a force of half a dozen men along the way. Ceda barked out orders, sending other men in every direction to seek out the enemy and seal off their escape.

More shots sounded, along with the burst of grenades.

'M206s,' Ceda said with a wry smile, his nose sniffing the air like a badger venturing out of its sett. 'I like these men.'

He broke into a jog, shouting for his men to follow him just as the rocket from Jerry's M72 detonated in the courtyard some way away ahead of him. It was a grisly picture that greeted him when he arrived. The rocket had brought down part of the stonework above the door-frame and two men beneath it had been virtually decapitated. Their skulls were crushed and their brains lay on the dusty floor about them. Ali took one look and retched.

Someone shouted, 'They're making a break for it!'

Ceda darted forward instantly. 'Keep after them. Don't give them any breathing space. Hound them into the grave!'

But as he stepped into the courtyard he saw a sight that froze him on the spot. To one side a body lay face down in the debris and rubble. In an instant he was kneeling at its side.

'Uncle!'

Gently he rolled Uncle Bandram over. The eyes turned towards him and the lips moved. He put his ear close to the bloodied mouth to catch its words.

'Avenge me, my nephew. Avenge all of us. I had hoped to do it myself, but now it's up to you and Ramesh. Get even with Sanji. Do this for me.'

Ceda fought to hold back his tears. 'You'll live to do it yourself, Uncle,' he said, not really believing his own words.

Gilma Bandram smiled and shook his head, coughing up blood with the effort of speaking. 'No. It's up to you now, Ceda. See to it. See to it.'

His eyes froze and set, the life exhaling from him into the cordite-filled air of the courtyard.

Ceda looked at the men around him. All were staring with disbelief at the body in his arms.

He reached down and closed the eyes, laying his uncle back in the dust and draping his cloak about him, covering the face.

'What are you all staring at? Haven't you seen a corpse before?' he barked at them. He could feel his anger rising now, threatening to blot out reason. He had to fight it, suppress it, transform it into an ice-cold, iron determination. Anger alone had never achieved an aim. It was only as a springboard to other emotions that it could serve a purpose.

Looking up he could just see where the infiltrators were leaving the platform and even in the poor light that shone around the courtyard from the few bulbs he could tell that their movement was that of professional soldiers. His own men were good, but with such an enemy as this trickery and cunning were the best weapons. He would do best to outwit them and outmanoeuvre them. He had to use his advantages rather than allow them to dictate the pace and the course of the fight. Closing with them would obviously result in heavy casualties. They had already proved as much. They were equipped with the most modern of weapons and knew all too well how to use them to maximum effect. But if Ceda could only box them in, force them out into the open, wear them down without closing to close quarters, then he would see just how good they were.

'Ramesh,' he shouted. 'I must speak to Ramesh.'

In response two of his men went away in search of his brother. The others, seeking to avenge the death of Uncle Bandram, surged forward, only to be met by a hail of fire from Don's fire team.

'No, you fools! Can't you see that's exactly what they want? Stay where you are and engage them with fire. I have other plans for our friends.'

In accordance with his instructions, some of the men started to work around the edge of the courtyard, and as soon as they could they reached the other doorways on the far side and disappeared through them, looking for a way round to the rear of the enemy position. Then, a few minutes later, some of the men arrived back with an armful of RPG7s and spare rockets.

'Well done,' Ceda congratulated them. 'A purse full of gold for the man who scores the first kill.'

Instantly the men were in action, fitting the rockets on to the launchers, aiming and firing. The rockets arced across the courtyard and slammed into the stonework around the retreating SAS patrol.

'Reload and fire again!' Ceda shouted.

Another volley followed the first, but this time the SAS had seen the new danger and their automatic weapons spat back at them, bullets hosing the ground until one of the RPG7 firers tumbled over, dead. The man beside him retrieved the weapon and prepared it to fire, aiming for the SAS light machine-gun. His rocket streaked towards its target but instead of the M249 it found in its path the doubled-over figure of Geordie frantically fighting to clear a stoppage from the breech of his M206. The rocket burrowed into the ground at his feet, exploding upwards and lifting him into the air. When Ceda saw the body flung aside like a puppet he cheered and slapped the firer on the back.

'Now another! Give me another!'

But the SAS men had vanished into the building. Ceda cursed and urged his comrades to follow up.

'But remember, don't get too close to them. Like any cornered rat they are at their most dangerous when in a tight corner.'

He was about to follow them himself when a man appeared at his elbow. Ceda turned to him impatiently.

'Yes, what is it?'

The man smiled proudly. 'Ramesh. I have found him.'

'Well? Where is he?'

Something in the man's eyes held Ceda back.

'He says you are to let them escape.'

Ceda stared at him as if he was mad but the man repeated his refrain, adding, 'Ramesh says to trust him.'

All for going on, Ceda nevertheless paused to consider his brother's enigmatic message. Ramesh had never let him down before. Their mutual trust and support had got the two of them out of a multitude of scrapes in the past, and in his heart he knew that he had no alternative. If Ramesh had discovered the infiltrators' weak point, then Ceda would do well to heed his advice.

Turning to Ali, he shouted, 'Hold the men where they are.'

Ali looked at him questioningly, but Ceda barked back, 'Do as I say! Now!'

While the rest of the patrol sought out the cover of temporary fire positions, Don went quickly into the room to confront Eli.

'We haven't much time. Come with us and stick close to Jerry here.'

He thrust her towards Jerry, who had been briefed to look after her.

'How do you expect to get out of here?' she asked in amazement.

'Don't worry about it. That's my problem. You just keep your head down and do as you're told.' He turned to Gavin. 'You and Jimmie take point. How's Geordie?'

'Dead.'

Don took it in but carried on. 'Jerry, stick with me. Rod and Tom, bring up the rear. You two have got the bulk of the fire-power now. Make full use of it. Give them plenty of stick and keep them off our backs. Any questions? Right. Move!'

Leading the way back to the walkway where the ropes led down the cliff face, Gavin steered a roundabout course that avoided the courtyard, which was now awash with the enemy. By now he had a fair idea of the layout of the stronghold and it was not too difficult a task to find the route back to their entry point. As they went, Rod and Tom burned through their ammunition. They had left a full resupply back with the bergens for the return march, should they need it, but for now they were determined to give the best possible account of themselves.

While Rod hosed down anyone who was stupid enough to show his face, Tom popped off a series of 40mm grenades into the more distant targets, seeking to establish a good spread of fires throughout the complex in the hope of diverting attention away from their flight. In some of the rooms his grenades found plenty of furnishings and bedding to catch alight and within minutes flames were sprouting from several of the windows as the fire spread, unchecked by the fort's inhabitants, who had other concerns.

'We've got to break clean before we dare start down the ropes,' Don said as they neared the walkway.

'I think I've got just the thing,' Gavin replied.

He took a satchel from around his shoulder and darted back and found a narrow archway. Then, crouching down, he opened the satchel and withdrew prepared packs of plastic explosive, which he began to set in place around the overhanging arch and adjoining walls.

'This should take them a bit of time to clear,' he said as he unreeled the electric cable and wired it into the firing box.

'Take cover, everyone!' he yelled when it was ready, and as soon as the last man was out of sight he pressed the button. An almighty roar filled the air and the ground rocked beneath their feet as if an earthquake was taking place. As the air cleared, Don saw that the archway had disappeared, its place being filled by a pile of rubble that any would-be pursuers would have to burrow through.

'Good work. Now fix up some remote claymores and we'll be on our way,' he said.

Aided by Jimmie, Gavin set up a pair of the devices, laying their cables across the path and drawing them taut to act as trip-wires. In this way, even when their pursuers had managed to get through the rubble they would stumble straight into the next trap, setting off the two-directional anti-personnel mines and releasing the barrage of steel ball-bearings in among them.

'Time to go!' Don commanded.

They set off down the walkway until they came to the point where the ropes had been left. Jimmie skipped over the parapet, found his footing on the outer edge and felt for the ropes.

'Got 'em.'

One by one the men slid over the edge and leaned out into the darkness, Jimmie handing them the ropes. Jerry helped Eli.

'I don't suppose you've ever done any climbing?' he asked hopefully.

'Me? You must be kidding,' she answered, her eyes wide and her voice starting to quake.

He cursed under his breath. 'Might have guessed. Here,' he said, turning his back to her and bending at the knees, 'Hop on. We'll go down piggy-back.'

Eli peered down into the darkness.

'Don't look! Just do as I say.'

She took one look back into the body of the smoking fortress, listening to the shouts, explosions and bursts of gunfire, and did as Jerry had instructed, linking her arms about his neck and clasping on tight.

'Grip me round the waist with your legs, like horse riding. Just don't throttle me, that's all I ask. If you do, we both fall.'

Last over the parapet, Tom scattered a handful of tiny anti-personnel mines the length of the walkway to dissuade anyone from coming too close. It would take some care to clear them in the dark and by that time, he sincerely hoped, the surviving members of the patrol would be safely on the ground.

The descent was considerably smoother than the upwards climb as the ropes had been fixed securely in place and would be abandoned there once the SAS men had made use of them. However, should anyone decide to follow them down, Tom had been instructed to sow a more comprehensive anti-personnel minefield at the bottom, combining it with further claymores and trip-wires.

First to reach the valley floor was Don, and as each man arrived thereafter he directed them into positions of all-round defence until the last member of the patrol was accounted for and they were ready to set off. Shaking out into formation, everyone did a hurried check of weapons and equipment, reloading with full mags, ensuring pouches and webbing were fastened, and taking a quick sip of water from the canteens in readiness for the night tab to the RV, which they knew would be fast and furious.

'All set?' Don said quietly, casting around the patrol and receiving the thumbs up from every man in turn. 'Move now.'

He rose from the ground and the patrol, as one man, rose with him. Jimmie and Tom never heard the bullets that cut them down.

It was as if a hailstorm had been unleashed, but instead of the harmless balls of ice it was lead stinging the air and pockmarking the sand at their feet.

'Ambush!' Don screamed at the top of his voice, hurling himself on to his stomach and firing off a burst from his Colt Commando in the approximate direction of the enemy.

In accordance with standard anti-ambush drills, every man who was still able blazed off a series of bursts, at the same time wriggling backwards into the nearest available cover. Rod got into the rocks first, flicked down the bipod of his M249 and fired a steady stream of lead at each of the enemy's muzzle flashes coming at them from out of the dark. Jerry pushed Eli down beside the buzzing machine-gun and then retrieved Tom's M206, discarding his own M16 and starting to fire off 40mm grenades at every likely position where an enemy might be located.

Don pulled the pins on two white-phosphorus smoke grenades and signalled for Gavin to do the same. Then, when both men were ready, they threw together, achieving a good spread with the four grenades that covered the front within seconds with a thick, noxious blanket of white smoke.

'Move!' Don shouted.

At his command everyone fired off another burst and then broke out, each man running in a different direction with the intention of making his way independently to the RV, where the bergens lay in wait. However, as Jerry was burdened with the extra responsibility for Eli, Don stuck with him, leaving it to Rod and Gavin to peel off to either flank and confuse the enemy as to what was happening.

As Gavin and Rod went, veering in opposite directions, Don could hear them shouting until even he began to believe that a substantial force was counter-attacking the ambushers. He and Jerry on the other hand, held their fire, preferring stealth to mask their withdrawal behind the dense smoke-screen. But Don knew that they had little more than seconds before it cleared and then they could expect the enemy to follow up into the killing area to check on the dead and search for survivors.

As Jerry ran, he half pushed and half pulled Eli after him, urging her in whispers to keep quiet and run for her life. Don brought up the rear, sweeping his Colt Commando from side to side, safety switch set to fully automatic, finger on the trigger, ready to blast anything that moved. From further off in the night they continued to hear the sounds of Gavin and Rod, the M16 and M249 replying to the blazing Kalashnikovs, SLRs and GPMGs that seemed to be sprouting from the ground like the spirits of the dead.

They ran for what seemed an age until Eli collapsed gasping on the rock-strewn bed of a dry river.

'That's it. I'm all in,' she gasped. 'I can't run another step. Leave me here and save yourselves.'

Jerry knelt beside her. In the dark she could see him smiling. 'You're just after another piggy-back, aren't you?' he said.

Then he helped her to her feet and she got on to his back again. 'Better take this, boss,' he said, handing the M206 to Don.

They ran on, Jerry hobbling along and Don continuing to provide the cover. When they were well clear of the killing area they stopped and Don took a compass bearing to get a fix on the RV.

'It's about another five hundred yards. Can you manage it?'

'No problem. She's as light as a feather.'

A fresh burst of firing far off on their right indicated that the ambushers were pursuing one of the other two SAS men, and a second later the familiar chatter of the M249 identified the unlucky recipient of this attention as Rod. Jerry and Don swapped glances, both looking away and pressing on as the M249 went suddenly silent after a crescendo of Kalashnikov fire.

It was another fifteen minutes before they arrived at the tumble of rocks where they had stashed the bergens. Jerry set Eli down, stretching and rubbing his aching back muscles and stamping to loosen his joints, which were protesting at the furious pace and the extra load.

'So I was as light as a feather, was I?' Eli smiled.

'Well, almost,' he conceded.

Don dived into the pile of bergens, flinging Jerry's at him and digging out his own.

'Do you want me to set up some claymores?' Jerry asked.

'No way. Gavin could run right into them. I want to kill as many of the terrorists as you do, but not if it puts Gavin at risk.'

When they had sorted out their kit and each had a drink of water, they settled down to wait for five minutes to see if any of the others had made it. Don checked his watch impatiently every few seconds until at last the five minutes were up and they were prepared to go.

'Going without me?'

They looked up in surprise as Gavin tottered into the circle of rocks. He collapsed exhausted on the ground, gasping for breath. Jerry rushed to check him for wounds but Gavin waved him away.

'I'm fine. Just a bit knackered, that's all. But I think Rod bought it.'

'I know. We heard the firing.'

Gavin wiped his face with his neck cloth. 'He was quite close to me at one point and I think that's when they surrounded him. I caught a glimpse of him in the light of some flares they were using. He was standing alone firing from the hip until his box mag emptied. That's when the bastards cut him down.'

'You're sure he was dead?' Don asked.

'Sure. I saw the fucking rounds hit him.'

Don swore and turned away. The mission had been a bloody disaster. There were only three of them left out of the eight-man team, and although they had rescued the hostage they still had to make it across the border. The enemy were in hot pursuit and it would be daylight in a few hours.

'We'd better get moving,' he said at last. 'I'll take point. Gavin, you bring up the rear, and Jerry, watch over Eli. Here' – he handed back the M206 – 'you're the heavy artillery from now on.'

They all replenished their stocks of ammunition and now that the last man was accounted for Don gave Jerry permission to booby-trap the RV and the unused bergens. He went about it with a will, sowing anti-personnel mines, laying claymores and trip-wires, and placing grenades under the packs and the surrounding rocks, removing the pins and balancing them as Gavin had demonstrated in the stronghold with the bodies.

'There,' Jerry said when he had finished. 'That ought to do it.'

They set off with two hours to spare before first light, blazing a furious trail across country on a simple compass bearing that led straight to the frontier's nearest point. It was unsubtle and even dangerous, but Don reckoned that the priority now was to reach friendly territory by daylight. It was true that they could hide up throughout the next day if they were unable to make it, but that increased the chances of their being found by the terrorists. Also, he didn't know what sort of rapport they had with the local military commanders. He hoped that the two would have nothing to do with each other, but he couldn't rule out the chance that the terrorists might be able to call on reinforcements in the form of army patrols, helicopters, vehicles and tracker dogs.

Eli struggled to keep up, and with reluctance Don eventually decided to slow the pace, judging that they would make better speed with Eli walking by herself than with her being carried by the men in turn. Piggy-back rides were all very well over a short distance, but on a difficult night exfiltration under duress were not to be recommended as an efficient mode of transport.

The ground changed as they marched, switching almost unnoticeably from the barren rock of the fort's surrounding area to the rolling hills and forbidding mountains of the border zone. Every so often they stopped to catch their breath and have a drink of water. At each halt the three men broke open packets of glucose sweets, pushing the succulent capsules into their mouths and drawing on the instant energy. Jerry handed a fistful to Eli.

'Suck one. It goes straight into the bloodstream and feels like a kick in the backside.'

She cautiously popped a capsule in her mouth and felt the sweet crumble the moment it came into contact with her tongue, the glucose washing round her mouth and bringing her wide awake.

'That's terrific,' she enthused, and popped in another.

'Save some for later. We've got a long way to go yet,' Jerry warned.

It wasn't long before Don noticed a lightening of the eastern horizon, and strangely enough it was only then that he realized how exhausted he was. It was not simply from lack of sleep or the physical effort of the attack and then the flight, but more from the stress of high-intensity combat, a tiredness that no amount of training could ever diminish.

Slowly, the razor-thin line of purple brightened and spread, cutting the night in two, pushing the sky up into the heavens once again, locking away its stars for another day and throwing a pale, watery light across the barren lunar landscape. Against this backdrop of mountains and steep forests, valleys and cascading streams, four tiny, stick-like characters clawed their painfully slow way.

Suddenly they heard the noise of the engine. Instantly they were on their bellies, wriggling forward into a ditch that widened and deepened into a dry river-bed. Over the far lip they heard the sound of a vehicle, a jeep, bouncing across country and coming closer.

'Sounds like he's alone,' Don whispered.

'Shall we take him?' Gavin asked.

'Might have to. Let's take a look.'

They crawled forward until they came to a patch of bone-dry scrub grass. Shielding their face behind it they peered cautiously over the top and saw the jeep coming straight at them. Don and Gavin looked questioningly at each other and Don waved Jerry forward with his M206.

'Don't fire unless I give the order. They might not see us.'

Jerry checked that the grenade launcher was loaded and ready, brought the butt into his shoulder and flicked up the sight. But when the jeep was about thirty yards off it skidded to a halt. The dust cleared, the doors opened and four men got out. The tallest of the group spread a map on the bonnet and they launched into a heated debate, pointing at the far valley towards which Don and the others had been heading.

'Looks like they're trying to figure out where the border is,' Don whispered.

Eli had crawled up beside them and stared in terror. 'That must be Ramesh. He's the image of his brother. I'm sure of it.'

'Ramesh Bandram?'

'It must be.'

Thoughts raced through Don's head. Eventually he said to Gavin and Jerry, 'Do you reckon you can pick off the two guys on the left?'

'What are you up to, boss?' Gavin asked suspiciously.

'If we can take a hostage of our own I reckon we might just persuade them to leave us be.' He slid out the retractable butt of his Colt Commando. 'I can take the third guy if you two can tackle his mates.'

Gavin stared in disbelief. 'And what about Bandram? Do you think he's just going to sit there while we slaughter his men around him?'

'Of course not. That's why the moment I've dropped his mate I'm going to bring him down with a wounding shot.'

A sly grin spread across Gavin's face and he checked the sight on his M16. 'At this range I should bloody well hope I could put a round between my target's eyes.'

'Nothing fancy. Just kill him. Don't take any risks.'

When all three men were ready, Don steadied his breathing and sighted on his target.

'On my shot, lads. After the count of three. One . . . two . . . three . . .'

The three shots rang out as one and across the thirty yards of rocky shrub three bodies crumpled around the jeep. Instantly Don switched his point of aim and just as the fourth man understood what had happened he fired again, a single shot that struck home exactly as intended, winging him in the upper arm. Before the wounded man had even hit the ground the three SAS men were up and running, Don heading straight for the jeep in a beeline, the other two swinging out to left and right in an arc. The man Don had shot had left his weapon in the jeep and by the time he had recovered from the shot and started to crawl towards it, Don was closing the last few yards and bringing the still-smoking muzzle of his Colt Commando to bear.

'Don't even think about it,' Don growled, half to himself.

The wounded man lay in the dirt, his wound slight but bleeding a lot.

Don came up in front of him as Gavin and Jerry arrived and checked the others to make sure they were dead.

'What's your name?' Don asked.

Jerry started to translate the question into Urdu but halfway through the man smirked.

'Save your breath. I speak English.' He glared at Jerry with contempt. 'Probably better than you do.'

'So what's your name then?' Don asked again, aiming his Colt Commando at the figure on the ground, his finger tightening on the trigger.

The man tossed back his head, ignoring the pain of his bullet wound.

'I am Ramesh Bandram. And none of you will get out of Pakistan alive.'

14

When Don had dressed Ramesh's wound he hauled him to his feet.

'What about taking the vehicle, boss?' Gavin asked.

'No. It's too visible now that the sun's up. We'll move on foot as planned.'

He stuck the muzzle of his Colt Commando in the small of Ramesh's back and shoved him forward.

'Walk.'

'You don't really think you can get away with this, do you?'

'You'd better hope we do, for your sake.'

'My brother and the rest of the men are right behind us.'

'Then we'll have a nice little reception waiting for them, won't we? Now that you've been kind enough to warn us.'

They set off, Don leading the way with Ramesh, Jerry and Eli walking behind, and Gavin bringing up the rear, keeping a watchful eye on the horizon for any approaching trouble. The border was getting closer by the minute and Don again forced the pace. As he walked, Ramesh turned his head and asked, 'How much do you know about Sanji?'

Don poked him in the back with his gun. 'Shut up and keep moving.'

But Ramesh wasn't to be silenced. 'You're a professional, I can see that. Your men have fought well. The ones back there died well also. You deserve to know the truth.'

'And I suppose you're going to tell it to me?'

Ramesh laughed. It was the laugh of a man who has long since conquered fear and Don couldn't help respecting his prisoner. 'There are always several versions of any truth, all of them partially wrong and partially right. I suspect your bosses have only allowed you to know the minimum required to do the job.'

If only you knew how right you are, Don thought bitterly.

'I have been a soldier myself. I know how we get used by the hidden men, the faceless ones. They're the soldier's real enemy. They send him to his death for reasons he is never allowed to hear. He just gets the public version, which is little better than an outright lie.'

He turned and winked at Don. 'I can see you know what I mean.'

Gavin called from the back. 'Do you want me to gag him, boss?'

'No,' Don said thoughtfully, and then to Ramesh, 'OK then, let's have it. Give me your version, the truth as you see it. Tell me about Sanji.'

Ramesh glanced back at Eli, ignoring her look of hatred. 'In 1947 Sanji was a minor official in the British administration that was preparing to quit India. As you know, at that time there was no such state as Pakistan, the country was all one, Muslims and Hindus living alongside each other. Then Pakistan was formed as the future homeland for the Muslims and the great treks began. Muslims who had lived in India for generations had to leave their homes and trek north, while Hindus who had lived for millennia in the states that were to become Pakistan travelled south. Some saw it as the only solution to the internal strife of the country that the British had kept together with the might of the army, but others saw it as the greatest disaster to befall us. Gandhi himself thought that, given time, the two religions could co-exist. But it was not to be.'

He paused, the emotion taking hold of him.

'You can hardly blame Sanji for any of that,' Don argued. 'You yourself said that he was only a minor official.'

'Of course I don't blame him for that. Perhaps the great separation had to be. I don't know. But what I do know is that it was the hot summertime, tempers were short and people were desperate. Terrible things started to happen. The killings began. No one knows where or how it started, but within no time at all Hindus and Muslims were killing each other.'

Don felt his flesh crawl as he got a suspicion of what was to come.

'When our dear, nice little Mr Sanji was not working conscientiously in his office, he was doing other things. Abominable, unspeakable things. Secretly, he was the head of an extremist organization that set out, not so much to ensure that the Muslims from his district of Delhi all fled to Pakistan, as to exterminate them *en masse* before they even had a chance of leaving.'

'I don't believe it!' Eli screamed at him, running forward and throwing herself upon him. With his good arm Ramesh thrust her off until Jerry could get control of her. 'He's lying,' she shouted to Don and the others. 'Don't you see it?'

'I said he could say his piece, Eli. I'll see your grandfather has ample opportunity to contradict him,' Don said gently.

Ramesh nodded his thanks and continued. 'He worked as an office clerk for the British by day, and by night he roamed the streets of the Muslim districts at the head of his gang, hunting down innocent women and children and putting them to the sword.'

Behind him Eli was weeping as Jerry walked with one arm around her. Every so often she muttered, 'He's lying. It's all lies. It must be.'

'Among those that he killed was a young married couple. Their name was Bandram.' He turned and looked sadly at Don. 'They were my parents. Ceda and I were only babies. Our Uncle Gilma found us where our mother had hidden us in the family house. He saved us and took us to his home, only to find that Sanji and his gang had been there too. They had killed my uncle's wife and children. Now do you see why we want him? It has taken us all this time to track him down.'

Don's pace slowed and he stared into the harsh light of the morning sky, trying to sift the facts. Ramesh's story had the ring of truth about it. He could feel it in his bones.

'If what you say is true, it's terrible. Yet it doesn't excuse the kidnapping of an innocent girl and it certainly doesn't excuse what your brother did in Britain. That was every bit as barbaric as the things you're accusing Sanji of.'

Ramesh sighed. 'It was never our intention to hurt anyone else. I can only assume that when my brother found himself so close to Sanji and yet saw the prospect of the evil bastard slipping through his fingers, his desperation got the better of him. I know that is no excuse and he will have to pay for it.'

They had come over a rise where the track led between tall, wind-blasted pines. In front of them the ground sloped down towards a broad stream that shone like glass. Ramesh pointed at it.

'There. That's what you want. That stream marks the border. On the other side of it is India. Cross that and you're free.'

Suddenly there was a warning shout from the back and Don spun round to see Gavin doubling towards him.

'Trouble. Look.' He pointed back to where two vehicles were hurtling towards them, clouds of dust rising from the wheels.

Don quickly estimated the distance to the border. 'Come on!' he shouted, pushing Ramesh forward and urging the others on. 'Run for it.'

As Gavin ran beside him he panted, 'There's no guarantee Ceda will stop at the stream. They cross it often enough anyway. It probably means fuck all to him.'

'I'm not aiming for the stream. That outcrop of rock just short of it should provide us with good cover. We can fight him off from there. With luck the Pakistani border guards will hear the shooting and come to investigate, and when they do, he'll bugger off and we can nip across. Even if the border means nothing to the Bandrams it bloody well will to the Pakistani authorities.'

They reached the outcrop as the vehicles were screeching to a halt on the crest a hundred yards behind them. Diving into the cover of the rocks and the few trees, Don, Gavin and Jerry turned their weapons on the men pouring out of the jeeps.

'Don't shoot until they do. We'll try and do a deal.'

Ceda was the first to address them. He had found Ramesh's jeep and the three dead men, but as his brother wasn't among them he guessed what had happened. Standing in the open, he hailed Don, demanding that Ramesh be freed.

'Cocky bugger, isn't he?' Gavin said, taking a bead on him, his finger itching on the trigger.

Don stood up and took a step into the open, where Ceda could see him.

'I'll do a deal. I'll let your brother go if you come over here and surrender.'

'Now why the hell would I want to do a thing like that?'

'Because you murdered innocent men in my country.'

'It's war, Mr SAS man. There are always casualties in war.'

'Like your parents? Was that war? Was their death justified?'

Ceda took a step forward, reaching for his gun. 'So Ramesh has told you?'

'Yes.'

'And?'

'And I'm very sorry but your argument's not with the girl nor with us. Nor was it with the men you killed in Britain. So the choice is yours now. Either you give yourself up, or Ramesh comes with us to answer for your crimes.'

Without realizing it Don had inadvertently moved further away from the cover of the rocks and as he finished his last demand, he saw the flash of a gun barrel from behind Ceda, but too late to avoid the bullet that knocked him flying. The next second Gavin was returning fire, the dirt at Ceda's feet kicking in tiny spurts. Gavin cursed his shooting and adjusted his aim, but not before Ceda had flung himself clear.

Behind the vehicles Ceda turned in fury on Ali, the gun still smoking in his hand.

'Who told you to fire?' he screamed at him.

Ali shrugged. 'It was such a clear shot. It was a chance we couldn't afford to miss.'

'Wrong,' Ceda replied evenly, his eyes ice-cold. 'This is the chance we can't afford to miss.'

Ali watched in horror as Ceda brought up the muzzle of his revolver and aimed it straight between his eyes. The finger was tightening on the trigger and he threw himself sideways, flinching from the shot. But Ceda had predicted it and the gun followed the target, only firing when Ali peeked again from behind his cringing arms to see if all was clear. The body flew backwards and lay still. Ceda stared at it without emotion and then spat, his spittle as accurate as his bullet.

On the ground near the rocks, Don rolled on to his stomach, nursing the wound in his side and starting to crawl. A hail of bullets blazed out from Gavin and Jerry, providing just enough suppressive fire to see him back into cover. While Gavin continued to fire single aimed shots, placing them carefully wherever he could see movement, Jerry slid across and examined Don's wound.

'It's not as bad as it looks. Just cut the flesh.'

'That's terrific news, 'cos it feels a fuck of a sight worse,' Don said, wincing as Jerry splashed water on it.

Ramesh shook his head in disgust. 'Barely a hundred yards and Ali couldn't even get that right.'

Gavin reached for the M206 and flicked up the sight, bracing himself to fire the grenade launcher. The small black grenade popped from the barrel and sailed towards one of the jeeps, Gavin holding his breath until he saw it strike the vehicle dead centre. With a huge gout of orange flame the jeep exploded, the fuel tanks igniting and erupting, rocketing parts of the shattered vehicle into the sky.

'Bull's-eye!' Gavin chortled, popping out the smoking empty casing and reloading to engage the second vehicle.

Fortunately for Ceda and his men, they had taken cover away from the jeeps and as they watched the destruction of their transport in horror, they poured a heavy fire down on the SAS patrol in frustrated anger. Gavin ducked out of the line of fire, the lead stinging and spitting around him and the moment the onslaught eased off he rolled into a firing position again, sighted on the next jeep and squeezed the trigger. Once again the grenade arced through the sky to score a direct hit, the second jeep bursting asunder.

'I'm getting quite good at this,' he said to Don with a wicked grin.

But Don had other problems on his mind. The stream and border were still some way behind them and the open ground was amply covered by Ceda's men. There would be no withdrawal to the relative safety of India before last light, and it was highly questionable whether they could hold out that long. Ceda could sit back, conserve his ammunition and wait for the SAS men to drop their guard or try a break for freedom. They were locked into a stalemate that only an outside agency could break.

It was another hour before such an agency arrived on the scene, and when it did, Don and his men were the most surprised of all.

From the Indian side of the border came the sound of vehicles and moments later a small convoy of four Land Rovers wove their way into the valley at Don's back, making laboriously for the frontier stream. Don took out his binoculars and focused on the lead vehicle.

'I don't fucking believe it,' he muttered.

'What's that?' Gavin asked as he searched for another target for his M206. 'Has the cavalry arrived?'

'If Tony Briggs counts as the cavalry.'

From his hollow where he was being guarded by Jerry, Ramesh sat up and stared in dismay. 'Did you say Briggs?'

'The one and only Sir Anthony,' Don answered as he watched the Land Rovers draw to a halt across the stream and the occupants debus. Apart from the tall figure of Sir Anthony he could make out half a dozen men in civilian clothes, all Westerners and, from the look of them, Intelligence service. 'Too heavy to be SAS,' he said contemptuously.

But the greatest surprise was when a small, diminutive figure eased out of the rear vehicle.

'Well, well, well. Looks like your grandpa's come to fetch you, Eli,' said Don.

'What?'

Instantly Eli was at his side, disbelieving until he had handed her the binoculars and showed her where to look.

A slow smile spread across Ramesh's face. 'Now you will be able to ask him if what I said is true.'

'I don't need to,' Eli said defiantly. 'I know my grandfather, and I know it's all lies.'

Don drew her back. 'Unfortunately no one's going to prove anything until we've worked out a way to get over the border. If we try it now Ceda and his chums will cut us to pieces.'

Help came from an unlikely source. No sooner had the party debussed than they advanced right up to the stream and Sir Anthony addressed Ceda Bandram through a loud hailer.

'Mr Bandram, I don't propose to beat about the bush. None of us can afford to spend more time here than neces- sary. You can expect the Pakistani border guards at your backs at any moment, and I can expect similar rough treat- ment from the Indians. My contacts have run dry and I've no more favours to call in. You've got something I want, and I've got something you want. We can do a swap.'

In his hideout among the rocks Don stared at Gavin in amazement. 'The bastard's doing a deal! He's going to give them Sanji in return for us.'

Sir Anthony continued. 'It's not my choice.' Don saw him turn briefly to Sanji. 'Mr Sanji has threatened to make every- thing public unless I allow him to give himself up to you.'

There was a pause while Ceda considered the offer, and after a while he stood up and shouted back, 'All right then. Send him across the river and when I have him I'll let your men go.'

'And the girl.'

'Of course. The girl too.'

Don watched with mounting disquiet as Sanji set out towards the stream. Something wasn't quite right and he didn't like it one little bit. It wasn't like Sir Anthony to give in to terrorists, yet here he was doing a deal with them.

Again the loud hailer crackled into life. 'Captain Headley, move with your men and the girl down to the river now.'

Don gathered up his weapon, wincing at the shot of pain in his side as he moved. He stuck the barrel of his Colt Commando in Ramesh's back. 'Come on. You're coming too.'

'That wasn't part of the deal,' Ramesh protested.

'It's part of my deal. Now move!'

Reluctantly Ramesh got to his feet and with the rest of the group, left the safety of the rocks and walked slowly down towards the river. As they walked, something tugged at Don's mind.

'Tell me,' he asked Ramesh. 'If you know so much about Sanji, how was it that he ended up in Britain so soon after Independence? He was a minor functionary, a man of no influence or status. How come he suddenly disappeared, only to reappear a British citizen who was then able to found a prosperous business?'

Ramesh shrugged. 'He must have had powerful friends.'

'A clerk with powerful friends? I'd say that doesn't quite fit.'

'OK then, it must have been in someone's interest to hush it all up.'

'Perhaps. But whose?' Don asked, directing the question as much at himself as at Ramesh.

On the slope behind them Ceda and his men had emerged from their cover and were moving swiftly down to claim their prize of the hated Mr Sanji.

'Well, he was working for the British.'

'Yes, but there's no way they'd have colluded in any massacres. The British administration did all it could to keep the two factions apart and prevent the bloodshed.'

Ramesh's mind was racing now too, catching Don's thread and tracing it to its terrible end. Something rattled deep in his own mind and the nearer he came to the boundary river the clearer it became.

'Just now you mentioned the name Briggs.'

'Yes. What of it?' Don asked.

Ramesh shook his head as if to clear it. 'I know it sounds stupid, but there was another Briggs, I think. Back in 1947.' He looked up at the sprightly figure of Sir Anthony. 'But it couldn't have been him. Surely. The Briggs I heard of was already old in 1947.'

Don stopped dead in his tracks. 'Another Briggs?'

It was as if Don's hesitation was the trigger. One moment they had been walking towards the river and freedom, the next they were in the centre of a hail of lead. Instinctively Don flung himself to the ground and as he looked up he saw that the men who had accompanied Sir Anthony were no longer standing watch, but were kneeling in fire positions, each man blazing away with an M16.

'Gavin!' Don screamed. But the sergeant had been cut down in the first onslaught.

Jerry crawled forward and wrestled the M206 from the dead man's grasp, shouting, 'What the fuck are they doing? I thought they were on our side?'

Behind him Eli lay flat on the floor screaming in terror. Don glanced up the hillside at their back and saw that Ceda and his party had been targeted as well. Sir Anthony's men had caught the lot of them, Bandrams and SAS, in their lethal ambush. Even Sanji had been scythed down in their murderous fire and now lay on a dry bank of pebbles in midstream, face up and motionless.

Ramesh wriggled up beside Don. 'Give me a gun. For God's sake at least let me defend myself!'

Don drew his Browning and handed it across with its spare ammunition clips. With his good hand, Ramesh took the pistol and rolled several paces away from Don before coming up and returning fire, using carefully aimed shots despite the incoming torrent from Sir Anthony's men. On the hill behind them Don saw only the prone still form of Ceda Bandram, with several of his men lying lifeless around him. All had been taken by complete surprise in the opening hail of bullets.

Frantically Don searched for a way out. And then he had it.

'Jerry, pass me the last M72 rocket.'

'What's on your mind?'

'Just do it!'

Jerry reached for the khaki tube, snapped it open and armed the rocket. As he handed it over Don said, 'If I don't make it to those rocks we're done for. Put your hands up and surrender.'

Jerry stared at him dumbfounded. 'They won't take a surrender. They'll cut us down.'

'Do as I say. Trust me. I don't think they'll harm the girl. And anyway, they'll kill you if you stay here. It's worth a gamble.'

Jerry looked at him doubtfully but nodded his agreement. He was a soldier and he would obey his commander's order, even if it was the last one he ever received.

Don took hold of the rocket and braced himself to run, fixing his eyes on the far spread of rock that would give him a good shot down the line of vehicles. He gathered his knees under him, took three deep breaths to steady himself, then burst from cover.

'Get some covering fire down!' Jerry shouted, blazing away with the M206. Ramesh fired off a whole clip, dropping it out and snapping in a replacement to continue.

But Don had set himself a difficult target. It was a long way to the rocks and within a second of leaving his position the Intelligence agents had him in their sights. Bullets bit into the ground all around him. One of them tore at his webbing belt, and another ripped through the sleeve of his jacket. Then the unthinkable happened. Jerry heard a cry of pain, and looking sharply round, he saw Don tumble, fall and come to rest, still a good ten yards from the rocks. His eyes were open and staring, fixed on the river. Eli screamed.

'You bastards!' Jerry shouted, burning through his last clip of ammunition until the firing pin clicked on an empty chamber. He hunted around for more but Gavin's body with its extra ammunition pouches was out of reach and a moment later Ramesh fired off his last round. He turned and looked at Jerry.

'I guess it's time to put your boss's judgement to the test.'

Desperately Jerry tried to think of an alternative, but it was no use. There was none. It was possible that a couple of Ceda's men might still be alive, but they were keeping their heads down and in no mood to risk their lives to save even Ramesh.

'OK then.'

He turned to Eli. 'Got anything white?'

'You can't be serious?'

'Have you got a better idea?'

She dug into her pocket and pulled out a yellow handkerchief. 'Will this do?'

He took it and tied it to the muzzle of the M206. 'Well, here goes.'

Waving the weapon aloft, he shouted down across the river. The firing stopped and the voice of Sir Anthony replied.

'That's more like it. Stand up, all of you, and make your way down to the stream now.'

Jerry started to his feet.

'This is madness,' Eli said, following his lead. 'He'll have us all killed.'

Ramesh was the last to stand and then together the three of them walked slowly down towards the border. As they went, Eli looked at her grandfather's body and started to sob. From behind the row of vehicles Sir Anthony and his men emerged, their M16s levelled at the three individuals now in the open and at their mercy. Slowly the two sides drew together until they were standing on opposite banks of the stream, separated by only a few yards of clear, shallow water.

'So here we all are,' Sir Anthony said pleasantly, a Walther PPK pistol in his fist. Jerry couldn't help thinking how out of character it looked. Sir Anthony would have been much more comfortable wielding a pen, doing his killing from a distance with cunning and deceit as his ammunition.

'We are surrendering to you in good faith,' Jerry said. 'I don't know what game you're playing, and I'm not interested.'

Sir Anthony raised his eyebrows. 'Really? That is good of you, you miserable little upstart. Who do you think you are to judge me? A bloody squaddie.'

'At least I'm not a traitor. I don't murder people who've put their lives on the line for a mission.'

Sir Anthony feigned a yawn, covering his mouth with the back of his hand. When he had finished he said to his men, 'Kill them,' and turned to walk away.

Jerry braced himself involuntarily for the impact of the bullets in his flesh, every muscle tensing as if that alone could repulse them. But as he did so he saw the expression on Sir Anthony's face change from smug boredom to alarm. He glanced round to see what had caught his attention. Beside the far rocks, Don had risen into a kneeling position. The M72 tube was over his shoulder, his fingers pressing down on the firing button. It was the backblast that Jerry saw first, the cone of flame and smoke erupting from the rear of the tube as the rocket powered out of the front. Then, as the slender warhead streaked across the intervening space, Jerry traced it in horrified fascination, all the way into Sir Anthony's chest, where the nose cone crumpled on his sternum, detonating the charge and blowing him to pieces.

Without thinking, Jerry swung down his M206 and levelled it at the six agents. But all of them had flung themselves to the ground at the blast of the exploding rocket, shielding their faces in their arms, and when they looked up it was to find themselves covered by Jerry's M206 and Don's Colt Commando, little realizing that the two SAS men had not a bullet left between them.

'Stay on the ground!' Don screamed. 'One move and you'll be confetti like Briggs.'

Ramesh waded through the stream and flung away the agents' weapons, keeping one for himself. 'I've got them now,' he shouted back.

With a sigh of relief Don lowered his Colt Commando. He grinned across at Jerry. 'For a moment there I didn't think you were going to surrender like I said.'

Jerry shook his head and started to shake with laughter. 'Surrender! Of all the stupid fucking orders. If I'd only known . . .'

'If I'd told you my plan you wouldn't have been convincing enough for someone as smart as Briggs.'

While Don secured the agents, tying them with rope from the Land Rovers, Ramesh and Jerry checked on the casualties. Back up the hill Ramesh found Murap kneeling over the body of Ceda. His eyes were open and his teeth were set in a grimace of pain.

'He was hit in the first volley of fire and I couldn't get to him,' Murap said weeping.

Ramesh stooped and closed his brother's eyes. One by one the scores were being settled. Sanji was dead, and Ali, and now the British policemen had been avenged with the death of Ceda. He looked out across the rock-strewn ground and saw Gavin's body. Briggs had been slain and with him, Ramesh feared, had died the reason for his betrayal. Why had he tasked the SAS with the mission, only to betray them and have them cut down by his own men? It was a question that Ramesh was no longer interested to ask. With his brother and his uncle dead, he felt more alone than he had ever done in his life.

'Come, Murap. It is time to go home.'

15

The purr of the engines had lulled both Jerry and Eli to sleep. From his seat by the window, Don looked at them and smiled. Their heads had tumbled together and in Jerry's lap their hands were joined. He had to admit that they made a handsome couple.

Outside night was falling, the sun slowly sinking in the west and shooting out orange rays that spanned the entire horizon. It would be a peaceful night, he felt. He himself was longing to sleep but there were too many ghosts that cried out to be laid to rest. Good men had died, and a serious reckoning lay ahead on their return to Britain. Procedures would have to be examined to discover how it was that Briggs had managed to mount the operation without the knowledge of his superiors. And there would undoubtedly be questions from the Indian government about the six British agents found wandering naked near the Pakistani border in Kashmir.

It had been the note found on Sanji that had proved to be the final piece of the puzzle, clarifying Briggs's role in the affair. Eli had found it and Don wondered if she would ever get over her grandfather's confession, which had corroborated everything that Ramesh Bandram had said of him. But more than that, Sanji had written of the other Briggs, the one whose name had sparked a faint memory in Ramesh's mind.

In the dark days of 1947 countless people had died, innocent people of every race and creed. One such had been Vivienne Briggs, the wife of Arthur Briggs, Sanji's boss in the last British administration. She had been caught and murdered in a riot orchestrated by none other than Uncle Gilma Bandram. Arthur Briggs had come to know of Sanji's activities with an extremist terror group of his own, but rather than report him to the authorities, he had concealed the fact, on condition that Sanji's men perform an act of revenge on his behalf. The murders had duly been carried out, and once it was thought that the last of the Bandrams had been accounted for, Arthur left India for the last time. With him went his young son Anthony.

The full story had only been made known to Sir Anthony by accident, during the talk between him and Sanji in the car on the drive away from the safe house. A check of the facts had confirmed the shocking coincidence that had brought the two men together, the ex-terrorist Sanji and the British Intelligence mandarin, their fates inexplicably linked.

Desperate to preserve his father's honour, Sir Anthony had settled on his course of action, blind to the consequences to the innocent members of the SAS team involved. Everyone concerned with the whole shameful business was to have been eliminated, and only Don's cunning and skill had stopped him from getting away with it.

Don pressed the button in his armrest and levered his seat back, stretching out his legs in an effort to relax. They had been good men. Tom and Jimmie, Taff and Geordie, Rod and Gavin, the old hand. They had all done their duty as ordered, carrying out the mission though it had cost them their lives, proving once again that the Regiment could rely on the finest of soldiers whenever the need arose.

He stared out of the window, the sun's last glow quenching itself in the vast expanse of the Arabian Sea. What had made Sanji recant after all those years? he wondered. Perhaps the weight of what he had once done had finally burned into him the guilt that he had managed to suppress all those years before. It had been a great wrong in a time of great wrongs. Crimes had been committed by people on all sides. Perhaps the message was that it would never be in the nature of such an evil to be laid to rest. However strong and resilient the young perpetrator might believe himself to be, however untouched by his crimes, in committing the evil he was unwittingly sowing the seeds of self-destruction in his own heart. Sanji, Uncle Bandram and Ceda, and finally Briggs himself – the seeds had borne their terrible fruit, and the evil come home to rest.

Evil would always beget evil, Don thought. It was only to be hoped that there would always be men good enough and willing to fight it.